A CUT ABOVE THE REST

A CUT ABOVE THE REST

When Dodie Fanshaw goes to stay with her daughter Elena, she is expecting a sedate village on the banks of the River Thames, but then a mermaid clambers out of the river and into Elena's garden. Well, not a mermaid exactly, but a mysterious, sopping-wet girl. When they call on Elena's neighbour, novelist Rick Wilbraham, they find Anna, his girlfriend, hysterically clinging to Rick's lifeless body. A literary puzzle, but what genre is the motive? It could be Romance, might be Financial Thriller – and the mermaid? Well, that's just pure Fantasy...

A CUT ABOVE THE REST

by

Marina Oliver

Dales Large Print Books
Long Preston, North Yorkshire,
BD23 4ND, England.

British Library Cataloguing in Publication Data.

Oliver, Marina
A cut above the rest.

A catalogue record of this book is
available from the British Library

ISBN 1-84262-483-0 pbk
ISBN 978-1-84262-483-8 pbk

First published in Great Britain in 2004 by
Severn House Publishers

Published in Large Print 2006 by arrangement with
Severn House Publishers

Dales Large Print is an imprint of Library Magna Books Ltd.

Printed and bound in Great Britain by
T.J. (International) Ltd., Cornwall, PL28 8RW

One

'You said Markenlea was a peaceful, sedate village when you moved here,' Dodie Fanshaw said accusingly.

She'd thought it idyllic when she'd arrived the previous day. The large green was surrounded with clusters of thatched cottages, a squat-towered Norman church, and several gracious old houses. Some more modern villas sat among the older ones bordering the Thames. And she had high hopes that Elena might be contemplating marriage at last.

Elena, busy with the coffee filter on the far side of the big kitchen, laughed. 'That racket last night wasn't typical, Mum. It's the first disturbance I've heard since I moved in, and I've been here over three months, since March.'

'It sounded like an orgy,' Dodie insisted. 'I was quite envious, it's a long time since I got involved in an orgy.'

'Come off it! I don't believe half your tall stories about your past. It wasn't nearly as lurid as you claim. You're almost respectable.'

Dodie chuckled. 'I'm not telling you everything. It might give you ideas. That can wait for my memoirs. But that's not the point. There's a mermaid in your garden.'

'A what?' Elena left the coffee to drip and came to stand behind her mother's chair in the big bay window. 'Good grief!'

The girl walking slowly across the lawn, her long green skirt clinging to her legs, her skimpy pink T-shirt outlining her ample breasts, and gleaming swathes of black hair plastered across her face, did bear some resemblance to Matthew Arnold's mermaid. The placidly flowing river behind her was hardly the sea, dotted as it was with pleasure boats and racing skiffs, willow trees fringing the far bank, and a blaze of colour all around her in Elena's garden. Elena sighed and moved across to the door.

'I don't know what it is about this stretch of the river, but that's the third shipwrecked rower I've succoured so far. Hello,' she added to the sorry-looking girl who was hesitating at the edge of the terrace. 'Need help? Were you on your own, or is there anyone else?'

The mermaid sniffed, and somewhat fruitlessly tried to wipe her face dry with the edge of the sopping T-shirt. She glanced nervously behind her, then shook herself, and seemed to register Elena's question. 'Anyone else? Oh, no! I was alone. The boat caught in some weeds, I think, and tipped up.' She gulped, and brushed angrily at her eyes. 'I got on to that island, then managed to swim across. I can't swim very well, I was so glad it wasn't far. May I – but I'll drip all over your floor!'

'Don't worry, the kitchen's tiled. Come in and strip off while I get you a towel.'

'There's no need, honestly. If I – or perhaps you'd do it for me – I need to call someone to come and fetch me.' She shivered and began to pick off some shreds of river weeds that clung to her clothes. 'I lost my sandals. I can't go back to – walk back, in bare feet.'

'The local taxi-drivers won't bless you for soaking their upholstery, either.'

'Oh yes. I hadn't thought of that. Nor – nor my friend. Whatever can I do?' She glanced across at the Aga. 'Perhaps they'd dry on the rail?'

'I can rinse your clothes and put them in the dryer, while you have a cup of coffee,' Elena suggested.

The girl hesitated, sniffed again, this time at the aroma of coffee which reached her as Dodie was filling three mugs. She swallowed nervously, then came up to the doorway. 'If you're sure? I was going to ring a friend, but he – well, his car's a new one – new to him, I mean, and anyway I'm not sure he's at home. I don't know what to do. I'd better get a taxi.' She stifled a sob and brushed wet hands across her face.

Elena persuaded her to come in, and led

her, protesting through her tears that she was frightfully sorry to be such a nuisance, through the dining room and into the shower room across the hall. 'Strip off those wet things. There's a towel, and a spare robe, shampoo, a comb. Take a shower, you're shivering. Look, have your coffee in there, and chuck out your clothes so that I can start them drying.'

Dodie watched her daughter organizing the child – she was not very old, nineteen or so, perhaps. But the gap in sophistication between her and Elena was far more than the half dozen or so years in age. It was good to be with her daughter again, after several months abroad, though she admitted to herself she was worried about the reason she'd had to come to England. And this house out in the country Elena had moved to was far better than the London one would be at this time of year.

It was a charming house. A row of centuries-old cottages had been converted to one house ten years before. Many of the internal walls had been knocked out, and the formerly dark and poky small rooms had been transformed into three double-aspect rooms and a large entrance hall, overlooking the village green and the river. Rose Cottage lived up to its name. Gloire de Dijon rambled over much of the front of the cottage, and the drive was bordered with a score or more varieties of hybrid tea and floribunda roses, all currently in full bloom and chosen, by the previous owner, for their abundant flowering and delicious perfume.

She sighed slightly. She'd have to stay in London when she went for the tests, but hopefully that would not be for more than one night. As Elena came out of the utility room she firmly banished gloomy thoughts.

Ten minutes later the girl, swathed in a thick towelling robe, was sitting at the table with them, sipping at a second mug of coffee, and looking anxiously towards the utility room where the dryer was churning noisily. She was quite pretty, despite the worried look in her eyes, Dodie thought. Her hair was beginning to curl into tendrils, and was not quite as black as it had seemed. She wore a ring, a small diamond solitaire, on her engagement finger and constantly twisted it round, pushing it nervously up and down.

'Do you live locally?' Dodie asked. 'Here, have another biscuit.'

The girl stretched out her hand, then shook her head. 'I – no, thanks. I – I'm on a diet. No, I don't live near here. I just – it's such a beautiful day, I thought I'd come and take out a boat. But I'm not a very good rower, and–' Suddenly she gasped, put her face in her hands, and began to shudder. 'I'm sorry! I'm so sorry!'

'It's the shock. Here's some brandy, that'll

help,' Elena said, forcing the glass into her hand.

She blinked at it, took a tentative sip, then another, and then tipped the brandy down her throat.

'Thanks. That's better. I'm sorry to be such a fool. Are my clothes dry yet? Can I ring for a taxi? I really am grateful, but I'd better get out of your way.'

'A few more minutes, and you can dry your hair while you're waiting. I'll fetch my hairdryer.'

'Did you lose your purse?' Dodie asked as Elena left the kitchen. She'd noticed there were no pockets in the girl's skirt.

She looked blank for a moment, then shook her head. 'No. Well, yes. I suppose I did. I remember, it was on the other seat. But it doesn't matter, I only had a couple of pounds in it.'

'No return ticket? To wherever you came from?'

'Ticket? I suppose so. But if I go by taxi I won't need it, and I couldn't – can't go by train.'

'Can you pay for the taxi when you get home?'

'No problem. It's not very far, and my – yes, there's someone there who'll pay.'

'Your parents? Or your fiancé, perhaps?'

'My fiancé?' She looked startled. 'I haven't – he's not–' She closed her eyes and took a deep breath. 'No.'

'It's fortunate you didn't lose the ring, it seems rather loose,' Dodie said, nodding at it.

The girl looked at it blankly, and jerked away her other hand. 'It's not– Oh, it sounds as if the dryer's stopped.'

She hurried into the utility room and, by the time Elena returned with the hairdryer, was dressed in her own clothes once more. After a cursory attempt to dry her hair while Elena telephoned for a taxi, she refused all offers of further help, and virtually ran down the drive when the taxi appeared, hopping occasionally when her bare feet encountered some roughness on the York stone paving.

'How very odd,' Elena said, staring after her. 'Do you think she'll be OK? She was still in a state.'

'Not enough to give away her name or address,' Dodie said. 'She was determined not to let us know that.'

'But why? What difference does it make? Unless she was hiding from someone.'

'I expect she was part of your orgy last night,' Dodie said, amused. 'Though I doubt if she's been on the river since then. Probably been in some love nest, and had to escape in a hurry when the man's wife arrived earlier than expected. What's on the other bank? Perhaps she had to swim for it, and there never was any boat.'

'There are fields across the river, with pampered little ponies belonging to the village children, There's a car park by the bridge, and riverside walks. That orgy was just Elizabeth, Rick's ex-wife.'

'Rick? Rich Ricky Wilbraham, your neighbour? The wonder-boy novelist everyone's raving about? Even before the book's been read by more than a hundred or so people?'

'Yes, our literary genius, if you believe the hype. But hardly a boy. He must be nearly forty.'

'Just one ex-wife? She was making enough noise for a dispossessed harem.'

Elena grinned as she stacked the mugs into the dishwasher. 'Don't exaggerate. One car, a few noisy hoots on the horn at midnight, and a few slamming doors.'

'Plus what sounded like a whole quarry of bricks being hurled about, and shattering glass.'

'I think that was Rick's conservatory. He's got a passion for orchids, and he told me Elizabeth used to resent the time he lavished on them. We'll find out when we go over. I'm going to change.'

Elena was half way up the stairs when the phone rang.

'I'll take that,' Dodie offered, on the bottom step, having lingered to gather up the wet towels the stranger had used.

'Hello? Hello?' the caller said loudly the

moment Dodie picked up the receiver. Grimacing, Dodie held it away from her ear. 'It's me. Is that you, Elena? Took you long enough to answer. I suppose it's too much effort to speak to your old gran.'

Dodie waved to Elena, who had paused and was grinning appreciatively, to go on up. 'I'll deal with her,' she mouthed, and Elena nodded and vanished into the bathroom.

'Ma, it's Dodie, not Elena, and I picked up the phone on the second ring,' she interrupted firmly. 'And stop getting at Elena. She visits you more often than I do! But if you start bullying the girl I'd not guarantee she'll go on putting up with you, you miserable old devil!'

She held the receiver much further away this time, grinning as she heard her mother complaining that she had always been an ungrateful and undutiful daughter. When Mrs Jackson wound down to a halt Dodie spoke again.

'I have to go soon, Ma, so don't waste time. And remember it's your phone bill, not mine.' Even though she pays it out of the allowance I give her, she added to herself. The reminder stimulated Mrs Jackson into recalling her reason for telephoning.

'You said you'd come and see me again soon,' she complained, her voice suddenly developing a faint, fragile tone.

'I was there three days ago. I came to see you the day after I landed. And if I remember rightly, you said you'd had enough of me to last you until Christmas,' Dodie enunciated slowly and clearly.

'Well, you don't usually take any notice of what I say,' Mrs Jackson said sharply, her vigour suddenly revived. 'When are you coming?'

Dodie sighed. One visit to her cantankerous mother was enough to last a year. She'd left home as soon as she could, but when she'd been in trouble, the old girl had supported her. She'd even cared for young Jake so that Dodie could go back to her acting career and the offer of a Hollywood contract. But the old girl was probably lonely now, despite her various pensioners' clubs and the company of neighbours who, like her, had lived in the same street in east London for most of their lives. Jake had vanished – they only heard from him when he wanted money – and Dodie spent much of her time travelling.

'I'm in London for the day on Tuesday,' she said reluctantly. 'I'll treat you to lunch.'

'I can't afford to give you lunch! What do you think I live on? My pension doesn't keep me in bread and milk. Of course, living the life of Riley, you won't care how much prices have gone up since you were here last.'

'In three days?' Dodie asked, but softly, then she raised her voice. 'I said I'd give you lunch. I'll pay for it. Me, out of my ill-gotten millions. I'll pay your bus fare up west and a taxi all the way home. We'll go to the Savoy or the Ritz, your choice.'

She dodged the squawk of protest that almost split her eardrums, and grinned. Her mother would love to go to either place, if only to be able to complain to her cronies at the extortionate prices, but would never bring herself to admit it.

'You may want to waste your money, but never let it be said that I helped you to do it,' Mrs Jackson said self-righteously.

'Right, I won't let it be said. Selfridges, Tuesday, meet you in the jewellery department at twelve sharp. Have to go now, there's someone at the door and Elena's out. Is that OK? Selfridges, Tuesday, noon, Jewels.'

And if that doesn't bring her, she thought as she firmly replaced the receiver on more protests, nothing would. Mrs Jackson, while eschewing expensive baubles, loved huge gaudy beads in garish psychedelic colours. And Dodie always gave her some after every foreign trip, and often when they met, as now, for lunch or shopping. She sighed. Much as she loved her mother, a little of her went a dreadfully long way, and she hadn't yet recovered from all the complaints and recriminations from three days before. If she loaded her up with gewgaws on Tuesday, maybe she'd be left in peace for a week or two.

Dodie, in a scarlet dress made of filmy, fine-woven silk, which was adorned with several floating panels, tucked a white silk scarf round her neck. She had a good tan from her winter travels, and in public maintained that white was best for showing it off. In private she admitted that low-cut dresses had an unfortunate effect on her ageing neck, despite her other substantial attributes. She consoled herself with the thought that thin women looked scraggy, and pulled the belt in another notch.

'Ready?' Elena called from the landing. Dodie picked up her purse and a wide-brimmed sun hat, sprayed on more perfume, and went to join her daughter.

'You don't look a day over twenty,' she said approvingly. 'But isn't it time you settled down with a suitable man? They don't all improve with age, like brandy.'

'I'm wearing well.' Elena grinned at her. 'And I'm not sure what a "suitable man" would be like. I don't seem to have met any.'

Dodie knew better than to pursue the topic. She was well aware that Elena was trying to make up her mind whether she wanted to marry the current boyfriend. She hid it well, but Dodie suspected she was missing him more than she would admit.

'I envy you being able to show those lovely long legs in a miniskirt. Your father was tall. I always preferred tall men.'

'But I doubt if his legs were such a good shape as ours, so come off it, Mum. Yours would still look good in the chorus line.'

Dodie chuckled. 'That was just a way in. You had to use whatever assets you had in those days. I became a serious actress,' she reminded her daughter. Well, a serious starlet, she added to herself. She'd never landed a really big part.

She considered Elena as they walked down the long drive. The younger woman had inherited her Brazilian father's dark complexion, and with Dodie's blonde hair she'd always looked exotic, stunning. Tall, she had an excellent figure, and the good fortune of never having to diet or exercise to maintain its lissome shapeliness. It was a pity she was so fussy about men. Dodie wanted to see her married, but until this latest one Elena had always insisted that she had plenty of masculine company, just didn't wish to tie herself down or live with anyone. And she didn't need a man for financial security, as Dodie in her own youth had. Her father had left her a fortune, and she made good money from her business, organizing large parties and weddings. Perhaps, Dodie thought with an inward sigh, that was what made her wary. She could only be sure a man with an even bigger fortune would want her for herself. Marcus Hurst was handsome, ambitious, clever, a computer whizz-kid, by all accounts, but he hadn't yet made a fortune. Dodie suspected Elena was worried that he might wish to use hers in order to finance some of his schemes. A pity this Rick Wilbraham seemed to be attached already.

Out of Elena's garden they turned left and went for a hundred yards beside a neatly trimmed beech hedge. Dodie once more admired the large village green, with ancient but well-restored old cottages and larger, opulent-looking houses scattered around it, most of them at least a couple of hundred years old. There was nothing like a picturesque English village on a sunny summer's day. At one side was a clapboard pavilion, cricket screens placed alongside ready, she assumed, for the next village match. The previous day had been peaceful, the local team playing away. Beyond it she could see the stocky church tower, the body of the church concealed by several ancient yew trees and a thick laurel hedge which also hid the ancient gravestones. At that moment the church clock struck twelve and a flock of rooks flew noisily away, cawing in protest. To one side was the local hostelry, The Plough. Once a busy coaching inn, its thatched roof held up by timber-framed walls which sagged precariously, it was still unspoilt by unsuitable modern additions. Already its car park was occupied by several vehicles, upmarket saloons, sporting types, and a showing of the latest country accessory, the four-wheel drive.

A pair of children on fat, solid ponies trotted across the green, and waved to them. Coming the other way were two women on sleek, elegant hacks. It was a storybook English country scene on the surface. Dodie wondered what passions and frustrations, sins and crimes, were concealed beneath.

They were a dozen or so yards short of an imposing gateway, its tall brick pillars surmounted by carved eagles, when Dodie's reflections were broken as an open-topped blue Mercedes swung out and then braked beside them. A woman with sharp features and short fox-coloured hair leaned out and whipped off her designer sunglasses.

'Elena? Going to see Rick?'

Elena went across to the car. 'Hi, Serena. Yes. I thought you'd be there.'

'Can't, crisis in the office. Give him my apologies and say I'll look in this evening.'

'Office crisis? On Sunday?' Elena asked.

'Our motto should be "We never sleep". It's worse than foreign exchange dealing. Specially with the modern curses of fax and e-mail. Contracts and problems flying at us from all over the globe, damned publishers sitting on manuscripts for months, then screaming for an answer yesterday. See you.'

She let in the clutch and the car leapt forward. A hand waved above the fiery head, and the car raced away in the direction of the motorway and London.

'Who was that?' Dodie asked.

'Serena Coates. Rick's literary agent, and if rumour doesn't lie as usual, she used to be something more. But why ask us to give her apologies to Rick when she's just been there herself?'

'Has she?'

'Well, she drove out of his gateway.'

They went through the gates and began to walk along the gravel. This drive was even longer than Elena's, and curved round a dense shrubbery of overgrown laurels. There was too little colour and it would look dark and forbidding on a wet winter's day, Dodie thought, and despite the heat, shivered.

'His mistress? Used to be? This gravel's the devil to walk on. But I suppose most people get delivered in their big cars. It's not designed for exercise freaks like us.'

Elena grinned. 'Stop complaining. It was no more than a rumour. He's reputed to be, in the old-fashioned phrase, a ladies' man. Serena's married to her business partner, though she still uses her maiden name, and they live on the outskirts of Upper Markenlea, just along the river. You saw how the town sprawls along the banks. And Rick has a new live-in girlfriend, Anna Terry. She's a writer too, I believe, though she'd only been here a few months, and I haven't met her very often.'

'Is Serena really so high-powered that she has to go to the office on Sunday?'

'She's high-powered all right. She got Rick some huge advance for his first novel. Now that's strongly tipped for the Booker.'

'The Booker? What's that?'

'Mum! You must have heard of the big prize for a novel, the one where there's always a well-publicized judges' row.'

'You mean that one with the books everyone buys and no one reads? The rows are orchestrated to make a few people buy the books to find out what it's all about. Just as theatre people organize a bit of juicy scandal if bookings for the play are slow.'

'Plenty of people have bought Rick's book, and it's only been out for a few months. I gather the sales have been remarkable for a first novel and they're printing a vast number of paperbacks for next month. Serena says she's going to get an even bigger advance for the next novels.'

Dodie pursed her lips in a whistle. 'So that's why he can afford to live in a huge riverside villa,' she murmured as the curving drive brought them past the shrubbery and opened into a wide space before a long, low house with an ornate pillared verandah running the full length of it, and an overlarge portico big enough for a Rolls-Royce to drive under.

'He was rich before. Made a packet in property, and got out before the market collapsed. He was involved in all sorts of schemes, I heard, huge town-centre redevelopments, and small renovation projects, as well as the normal house building. He bought this house a year or so ago, though I believe he wrote the wonder book somewhere else. Come on, we can go straight round. He says he always has his Sunday drinks parties on the terrace at the back, though I've only been to one before.'

'No cars here. We're the first, unless all the others walk. Are they the local worthies?'

'Last time he had people from London too.'

'Where's his orchid house?' Dodie asked as they walked past the side of the house, on to a terrace paved with old York slabs, and edged with a stone balustrade on which tall urns perched.

'On the other side. It opens out of the room he calls his study.'

'And I suppose he gains literary inspiration from talking to the flowers,' Dodie said, chuckling. 'Or they dictate the story to him. I wouldn't be surprised by anything in this quiet little village. But he'll be writing the second book now, won't he?'

Elena nodded. 'I overheard Anna a few days ago, talking to Mrs Weaver in the shop. She was asking how it was going, and Anna said the first draft was almost finished.'

Dodie paused to look at two pairs of French windows which stood open. She could see what looked like antique dining furniture in one room, and half a dozen squashy white leather settees in another. On the terrace several conversation groups of green-stained wooden tables and chairs were scattered about. They were interspersed with terracotta pots crammed with exuberant pelargoniums of every shade from white to deepest red.

'Flashy,' Dodie muttered. 'Like his book, from all I've read in the reviews. Everything there from sex, violence, pathos and wicked capitalists, all excused by ostentatious political correctness but a bit over the top, like a feminist perchild.'

'Per-what?' Elena demanded, amused.

'Child. After all, a son in person is masculine, and that's not gender-correct.'

Elena laughed. 'What's been bugging you? Too much female company in Bermuda?'

Dodie grinned. 'Probably. I need some male company, so where's this clever neighbour of yours who doesn't need a fortune but snaffles big advances from the mouths of starving hacks in garrets?'

'Perhaps he's by the pool. This end of it, and the changing rooms, are hidden from up here,' Elena said, walking past the balustrade to the far side of the terrace.

Only the far end of the pool was visible, blue water lapping gently against the sides, the occasional larger ripple overflowing on to the brilliant white tiles which surrounded it. Curved flights of stone steps led down from the terrace to the lower level and what turned out to be a surprisingly large swimming pool. White plastic tables with multi-coloured parasols, loungers and chairs with matching cushions were scattered about, but there was no sign of their host, or any evidence of preparations for a drinks party.

'I wonder if he's on the lower lawn?' Elena said, puzzled. 'It's another level down, just above the river bank. I didn't think he used that much. I wonder if I should have my garden redesigned and terraced? It would be less effort than that slope.'

They walked past the pool and, without thinking, Dodie picked up a cushion which had slipped to the ground from one of the loungers, and replaced it. 'There's a towel here,' she said, 'and it's wet. He can't be far away. Perhaps he was tempted by the weather and had a dip, and is changing now.'

She glanced back at the twin pavilions, but both doors were open, and all the windows, and the only movement was curtains waving gently in the breeze.

They made their way cautiously down a steep grassy slope, and rounded a clump of shrubs at the bottom. In front of them, sticking up no more than a foot above the terrace, was a large boathouse, with a dozen or so steps leading down beside it to the path bordering the river. The scent of honeysuckle and lavender wafted towards them, but Dodie forgot about that as she saw the tableau on the grass. There was an overturned deckchair, and in front of it, sprawled face down, a man in swimming trunks lay with his head towards them. He was slight, almost boyish, with tight black curls, so that the bald patch on his head looked incongruous. Standing beyond him, turned half aside, was a tall woman in jeans and a long loose shirt. She was holding something, almost cradling it, in her arms.

Elena stepped forward. 'Anna? What is it? What's the matter with Rick?'

Dodie caught her arm. 'Elena, no!'

The girl turned round, looking dazed. She was holding a short, stubby metal garden stake, clutching the wide top where a printed plant label was slotted into it. The pointed end, which tapered sharply, was covered in blood.

'Rick. He's dead,' she said, puzzled, and then sank on to the ground beside the man and began to sob convulsively.

Two

Elena gave her mother an appalled glance, and they cautiously approached the girl.

'Anna? What happened?' Elena asked urgently.

The girl seemed not to hear, but after a moment she looked down at the stake still clutched in her hand, and with a gasp of dismay threw it away from her. 'No!'

'Is Rick really dead?' Elena asked, crouching down beside them while Dodie, whisking off her scarf, picked up the weapon and wrapped it up carefully.

Elena had managed to reach the man's arm. 'He doesn't seem to be breathing, and there's no pulse. I'll try ringing for an ambulance.'

Anna clutched at her. 'He's dead!' she gasped. 'That thing was in his back!'

Elena disengaged herself. 'Mum will look after you. I must try to get help.'

As she ran towards the house Dodie lowered herself to the ground beside the girl, trying to assess her. Was she shocked at the discovery, or guilty of violence and horrified at the result?

'You took out the stake – label, whatever it

is?' she asked.

Anna looked blank. 'Took it out? Yes, of course I did. That is, I must have done. I – I thought – I don't know what I thought! Oh, Rick! He can't be dead! He can't!'

'You shouldn't have touched it,' Dodie said gently.

'Why not? It might have saved him, but I was too late!'

She obviously didn't see the implications, and Dodie wasn't about to try and explain them. 'Did you see anyone else?' she asked instead. 'As you came here, I mean.'

'No. I've just got back. Oh, Rick! What shall I do now? I shouldn't have left you! I should have come back last night!'

With some difficulty Dodie prevented her from casting herself on top of the man, although Dodie was sure by now he was a dead body. She had to keep the girl talking. 'Where have you been?'

'Brighton. To see my parents. But what does that matter? Who did it?'

'The police will find out,' Dodie began, but as she spoke a man appeared from the direction of the house. He was tall, with greying hair, and pale, unhealthy-looking skin. He wore tight khaki shorts and a bright emerald-green T-shirt which strained over a large paunch. He was carrying a tray of bottles and glasses.

'I took the liberty, sir, of bringing – oh my

God, Rick, what's happened?'

Bottles flew in all directions as he dropped the tray and ran towards them. With a furious jerk he thrust aside the girl and tried to lift Rick into a sitting position.

'Leave him,' Dodie snapped, but the man was oblivious, almost shaking the body in his anguish.

'Rick's dead,' the girl muttered, and curled up into a ball, rocking herself to and fro.

'And you did it, you jealous little cat!'

Dodie was still trying to persuade him to let go when she heard breathless voices, and several people came running on to the lawn.

'What's happened?'

'Elena said there'd been an accident. Rick? Is that Rick?'

'Is he dead?'

'Frank, what's happened, man?'

'There isn't any pulse, but he's still fairly warm,' Dodie said as calmly as she could. 'I'm pretty sure he's past help. You'd better stand back, not trample all over the evidence.'

'Evidence?'

From the babble of consternation a calm voice followed by a small woman dressed in white slacks and shirt emerged. 'I'm a doctor,' she said as she knelt beside their host. 'Yes, it's too late,' she said after a minute. 'You'd all better go back to the house. Has Elena sent for the police too?'

'Police?'

'He can't be dead!'

The crowd – though when she looked again Dodie saw there were only four newcomers – burst into renewed exclamations.

'She did it!' The man in shorts pointed to Anna, who was still rocking, oblivious, on the ground. 'That jealous little scrubber stabbed him!'

'Frank, be careful what you say,' the doctor advised. 'Where's the knife?'

Dodie indicated her gruesome parcel. 'It's not a knife. One of those plant label things, like that one over there. It looks quite sharp, but it must have taken a hell of a lot of force to drive it in. I wrapped it up–' she began, but Frank interrupted her.

'He'd been swimming, and she came on him, helpless, and did for him. Oh, Rick!'

He seemed about to throw himself across the body, but the two men grabbed him.

'Gerard, you and Charles take him up to the house,' the doctor ordered. The remaining woman hovered uncertainly. She was breathing heavily and looking rather lost. The doctor glanced at her, and then turned her attention to Anna. 'What happened?' she asked quietly.

When Anna didn't reply Dodie explained. 'We can't do anything for Rick. Let's get Anna up to the house. Jane, give me a hand with her.'

'It's all right for you, Rachel! You're used to dead bodies!'

'Not stabbed in their backs,' the doctor replied grimly. 'Come on, help me. The police will want to see her if she's fit to talk.'

The police wanted to talk to everyone. After the body had been taken away they commandeered the dining room and interviewed Frank first. The others were asked to wait outside or in the sitting room. Anna curled up in the corner of one huge settee, shut her eyes determinedly and refused all offers of help or conversation. After an indecisive few minutes everyone else went outside to sit under the big shades on the terrace. The doctor foraged in the drinks cabinet and poured them all drinks.

'We need this,' she declared, sitting beside Dodie. 'I'm Rachel Dean. I live on the far side of the green. I know Elena, of course, and you must be her mother.'

'Yes. Dodie Fanshaw. Thanks, that's better,' Dodie sighed, sipping the brandy. 'Who is Frank? He behaved like a butler, saying "Sir" very formally and bringing drinks, though he didn't talk like that afterwards, and he certainly didn't dress like one.'

'Frank Rogerson. He's some kind of relative, second cousin or something. He had a breakdown and couldn't get a job, so Rick employed him as a general factotum. He does the garden, sees to the pool, and helps out generally.'

'I suppose he'll inherit as next of kin,' the man who'd been there first and now introduced as Charles Baxter, said in a low voice. 'Rick hasn't any other family, and he wouldn't have left anything to Elizabeth, she took him to the cleaners when they divorced last year. Could Frank have done it? I've never thought him especially stable.'

'Unless it was Anna. You must admit she's inclined to tantrums,' Jane Baxter said.

'Anna's all right. I don't blame her for getting mad at Frank when he called her names right outside the village shop,' Charles said, but at that moment Anna's voice, shouting hysterically, could be heard. Before the rest of them could move Anna rushed out on to the terrace, clutching a cushion to her chest, and flung herself into his arms.

'Don't let him get near me!' she shrieked. 'He killed Rick! He was mad at him, he did it, and now he's threatening me. Keep him off!'

A tall, broad-shouldered man with wildly curling hair and a deeply tanned face was standing in the doorway. 'Hello there. Why is Anna behaving like a banshee? What the devil's going on?'

'Piers? You may well ask!' Charles said, trying to free himself from Anna's convulsive grip.

'I am asking, in case you hadn't noticed. The front door was open, there are all sorts of tradesmen's vans out on the drive, and Anna's flipped again. Where's Rick?'

The doctor explained, and the newcomer sank down on to a chair. 'Ye Gods! Poor Rick! Who did it?'

'That is what the police are trying to discover,' Jane said curtly. She seemed about to speak again, then clamped her lips firmly together and moved her chair a little distance away as if to isolate herself from the group.

The doctor managed to calm Anna down and lead her back into the house, and after watching them go, Piers turned back to the group. He looked at Dodie and Elena and held out his hand. 'Good morning. I'm Piers Walls-Farmer, Rick's publisher.'

He looked far too much the outdoor type to sit behind a desk all day, Dodie thought as she shook hands. He turned to Elena, and his smile grew warm.

'I'm Rick's neighbour, Elena da Rocha, and this is my mother, Dodie Fanshaw.'

He held her hand for a few seconds too long, then asked, 'What's happening?'

'They're questioning Frank now,' Jane said, 'but it's just as likely to have been Anna. She was green with envy when Rick's book was such a roaring success.'

'And I was about to collect his next script. The first draft, anyway. We're down at my in-laws, and as it's only ten minutes away I decided to pop over. Poor Rick! What a tragedy!'

'For you or for Rick?' Gerard Dean, the doctor's husband, who had remained silent so far, asked.

Piers glanced at him and frowned. 'Of course for him, man! I may be a publisher, but I'm not heartless!'

'But his book promises to be a goldmine for you,' Jane said, 'and now there won't be any more.'

'No goldmine when you deduct the advance I paid and the one due for the second book.'

'That will all have to wait, I suppose,' Charles said. 'Even Wallaby Publishing can't speed up the police and the Coroner, let alone probate. And his heir might not choose to sell you the book.'

'You don't understand,' Piers explained, a bored look coming into his eyes. 'He's already contracted for the second. I have the rights to it. I just hope it's in a finished enough state to be publishable.'

'Do we have to divide the spoils before the poor man's even cold?' Gerard asked.

There was an uncomfortable silence. The newcomer frowned, then nodded curtly.

'I suppose I'd better get back, then.'

'I thought you avoided your mother-in-law, Piers,' Charles Baxter said. 'Why the sudden eagerness to return to her company?'

'I do normally, but she's broken her arm and poor Chloe's had to come and minister to her. Looks as though she'll have to stay down here, the old man's useless and they won't even consider a nurse, even though they could afford a dozen. Cheers.'

Before he could retreat, a police constable came to ask Dodie and Elena to go into the dining room.

'And the Detective Inspector would like a quick word with you, too, sir,' he added to Piers. The publisher frowned, then shrugged and sat down next to Jane.

'Interesting undercurrents,' Dodie murmured as they followed the constable inside. 'I wonder if they've had time to bug the terrace?'

'Mother!' Elena chided, both shocked and amused.

'This won't be a cut and dried case,' Dodie predicted quietly. 'There are too many passions swirling around.'

The interview with Detective Inspector Morton was conducted with brisk efficiency. He was a large man, but it was all hard muscle. His hair was black and thick, and he had hard blue eyes set in a rather craggy, almost ugly face. His nose had been broken at some time. Dodie put him in his mid-thirties. His strong personality completely overshadowed that of his companion, a mild-looking, thin man introduced as Detective Constable Bateson.

'Just a few questions for now,' he said. 'We'll take proper statements later on.'

Dodie and Elena described how they had found the body, and Dodie was congratulated, but with a rather suspicious stare, on her forethought in preserving the weapon without touching it.

'My portrayal of a private eye was my first big role,' she said sweetly. 'Pity the critics didn't think so or it might have led to a TV series.'

Detective Inspector Morton frowned slightly. 'I'm sure to have other questions later, but for now you may as well go home,' he said in conclusion, and they found themselves shown briskly to the front door.

Outside, as the door snapped shut behind them, they looked at one another with raised eyebrows, then began to walk down the drive. 'Don't they want us conspiring with the others?' Elena said, and despite the hot sun shivered slightly. 'I wouldn't like to be a criminal being interrogated by him.'

Dodie patted her arm. 'He looked more like a rugger player than a cop, but he's intelligent, I guess. I don't suppose we could have done anything to help if we'd been allowed to stay,' she said. 'That Dr Dean looked very competent, and they know

Anna and the man Frank better than we do. They'll do the good Samaritan bit.'

Elena grinned faintly. 'Rachel seems to run the village as well as her practice, even though she no longer lives at the Manor. The Baxters bought it a few years ago. Her family were squires here for centuries. She'll summon all the help needed. You don't think Anna could have done it, do you?'

'She looked shocked, distraught. I doubt if she could act that well. Tell me about her. There were clearly some jealousies flying around, and why was she so scared of that publisher chappie?'

'She's only lived with Rick for a short while, I think, though I believe she knew him for some time before,' Elena began, but at that moment they had to leap aside as an open-topped Mercedes was driven recklessly through the gateway.

The car slewed to a halt, spraying gravel, and a tall thin woman leapt out and grasped Elena's arm.

'It's not true! Elena, it can't be true! God, it can't be!'

'I'm sorry, Elizabeth, but I'm afraid it is. Rick's dead,' Elena said bluntly.

The woman stared at her, then blinked rapidly a few times, and shook her head. Without another word she got back into the car, reversed blindly out of the gateway, and shot off in the direction of the church.

'The grieving widow? Elizabeth Wilbraham? Or is a divorced wife a widow?' Dodie asked. 'None of my ex-husbands have died yet, so I don't know the protocol. That was Rick's ex-wife, I take it?'

'Yes.'

'Was that Serena's car? It was the same model and colour.'

'No. They both have one. Rick's gifts, I understand. When he gave one to Serena, I'm told as a parting present, Elizabeth insisted on having one too.'

'That must cause some confusion when they're driving around. He sounds like a foolish man,' Dodie said slowly. 'How had she heard so quickly?'

Elena laughed, unamused, and began to walk again. 'In an English village news is transmitted faster than by satellite. And she lives only half a mile away, just along the river. I wouldn't be surprised if Frank had telephoned. I expect he went up to his own room when the police finished with him, and I know he has a mobile phone.'

Dodie was silent until they had almost reached Elena's gateway. 'Within hours we'll be overrun by the press, no doubt. Brandy's all very well for shock, but I need a strong gin and tonic to brace myself for the media invasion. Let's get lunch at the pub before they all descend. When they do, we won't be able to get near the place. And we might hear some gossip.'

'OK, but on a day like this the place will be swarming with townies come to sit by the river. There won't be many locals there.'

Elena was mistaken. The moment she and Dodie walked through the main entrance of the thatched, higgledy-piggledy building a couple of women appeared beside her.

'Elena! Is it true? Has Anna been arrested? I always said that little trollop would come to no good!' the short one with the scraggy neck exclaimed, seizing her arm.

'Did you really find the body?' the short plump one added, her eyes gleaming. 'We heard that you took the pistol away from Anna, and held her until the police came. I couldn't have been so brave! What was it like? Did he bleed much? Or was his head blown away completely? Was it dreadful? Poor Rick!'

Dodie grinned sardonically. 'Actually he'd drowned in the pool after drinking hemlock from a poisoned chalice and then been strung up on the branch of a tree,' she said conversationally. 'How do these incredible rumours get about?'

The women eyed her uncertainly. 'Somebody who saw the police arrive phoned us,' one said. 'What do you mean? They said he'd been shot. Wasn't he?'

'No. He'd been stabbed in the back with

one of those stakes used to label plants. There was no pistol. We found him. Anna had taken out the stake, she'd found him first and was so shocked I imagine she thought taking it out would stop him dying. That's fact, not rumour. Now, excuse us, but we really need a drink.'

Dodie turned away and walked towards the bar. 'Sorry, Elena, hope they aren't your bosom pals. I can't bear ghouls.'

'A couple of bored women with no interests except malicious gossip,' Elena said softly. 'But I thought you wanted gossip?'

'Gossip about people, not lip-licking speculation,' Dodie replied. 'Where's the best place to hear some, the bar or the terrace?'

'Through here,' Elena said after they'd ordered drinks and bar snacks, and led the way through a low archway into a dimly lit room where none of the sun penetrated. 'This is where the locals come to get away from the others.'

'Who all want to sit outside being rustic, no doubt,' Dodie said scornfully, looking at the unevenly plastered walls and blackened beams.

Tables made from thick planks of highly polished wood, surrounded by cushioned stools and benches, took up so much space it was difficult to squeeze past to a couple of empty places. One glance told Dodie these people were not townsfolk out for a day beside the river. There were a couple of ruddy-cheeked men in check shirts, probably farmers, accompanied by plump women, but most were dressed in casual, expensive clothes, not tourist gear.

The hum of conversation ceased abruptly, then a few people tried to resume their conversations, pretending to ignore the newcomers. One of the farmers was more open.

'Is it true Mr Wilbraham's dead? Murdered?' he asked. 'That's what we heard, but no one knows the truth of it.'

Elena nodded. 'It looks like it, he'd been stabbed.'

'Poor devil. He was a randy old sod, but there was no harm in him. He was always ready to cough up for the church restoration or the cricket club. More than that wife of his, even though she'd been born and bred here.'

Three

Dodie and Elena were lying on softly cushioned garden loungers on Elena's lawn. By the time they had finished lunch, a couple of television vans and several photographers had made camp opposite Rick's house.

Elena had managed to shut and lock her driveway gates before they'd been spotted, much to the disgust of some reporters who'd pleaded for inside knowledge.

Dodie was thinking about her appointment with the specialist in two days time, and hoping the tests he was suggesting would not involve a spell in hospital. She loathed hospitals.

Elena was browsing lazily through the Sunday papers. Suddenly, throwing down the last section, she sat up. 'Honestly, I never even open most of the bits of this paper!'

Dodie opened her eyes. 'Mm? You know, they ought to pass a law insisting on siestas when the weather's as hot as this.'

'It's OK, you weren't snoring.' Elena chuckled.

'I never snore. Not once did my snoring figure in any divorce. What did you say, when you so inconsiderately deprived your ancient mother of a well-deserved after-lunch snooze?'

'Did you find out anything useful at the pub? Get the gossip you wanted?' Elena asked.

Dodie sat up and swung her legs over the side of the lounger. She looked at her ankles complacently. Poor legs couldn't be disguised, and hers were still good. She could use all the tricks she'd learnt during her stage and film career to make good other deficiencies. For a moment she wondered whether she ought to go in for some kind of exercise, try to get back a sylph-like figure such as those possessed by geriatric keep-fit instructors on TV, then she shook her head. Too much time and effort involved. And too few scones and cream.

'A bitchy lot, your local women. They seemed to know all about Mr Wilbraham and his love life. Is it true, what that red-haired one was hinting, that Serena Coates broke up his marriage?'

'It could be. I wasn't here then, but I've heard rumours, and she and Elizabeth certainly avoid one another. But he and Serena broke up several years ago, and she married Daniel North. Rick may have been working towards the split from Elizabeth before then, but they didn't get divorced until a year ago. From the gossip, there was a big row over money. Serena and Daniel both seem to get on well with Rick, but woe betide any unwary hostess who asks Elizabeth to the same function as any of them. If ever they meet there's a race to see which one of them walks out first, even if it's only the village fête. Makes life difficult.'

'Do the village worthies side with either of them?'

'I think they did, at first. Elizabeth has lived here all her life, and Serena's a relative newcomer. She's only been here a matter of a dozen or so years, though I believe she was born not far away.'

'Do any of Elizabeth's family live here still?'

'No. Her father was the vicar for ages, and when he died her mother went to live in Canada with Elizabeth's brother. I think people were surprised Elizabeth didn't go too, after the divorce.'

'It would certainly have been more comfortable all round.'

'Instead she bought a house just on the village outskirts, about half a dozen plots further along the river, not far from Serena's. Hers is technically in the next parish, but there's only a couple of fields between.'

Dodie yawned. 'Tell me about Anna. You've met her around the place. What's she like?'

Elena thought for a moment. 'She's shy, I think. She doesn't go out of her way to meet people, and she always seems a bit wary when you talk to her. Some people interpret that as stand-offishness, but I don't think it is. And once or twice I've heard her yelling at Rick. She seems to have a pretty volatile temper.'

'Enough to make her murder someone? Is she sensitive about being with Rick? Though I'd have thought no one cared these days.'

'No, but having his ex only a few doors away, even if the doors are pretty distantly spaced, might be a bit inhibiting. Not to mention Serena popping in all the time. And Frank detests her, as must have been obvious. She can't have an exactly comfortable time of it.'

'Was he faithful to her?'

'I think that's unlikely. From all people say he's always been like an alley cat. And I understand he spends quite a few nights in London without her. Even if she doesn't know for certain, she must suspect. But apparently she's the first girl he's ever had to stay for more than the odd weekend.'

'So there's something she has the others didn't. Just writing interests in common?'

'Somehow I doubt it.'

'I wonder why she reacted so violently to that publisher fellow? That was over the top.'

Elena shrugged. 'Reaction to the shock, perhaps? Hysteria? She'd probably just realized that Rick was truly dead. Before then she seemed stunned.'

Dodie yawned again. 'I could do with a cuppa.'

'I'll go and make it.'

Dodie lay back with her eyes closed, trying to recall every comment she'd heard in the pub about Rick Wilbraham and his women, but the sun was hot, especially for England, even in June, the lounger was comfortable, and she still hadn't recovered from jet-lag.

The sound of rustling bushes and voices dragged her from another snooze and she looked up.

Elena was standing beside her, holding a tray. 'Mum, here's Frank. He says the police have arrested Anna.'

Frank Rogerson, with his pasty face and straggly, greying hair, some bright gold laburnum petals on his hair and more attached to his clothes, loomed above Dodie. He still wore the same clothes he'd had on that morning, and his flabby flesh bulged around the hems of his shorts and sleeves.

Dodie sat up, blinking to dispel the sleepiness from her eyes.

'Anna?' she asked. 'Have they really arrested her, or just taken her away for questions?'

Frank shrugged. 'What difference does it make? They'll arrest her in the end. She did it. Those vultures from the papers and TV are just waiting for it. I had to push through the hedge so's to avoid them, or I couldn't have got here.'

'We can't be sure they'll arrest her,' Elena said gently. 'Tea, Frank?'

He shook his head impatiently. 'No. Thanks, but I don't feel like anything. I still feel sick when I think of poor Rick lying there, covered in blood. He was so good to me.'

'There wasn't much blood, actually,' Elena said thoughtfully. 'I suppose he bled internally. It wasn't as gory as I'd imagined it to be.'

'You said Anna was jealous,' Dodie said after a pause, sipping her own tea and resolutely ignoring the scones Elena was offering her. She found it hard to understand Frank. He was at the same time obsequious and truculent. Was it just the consequence of being a poor relation, the effects of his cousin's murder, or were there other causes? 'What did you mean?'

Frank looked at her. 'She was green with envy because he was going to get another huge chunk of the advance when his second book was delivered,' he said. 'She pretended to be a writer too, but she couldn't compare with him, and she distracted him. Rick was...' his voice broke, but he swallowed hard and managed to continue, '...one of the greatest! And now he'll only ever have two books for us to remember him!'

'I'm sure you'll have some memories others can't share,' Dodie said comfortingly. 'You're a cousin, aren't you? And about the same age.' She was flattering him: he looked much older. 'You'll have memories of when you were boys, young men.'

'No!' He shook his head and scrubbed at his eyes with a clenched fist. 'You don't understand. I never knew Rick until a year or so back.'

Dodie leaned over and patted his knee. 'Don't try to explain. It's too soon to talk.'

'But I want to! People can be vicious, and there are already some who say I took advantage of him.'

'I hadn't known Rick for long, but I can't imagine anyone doing that,' Elena said briskly.

Frank nodded, and bit his lip. 'No, he was clever, Rick, ready for all their tricks.'

'How did you meet?' Dodie asked.

Frank took several deep breaths and seemed calmer when he finally spoke. 'My mother moved away when she married and lost touch with the rest of the family. They didn't like my father, there was some unpleasantness, I think. Then, when Rick's divorce was in the papers, soon after he got that huge advance for the first book, she mentioned we were related. She and Rick's father were cousins, you see.'

'And you got in touch?' Dodie prompted when he sank into some private reflection.

'Not at once. Dad had left us years before. Never heard from him again. My mother was sick, and when she died I wrote to tell him. Rick, that is. He invited me to come here, and – well, we got on fine, and he suggested I made my home with him.'

'That was kind.'

'Just like Rick, always ready to help anyone down on their luck, despite what some people say.'

'Oh, do they?'

'Only those who envied him. He was a good businessman, and they resented him doing better than they could. And you always get the odd employee who's never satisfied, however well they're treated.'

'And were you? Down on your luck?' Dodie asked.

'I never got any qualifications. Had to leave school and get a job as soon as I could, to help out. I had to take anything going, any job, whatever was there. Then I'd lost my job, you see, while I'd been caring for Mum. Now it's harder to find work, unless you've got all sorts of letters after your name,' he added bitterly.

'And Rick offered help?'

'Yes. But I wouldn't take charity. I insisted that if I stayed I worked for him, and earned my keep. His gardener had just retired, but the old fellow hadn't been up to it for years, and the place was in a state, needed a lot doing. I did twice what he did, and soon got in good nick again. Then that little trollop has to come and kill him!'

He stood up abruptly, and with a muttered apology walked away from them. They watched him scramble through the hedge, and when he was out of sight Dodie took a deep sigh.

'He's not exactly prepossessing, is he? And from all I've heard of Rick Wilbraham I wouldn't have expected him to suffer someone like that around, who seems surly, and has a huge chip on his shoulder.'

'But he seemed to admire Rick.'

'And you think Rick would put up with the rest for the sake of some facile admiration? Was the famous author like that? Assuming he offered it to Rick's face, and wasn't just putting it on for our benefit. And he certainly has it in for Anna, and would probably like to see her on trial.'

'It would have been interesting to overhear some of what went on in that house,' Elena said.

'It sounds like the Garden of Eden,' Dodie said thoughtfully, 'but which of them was the snake?'

Elena frowned. 'Do you think Anna did it after all? I only saw her for a second or so before I went to call an ambulance, but she seemed so shocked.'

'I suppose if you'd stabbed your lover in a fit of rage you'd be shocked all right,' Dodie said. 'But I don't believe Anna did it. The police can't have arrested her so quickly.'

'They say most murders are domestic, and most are solved swiftly or not at all,' Elena said quietly.

Dodie shrugged. 'I can't believe Anna did it, and if the police do they aren't using common sense.'

Dodie was in danger of drifting off to sleep again, so she forced herself to fetch a writing pad from the house. Elena had vanished, having cleared away the tea tray, and everywhere was quiet. Rejecting the lounger, which was too comfortable, Dodie seated herself on a wooden bench and started to make lists.

'Opportunity,' she muttered to herself. 'Who could have been there? Anna, before we found her, and presumably Frank, before that.' She wrote down the names, then paused and nibbled the end of her pen until the taste of ink penetrated her absorption. 'Ugh. In books they construct neat timetables and work out who could have been where. Trouble is, I haven't enough information.'

'Talking to yourself won't help,' Elena said, laughing as she approached. 'What are you doing?'

'Where have you been?'

'In my bedroom, making a few phone calls.'

'Oh. To Marcus? I'm looking forward to meeting him. Will he be coming down while I'm here?'

'No,' Elena said rather abruptly. 'He's away, business trip, to Seattle,' she added. 'And before you ask, I'm not sure when he'll be back.'

Dodie tried not to react. Elena clearly didn't want to confide in her. She had bent down to pick up Dodie's pad.

'What's this? Suspects?'

Dodie sighed. 'Just people with the opportunity. The trouble is, there could have been a dozen people there without our knowing. How many ways into that place are there?'

Elena ticked them off on her fingers. 'The main gateway, the way we went.'

'And Serena was coming out of there. She may have seen someone.' Dodie took back the pad and wrote.

'There's a smaller gateway further along the road with a path that leads straight to the kitchen door,' Elena said. 'The kitchen's at the front, in the far corner, with Rick's study behind it. In the days when butchers and bakers and candlestick makers delivered, their boys used to go in that way on their bikes, I imagine. Then it's possible for someone to come along the river bank in either direction.'

'There isn't a public path. Your gardens go right down to the river bank.'

'Yes, but the bank right by the water is hidden from most of the houses, the gardens are so steep and several of them, like Rick's, are terraced. People can get along there without much risk of being seen from the gardens. In Rick's garden there's at least a dozen steps from where we found him down to the bank proper.'

'Still, it would be risky to come through the gardens in case people were down by the bank.'

'Not so difficult as you might think,' Elena said thoughtfully. 'Beyond Rick's house there are only a few more houses until you get to fields, and some of those are holiday homes. Not everyone comes every weekend, so probably some are empty. Then in one there's a very old man who's practically bedridden. He never gets down to the river, I'm sure. And a couple of sisters who always go to church, so their house would be empty then too. It wouldn't be a tremendous risk, and there are plenty of bushes to hide behind anyway.'

Dodie sighed. 'And someone could come from across the river in a boat. Like your mermaid. Where would she have hired her boat, and what's happened to it?'

'There are boatyards in both directions that hire out rowing boats and small motor boats.'

'So that's two more possibilities. As well as someone with their own boat, or even swimming across the river from the far side.' She began to pull herself to her feet. 'Let's go and see whether our mermaid's boat is lying abandoned somewhere.'

'It's stuck in some reeds a few yards out,

on that small island. A pair of swans were looking very interested. I went to look while you were asleep.'

'Resting my eyes,' Dodie corrected with a grin.

'I was ringing the boatyards to ask whether they'd lost one. So far there's none missing, but several were hired for the whole day and aren't expected back yet. The yards don't close till late in the height of summer.'

'It doesn't help, anyway,' Dodie said, returning to the major mystery. 'Lots of people could have got in by various methods. Who could have wanted Rick dead?'

'Anna, if they'd quarrelled.'

'Frank, ditto. What about Elizabeth?'

'She'd have no motive, since she's doing very well out of their settlement. I believe he agreed to a percentage of his income, and with his first book doing so well even in hardback that must be far more than he or she ever imagined it would be, and they'd expect it to get even better.'

'Women don't always consider that if they're hopping mad,' Dodie pointed out. 'What's Elizabeth like?'

'You saw her. She's dramatic, liable to fly into a rage, yet I suspect she never does anything without careful consideration.'

A cloud had covered the sun and Dodie shivered. 'We don't know enough. There could be all sorts of other people with much stronger motives. Did Rick employ a housekeeper?'

'Yes, but she doesn't live in. And he has a cleaning woman twice a week, Mrs Burns who comes to me on Fridays. And I happen to know they've both gone away on a cheap weekend break organized by the Women's Institute.'

'Was Rick generally liked in the village?'

'I think so. A bit of a philanderer, but they still liked him.'

'He was small and skinny, a bit like an elf with that funny little pointed beard, not the sort of figure women like, I'd have thought,' Dodie said reflectively.

Elena grinned. 'Not our type, eh? Perhaps it was the aura of money. Or power. That's supposed to be an aphrodisiac. He was generous, and as far as I know hadn't offended anyone.'

Dodie gathered up her pad and pencil, picked up her handbag and a wide straw hat she'd tipped over her eyes as she dozed, and stood up. 'I'm going in. Didn't you say we were invited out to a meal tonight?'

'Yes. I'd almost forgotten. The Deans. I'd better ring Rachel and make sure it's still OK.'

'So almost anyone could have had the opportunity,' Dodie mused as she walked towards the house. 'Who had a motive?'

'I wouldn't have thought Anna had been

with Rick long enough for him to make a will in her favour,' Elena said, collecting the cushions from the loungers. 'I doubt if Frank would be mentioned in a will yet either.'

'Does Elizabeth get anything?'

'I haven't any idea. You're more of an expert on divorce settlements than I am.'

Dodie chuckled. 'I got lump sums both times. None of this uncertainty about whether they'd live to go on shelling out, and no arguments about increases. That's why we're still friends.'

Elena grinned affectionately at her. 'I wonder what happens to the book?'

Dodie glanced sharply at her. 'Which one? The new one that he's just written?'

'Yes. That publisher chap, Piers Walls-Farmer, wasn't it, said it was only the first draft. Will that be enough? He'll still want to publish, I imagine, when the first book was such a success.'

'And the notoriety of a murder case will make the second one sell even better,' Dodie said. 'I suppose they could get someone else to finish it. A ghostwriter, don't they call it?'

Elena shuddered. 'How macabre!'

They had reached the house and Dodie went to soak in the bath. She was still sleepy, and her mind wasn't working at all efficiently. There was something she ought to have remembered, but try as she could, it refused to surface. She poured bubble-bath lavishly, and gave a deep sigh as she sank into the water. A confused medley of images floated on the surface of her mind – swimming pools, swirling rivers, mermaids on rocks, submerged boats and, causing her to shudder with sudden revulsion, daggers dripping with blood.

She sat up and began to soap herself with fierce energy. She had no intention of getting mixed up in a murder investigation. She didn't know any of the people involved in this killing. She'd never met any of them before today, and it had nothing to do with her. The police could solve it, and surely the police here in England would be conscientious enough, and clever enough, to find the murderer. Detective Inspector Morton looked competent and determined. She thought longingly of her house in London. Even in this weather it seemed more attractive than this riverside village now murder had appeared. Elena had asked if she wanted to go back to London. She'd persuade Elena to go with her, and if her tests proved negative they might even take a trip somewhere, Scotland or the Lake District. No, not the Lakes. She wanted to get away from water.

She was dressed in a loose-fitting dark-blue silk dress and applying eyeliner when Elena came into her room.

'Frank just rang,' Elena said. 'The police have released Anna, but she's refusing point blank to stay in the house with him. Apparently she's hysterical, and ran straight out when they brought her home. Frank thinks she's on her way here.'

Four

As she finished speaking there was a loud peal on the doorbell.

'Anna, presumably. Seems like our day for rescuing damsels in distress,' Dodie said.

'I can't turn her away, can I? She was accusing him, so I suppose she's afraid of Frank.'

A pale-faced Anna, who'd been leaning against the front door, almost fell on to the hall floor as Elena opened it.

'Thank goodness you're in! I had to climb over the gate, and they nearly caught me! Elena, please help me! I don't know what to do! I can't stay there! But the police say I've got to stay in the village. I want to go home!'

'You look exhausted. Don't worry, Anna, you can stay here.'

'May I? Oh, Elena, you've saved my life! I couldn't bear to be in the same house as Frank. I'd be too scared.'

'Scared? Of Frank, you mean?'

'Yes, of course. He must have killed Rick.'

'Why should he? I'd have thought he'd be better off with him alive,' Dodie said.

Anna frowned at her. 'He resented Rick being successful. Besides, I think he's mad. He was always wandering around the house muttering to himself. And every so often he'd go off by himself on his own, and never say where, or when he'd be coming back. Rick used to get mad at him, say he couldn't depend on him.'

'Did they have arguments?' Dodie asked quickly.

'Arguments? They had flaming rows, there was one the night before last, before I went away to see my parents. And the police let it out that Frank had broken some windows last night. I don't know where, I didn't stay long enough to see them.'

'The conservatory?' Elena exclaimed. 'Then it hadn't been Elizabeth? We heard glass smashing and car doors slamming.'

'I gather Frank was trying to blame Elizabeth, said she'd been round, and there'd been a more serious row between her and Rick than normal. I don't know, I don't believe anything he says.'

'Well, never mind that. You'll be safe here. But have you been with the police all afternoon?' Elena demanded.

'Yes. They had so many questions, and

they went over and over everything until I was ready to scream!'

'Would you like a drink? How about brandy? Or maybe you'd prefer coffee?'

'Brandy, please. I still feel so shaky. It hasn't really sunk in yet, that Rick's actually dead.'

She sat down in a large armchair, curling up with her arms protectively round her knees.

'But they didn't charge you?' Dodie asked as Elena went across to the decanter and poured out the brandy.

'They wanted to, but in the end they had to believe me. The doctor who came, the police doctor, I mean, not Rachel, said he'd been dead at least an hour, and I was on the train then.'

'You could prove that?'

Anna shook her head. 'Not directly. I didn't see anyone I knew on the train, or at the station. It's not very busy on Sundays. But Serena saw me walking to the village and gave me a lift.'

'Serena? That's less than half a mile from her house.'

'She'd been down to the station to the postbox there, she said. It's a big slot, and she didn't want to have to bend something, as she'd have to if she posted it here in Markenlea.'

'We saw Serena coming out of Rick's drive

just before we got there,' Dodie said. 'That was why she was there, then.'

'Yes, dropping me off, and I'd only just found him...' She sniffed and searched in vain for a tissue. Silently Elena handed her a box and she took a handful and blew her nose. 'Thanks. He wasn't in the house, and I'd just found him when you came, so there wasn't time, was there?'

Dodie didn't reply. She was considering Anna. The girl, despite her recent display of hysteria towards Frank, seemed much calmer than before. More questions would have to wait. She looked at her watch, and Elena nodded.

'Anna, let me show you the spare room. Did you bring a nightie or anything?'

Anna shook her head. 'I forgot. I wasn't thinking straight, I just wanted to get out of there.'

'Never mind, you can borrow one, and I'll find you a new toothbrush. Then I'm going to suggest a sleeping tablet, or you'll have nightmares. Mother and I are going to Rachel's, we'll only be a short way off. There's a phone extension in the spare room if you need us.'

'Oh, God, I'm ruining your evening! I'm so sorry!'

'No problem, but you'll feel better after you've had a good sleep. Have you eaten today?'

Anna shuddered. 'Lots of stewed tea, and a dried-up sandwich which I couldn't swallow. I'm not hungry. I couldn't eat.'

'You must try. I've got some soup, I'll heat that and leave it and there are some scones we didn't eat earlier.'

'I'll do that while you show Anna her room,' Dodie offered.

Ten minutes later she and Elena were walking across the green. They had slipped out of a side gate which was concealed from the press pack by a curve in the hedge, walked for a little way in the opposite direction, and were across the road before anyone saw them, or knew which house they'd come from.

'She was really frightened,' Elena said a little defensively. 'I couldn't do anything else.'

'Of course not. She was terrified, and presumably she believes Frank killed him,' Dodie said slowly. 'He had the opportunity, but he'd have to be a good actor to carry off all that angst. But what could he gain? I wonder if he is Rick's heir?'

'He'd be a fool to do it otherwise. He had a good home, an easy job, and from all I've ever heard he was pretty much destitute before he found Rick.'

'But they had the closest connections with Rick, in the domestic sense. It doesn't make sense for either him or Anna to do away with their home unless they stood to gain more from it.'

'Serena is out of it, if she and Anna were together.'

Dodie shook her head. 'Not entirely. If Rick died an hour earlier either of them could have killed him and been well away, back towards the town, long before they met,' she said slowly. 'Anna can't prove which train she was on, and I presume there's more than one, even on Sunday morning?'

'Yes, but Serena gains more from a live author and lots more books, and none from a dead one.'

'Unless she were jealous of Anna.'

'I'm sure that affair was over. Rachel will know. They are good friends, unlikely though it might seem.'

'Women can be jealous long after they've finished with a man. And they were working together.'

Elena nodded. 'No doubt we'll hear more tonight. And here we are, this is the Deans' house.'

It was a small but perfectly proportioned early Georgian house, overlooking the green close to the cricket pavilion, with a short path between closely mown squares of grass. Elena had told Dodie it had originally been the dower house belonging to the Manor. They had barely opened the gate before Gerard appeared in the doorway, a welcoming smile on his face and a bottle of champagne in his hand.

'Come in, come in,' he welcomed them. 'I opened this, thought we needed cheering up.'

'I told him it looked too much like a celebration,' Rachel said, appearing beside him. 'We're sitting outside, it's such a lovely evening. Come right through.'

An elderly couple were already there, seated on elegant wrought-iron garden chairs. Rachel introduced them as Dr and Mrs Carruthers, her former partner and his wife.

'Philip took me on when I'd qualified, and took me in hand, taught me far more than medical school,' Rachel said affectionately. 'And Patricia used to be a nurse, and taught me how to get my own way with patients and not let them know it wasn't all their idea.'

'You always get your own way, with everyone, not just patients,' Gerard said, laughing. Rachel frowned slightly, then shrugged.

Dodie glanced sharply at him. He was handsome in a big, blond manner, and looked athletic. He wore casual but beautifully cut slacks, and a thin silk sweater, and she could see the muscles of his legs, as well as those on his arms. Had he meant his comment as a joke or was there something more serious underlying his remark? She recalled Elena's comment that Rachel ran the village, from her position as the daughter of a long line of village squires. What sort of marriage was this? She must find out more about Gerard's own background.

Just then a girl who promised to be the image of Rachel in a few years came out of the house carrying an ice bucket. Rachel smiled at her and introduced their daughter, Charlotte.

She was about twelve, Dodie judged, and seemed free of the usual adolescent gaucherie.

'Hello. I saw you this morning, I was riding across the green with my friend Emily Baxter.'

'Charlotte's pony-mad,' Gerard said in mock despair. 'I seem to spend most weekends taking her to meets and gymkhanas.'

'It wouldn't take so much time if I didn't have to graze Muffin right on the far side of the river,' Charlotte said. 'Why can't we find a field nearer the house?'

Rachel sighed. 'Not now, darling. You know there isn't anywhere available.'

As they sipped the champagne Dodie steered the conversation. Dr Carruthers, she discovered, had retired from the practice ten years earlier, and they had moved to live in Devon. They were visiting a daughter who lived in Henley, and Rachel had taken the opportunity to ask them over.

'Tell me about this excitement you had this morning,' Dr Carruthers asked when Rachel, with a murmured excuse, took Charlotte with her, saying she needed to check the oven. 'We heard it on the local radio as we were driving over.'

'You didn't know him?' Elena asked. 'I understood he'd lived in the area all his life.'

'He lived in Upper Markenlea, then Reading, I believe, but he was never my patient,' Dr Carruthers said. 'No, we've hardly been back in the past few years. I never met the poor man, though of course I've read his book.'

'Poor? He was rich,' Gerard put in. 'Persuaded other suckers to invest in get-rich-quick schemes, and then got out when he saw the bubble bursting, leaving us to find out the hard way you can't get rich quick.'

'You lost money?' Dr Carruthers asked, surprised. 'I thought you were the ultra-cautious type of fellow.'

'I am, usually,' Gerard said ruefully. 'I didn't lose a lot, but I don't like losing anything. Who does? Have some more to drink.'

'What sort of scheme were you interested in?' Patricia Carruthers asked. 'We were approached by someone we met at a charity concert, with a plan for some kind of investment importing rare animals like ostriches for meat. It sounded highly unlikely.'

'There's quite a lot of speciality meats around now, but it wasn't exactly tactful to tout that idea round at a concert to support conservation,' her husband snorted. 'I suppose Rick Wilbraham's schemes involved property speculation?'

'Yes, office blocks, housing, even a private hospital, as well as health clubs and hotels. He had fingers in every pie. He persuaded me to invest in a health club. I did it mainly because I thought it would increase my business, not to make a profit. I'm a physiotherapist, mainly sports injuries,' he explained to Dodie.

'What went wrong?' she asked. 'I thought the world was full of fitness freaks these days.'

Gerard smiled ruefully. 'He got the foundations in, and then sold his share to someone else just before the bottom dropped out of the market, and this fellow was bankrupt within weeks. That meant we all had to sell out at a big loss. Rick said he'd meant to warn me to get out too, but his secretary had lost the letter he sent.'

'Hard luck, old chap.' Dr Carruthers heaved a sigh. 'So what happened to him? We heard he'd been stabbed. Is that true?'

Rachel had come back from the kitchen. She was standing behind her husband, her hands on his shoulders.

'Sorry, but I'll have to break it up. The

soufflé's ready and won't wait. Rick was stabbed, but my bet's on him having drowned.'

'That was interesting,' Elena said as they strolled back across the green through the soft summer night. There were a couple of street lamps near the road, but most of the faint illumination came from a full moon. The television vans had gone, and Elena unlocked the gates, but left them closed. 'It seemed convincing, Rachel's idea that he'd drowned, and no doubt the post-mortem will prove it. I wonder, by the way, when they'll have the inquest?'

'Soon, won't they? It's usually a brief affair in this sort of case, then they'll adjourn until the police have solved it.'

'Or not, perhaps.'

'It explains something that worried me,' Dodie said. 'It wasn't a very suitable weapon, and it must have been grabbed on impulse. Besides, there was too little blood, and Anna's skirt was completely free of it apart from a smear where she'd clutched the stake to her. I'm sure that if she'd stabbed him when he was alive more blood would have spurted out.'

Elena shivered. 'But why should someone stab him when he was dead? It wouldn't mislead anyone for long. Was it sheer hatred, vindictiveness, or perhaps making sure in case he wasn't drowned after all?'

'And why take the trouble of heaving him out of the pool after he was drowned?'

'Might the drowning have been accidental?'

'Was it likely? Elena, you've been to his house before, used his pool. I assume he was at least a competent swimmer?'

'Yes, quite good, in fact.' Elena halted suddenly. 'Do you think he could have been hit on the head, perhaps, then thrown in, or even hit his head falling?'

'None of that explains why anyone should bother to get him out and then stab him.'

'No, I suppose not. But it would have taken quite a lot of strength for one person to heave him out. It's terribly difficult to pull anyone out of water unless they're cooperating, helping you. That surely eliminates some of the women?'

Dodie shook her head. 'Anna's quite tall, and so are Serena and Elizabeth. That would help, and Rick was very small for a man, probably weighed no more than any of them. I noticed, too, that the water level was very near the top of the pool, so he could have been rolled over the edge without too much trouble. Then it would be easy to drag him down to the next level. But why?'

'If that's what happened maybe whoever it was hadn't much time, and didn't want to risk being seen from the house. And if they thought there was any chance he might not be dead, or could be revived, they made sure. Using that stake must have been a sudden impulse, they grabbed it because it was there.'

'Now I remember what puzzled me,' Dodie exclaimed. 'I picked up a towel, and it was wet. Someone had used it, but not Rick. He was wet where he'd been lying, though the sun had dried his back.'

'So the murderer must have used it to dry himself.'

Dodie nodded absently. They walked the rest of the way in silence, let themselves in quietly, and went up the stairs. Dodie peeped into the spare room and reported that Anna was fast asleep, and had eaten only one of the scones.

'It looks as though she fell asleep almost at once. She must have been shattered. And so am I, so I'll be off to bed too. No doubt we'll hear more in the morning.'

It was late when Dodie woke, to another brilliantly sunny day. For a moment she thought it was the day of her appointment in Harley Street, then relaxed. That was tomorrow. So much had happened yesterday.

Her bedroom was at the back of the house and her window was open. She could hear voices on the terrace outside and, looking down, saw Elena and Anna sitting there with mugs of coffee.

She showered quickly, pulled on a loose caftan of fine cotton, and went to join them.

'How do you feel this morning, Anna?' she asked briskly. 'Better, I hope?'

Anna nodded and tried to smile. She didn't make a bad attempt, Dodie considered, and began to wonder just how deep the girl's attachment to Rick Wilbraham had been. Had she loved the man, or was it his money which had attracted her? Or quite possibly it had been his fame as a writer.

'I feel much better after a good sleep,' Anna said. 'I'm so grateful to you for taking me in, Elena.'

'No problem. Stay as long as you need. But afterwards, have you somewhere to go? A family? You'll have to think about getting a job, I suppose?'

'My parents live in Brighton, I don't really fancy going there, but I can go and stay with my sister, in Wembley. Then I'll have to try and get a job temping.'

'Is that what you did before? Secretarial work?'

'Well, yes, some of the time. But I also worked freelance, copy-editing for a children's publisher. I'd like to get into a publishing house full time, but it's not easy.'

'And then you met Rick. You were helping him with secretarial work, weren't you?' Dodie asked.

Anna flushed, and for a moment there was a bitter look in her eyes. She dropped her gaze swiftly, and took a deep breath. 'Yes,' she said after a long pause.

'What about your own writing?' Elena asked quickly. 'Were you doing children's books, or an adult novel?'

'Oh, nothing so ambitious. I did some short stories, but before I met Rick I was doing magazine articles. Not that I had much success. It was Rick who – who persuaded me to try a novel, but I hadn't got far.'

'When this is all over, no doubt you'll go back to it,' Dodie said, trying to be bracing.

She knew very little about the temperament of writers, but plenty about stage performers. They frequently drowned their sorrows in more and harder work. She winced inwardly. Talk of drowning was hardly tactful. It was fortunate she hadn't voiced the thought out loud. Then she reconsidered. Anna didn't yet know Rachel's suspicions. It would be instructive to see her reactions and, in the case of murder, one couldn't be too squeamish about offending the sensibilities of potential suspects.

'Last night Rachel said she thought it possible that Rick had been drowned before he was stabbed,' she said, watching Anna closely.

Anna looked at her and frowned. 'But

how? He was a good swimmer. He wouldn't drown.'

'Not unless someone helped him. Or it's possible he fell in and hit his head.'

'Then it could have been an accident,' Anna exclaimed, looking instantly more cheerful.

'If so, why was he dragged out and then stabbed?'

'Oh. Yes, I see. But in that case, whoever did it would have been soaking wet!'

'The mermaid!' Elena exclaimed.

'Mermaid?' Anna looked startled, and cast a wary look round the garden. 'What mermaid? What do you mean?'

Elena explained. 'A girl who scrambled up from the river yesterday afternoon. She said the boat had overturned.'

'And that was just before we changed to go to Rick's house. If Rick had been dead for an hour, that could fit in,' Dodie said thoughtfully.

'You mean she could have come by boat, then overturned it to hide the fact that she was soaking wet from the swimming pool?' Elena asked. 'Surely that's too complicated to be likely?'

'I'd like to know who she was,' Dodie said. 'That's more important.'

'Another of Rick's women?' Anna said, and this time her bitter tone was undisguised.

'He had many, did he?' Dodie asked, trying to inject as much sympathetic understanding into her voice as she could.

Anna shrugged. 'He didn't try to hide it. Everyone thought I was some sort of a special girlfriend because I moved into the house, but I wasn't there for that. Once he'd persuaded me to help him there, with the typing, he didn't bother. Half the time I'm certain he was with someone else in London. But I never knew who.'

'So another suspect, unknown,' Dodie said, looking at her curiously. 'Why were you there then?'

Anna shook her head. 'I'm not making sense. Sorry. That sleeping pill was powerful. I was helping him do research, type up notes, that sort of thing. It helped because I'm a writer too, I knew how to do it in a way that helped him best. I wonder what's going to happen now? Do you think the police will want to see us all again? Do we have to stay put, or do you think I could go up to London? There's something I have to do there. Someone I must see. And I suppose I'd better sign on at one or two agencies, to see if there's much work available.'

Five

'I'll drive you to the station,' Dodie offered when Anna, reluctantly, had given in to their insistence and checked with the police that they had no objection to her visiting London, so long as she was available for a further interview the following morning. 'I can be back before you need to leave for your appointment, Elena.'

Elena was gathering together papers and samples. 'You can drop me off, it's not far, and I can walk home. Mrs Burroughs said any time after nine, and as she's left it so late there'll be loads to decide. Honestly, fancy trying to arrange a huge wedding at only two months' notice! But can you go into the supermarket and get me a few things?' she added. 'The village shop's handy, but doesn't have a very wide selection.'

They set off, and Dodie glanced towards Rick's house as they passed the drive entrance. A lone reporter sat in his car outside, and a police car and a couple of unmarked vans were visible inside the gates. As they passed the further small entrance Frank appeared on an ancient bicycle.

Anna shivered. 'I'm amazed the police

haven't arrested him,' she muttered. 'It's so obvious! He was alone with Rick all night, no one else had been there until I arrived.'

'We can't be sure of that. Elena and I didn't see him, and we went down to where we found you because no one else was about. Anyone could have come in without being seen if Frank was in the kitchen. Did you look for him when you got back?'

'No. Serena dropped me in the drive, and I went straight in.'

'It's the next turning on the right,' Elena interrupted. 'Stop here, I can walk up the lane.'

Dodie did so, Elena waved farewell, and as she moved off again Dodie resumed her questioning. Fortunately Anna didn't seem to mind the inquisition.

'Was the door unlocked?'

Anna shook her head. 'No, but I have a key. I didn't need to ring. In any case, the French doors are usually open when it's sunny, I could have got in that way. Anyone could, if they knew the house.'

'Where would Frank have been?' Dodie asked.

'I suppose he was in the kitchen, getting glasses ready and so on.'

'Would that be his usual routine before a party?'

'Yes. Rick was glad to leave all that to him.'

'Was everything normal? Did you go upstairs?'

'I didn't have a suitcase. I keep spare things at my parents' house, and I usually only go down for the occasional night, so I don't need more than I can carry in my handbag or pockets. I dropped my handbag in the hall and called out but no one answered, so I thought Rick would be out by the pool. I went straight out. But he wasn't. I went down, he might have been getting a boat out. That's odd.'

'What is?'

'When I – found him, there was a deckchair by him. I didn't think about it then, I was so shocked. But he never sat in that part of the garden. He said it was too public, people on the river could see him.'

Dodie frowned. 'Yes, I remember. And there was only one chair. Why should he be sitting down there alone when he was expecting visitors? And there's another thing. It wasn't like the chairs by the pool, it was a collapsible type, I think.'

'It was one Rick kept for the boats. Sometimes he took people out on the river, and they might moor somewhere and have a picnic.'

'So they were normally kept on the boat or in the boathouse? Was that locked?'

'Yes, but the key was kept on a small ledge under the eaves. Frank used to moan all the time about it, tell Rick it was far too obvious a place, but he used to laugh, and say the boats were all locked or secured with padlocks, and those keys were up at the house. Even if someone didn't know it would be the obvious place to look.'

'So another mystery – if the murderer did it why plant a chair to make it look as though he'd been sitting there?'

'I wonder? No, it's crazy.'

'What is?' Dodie asked. 'It can't be crazier than what we have already.'

'It just occurred to me that maybe someone else had set themselves up there, broken into the boathouse, found the chairs, and decided to treat it as his own personal bit of lawn. And Rick might have found them, and there was a fight. If he drowned, as Rachel thinks, it could have been in the river, not in the pool.'

'But then surely he'd have been muddy, had bits of vegetation clinging to him? The mermaid certainly did. And if that happened, why not just let him float away? It's the same as the stabbing. Why draw attention to that when it could have been taken as an accident?'

Anna was silent for a moment, and Dodie, glancing at her, saw that she was frowning in concentration. Then she sighed deeply.

'Frank brought drinks down to him. He must have known Rick was there.'

'I expect he heard us talking, or had seen us from the house, going past the pool, and wondered what we were doing.'

'No, he'd more likely seen me,' Anna insisted. 'He wanted to frame me. That's why he stabbed Rick, to make it obvious it was murder, and he knew I'd go looking for Rick as soon as I got here.'

'Even if that's true, why?'

'He and Rick had been falling out more than ever lately, so he was afraid of being sent away.'

'What did they quarrel about?'

'Frank was pathologically jealous of everyone Rick had anything to do with, but especially of me. This way Frank not only killed Rick, he could get rid of me, make sure I didn't get anything from Rick's will, and he would scoop it all as his only relative.'

'Had Rick left you anything?' Dodie was surprised. From what Elena knew they had both assumed Anna's entry into Rick's life was too recent for any such change to have been made. And from what she had heard, he changed his women with too much frequency to consider leaving money to any of them.

Anna shook her head. 'I doubt it. We never even mentioned it. He wasn't old, he wasn't likely to die. I was under no illusions, Mrs Fanshaw. I knew Rick would tire of me soon, but Frank didn't know that. He may have assumed something though.' Her brow was once more furrowed with thought, and then she nodded. 'That must be it. I know he once overheard Rick say something about giving a percentage of his royalties to me. It was payment for the research I'd been doing. I – well, I helped a lot,' she said slowly. 'Rick thought that was fairer than a lump sum. But Frank could have interpreted it as a percentage of Rick's money, in his will.'

They had arrived at Upper Markenham station, and Anna, with a swift word of thanks, was out of the car before Dodie could ask if she would like a lift when she returned. She waved, and was swallowed up in the station. Dodie drove slowly to the supermarket visible just across the station car park and decided she would indulge in a coffee and Danish in their café before tackling the long list Elena had given her. She needed to keep her strength up.

Laden with her shopping, Dodie let herself into the house. Elena came to help her.

'Just a few things,' Dodie teased as she relinquished several carrier bags. 'I almost had to get a second trolley.'

'Gran rang.'

Dodie sighed. 'Now what? Can't she make lunch tomorrow?' she asked hopefully.

'She's heard about the murder, her friend the clairvoyant has seen you in some sort of deadly danger from dastardly crooks, and she knows the home counties are full of drug barons and escaped murderers and Great Train robbers, not to mention rapists and perverts who do things she wouldn't care to sully my innocent ears with,' Elena reported. She chuckled. 'She wants us to go back to the safety of London by the next train, and she's proposing to come and stay in the London house with us to protect us.'

Dodie groaned. 'At least meeting her would scare off any perverted rapist. Did you tell her we were well-protected?'

'I said I'd hired a couple of Rottweilers to patrol the garden, and let them loose in the house at night.'

'Wonderful! She's never forgiven that Peke for nipping her finger when she thought it was a furry toy that child was carrying.'

'But could you ring back, she said, so that she can believe you're not the body. Though she did say it would take a blind policeman to mistake you for a bearded little wimp of a man who had nothing better to do with his time than scribble stupid stories no one believed in anyway.'

'I take it they showed a picture of Rick on TV. Oh, well, better get it over with.'

Twenty minutes later Dodie flopped into a chair and watched Elena washing a lettuce.

'Did you convince her? Poor Gran, she can't help fussing.'

Dodie grinned. 'She gets worse with age. If I get half as bad in twenty years, push me over a cliff.'

'The plot thickens, the field widens,' Dodie said as she and Elena sat in the garden after lunch.

'All Rick's discarded women, you mean? As well as Anna, Serena, and Elizabeth, we could have unknown numbers of women, all mad at him,' Elena said. 'And there are all the people who lost money because of him, like Gerard.'

'I think I need to chat with some of them.'

'I'll make a list of the women Rick might have been entangled with,' Elena said, laughing. 'You can chat with all of them. And another of everyone who might have lost money through his schemes.'

'Well, you must admit village life is turning out to be less placid than you thought. Orgies, mermaids, murders, all virtually in your back garden! Not to mention all the other depravity. It makes London look like a haven of peace and purity.'

London was hot, stuffy, and unpleasant. Dodie had decided that, instead of making a fiendishly early start and travelling with all the commuters, she would spend a peaceful night in her town house, and take a civilized taxi to Harley Street on the following morning.

Elena ran her to the station to catch an early evening train. She went to her house to shower and change, and then met one of her former husbands for dinner.

Her first husband had been in the Army, and had died in Cyprus, rescuing a friend from an ambush. The third, Elena's father, had been killed by a terrorist bomb in his native Brazil. She had divorced the other two. But Dodie had parted from these husbands in a manner that enabled them to remain friends. She met them regularly, even stayed with them at their various houses around the world, and spent holidays on the richest one's yacht. She had no hesitation in demanding their help if she ever needed it, and they, despite their subsequent marriages or affairs, always provided it.

Over the melon she recalled the heady days when she and the Californian Joe Broughton had first met, during her days in Hollywood, and admired his still slim figure, full head of crisp brown hair, and broad shoulders. After two glasses of champagne she was beginning to recall episodes such as their honeymoon, and the first fine raptures of love and all that implied. She felt her cheeks flushing, and banished the images of satin sheets and vast, circular beds. Was he the one who'd had a mirror installed in the ceiling above their nuptial couch? Firmly she told herself it didn't matter, and turned her glass upside down, splashing the last of the champagne it held over the feet of the waiter who was about to top it up.

While eating the delicious Dover sole she forced herself to recall more mundane matters, such as the dozens of ruined dinner parties when he'd been unavoidably delayed at the office, and she'd had to make his excuses to their guests, barbecue the steaks, carve the joints or the birds herself unless she could entice a guest to take over, and the cancelled trips, which she had eventually decided she was cancelling for him only, and taking them herself. It was on one of these solo holidays, she reminded herself guiltily, that she'd first met Elena's father, though they hadn't married until some years later.

Refusing dessert, Dodie watched her former consort tucking into profiteroles, lashed with hurricanes of cream. And began to recall other of his less endearing habits, such as never picking up dirty socks or underwear. By the time he'd loaded several biscuits with mountains of very ripe Stilton she knew once more why she had divorced him. She couldn't abide people who ate so heartily and remained so slim. Next time, she promised herself, she'd meet him for lunch, and make sure it was in, at most, a soup and salad bar.

With her customary sweet smile, she

dissuaded him from escorting her home, saying she knew he had to go the opposite way to the Savoy, where he was staying. A taxi was perfectly safe, and besides, she had to get up early for an appointment in Harley Street. 'Women's troubles, dear,' she said loudly, as she was about to step into the taxi, knowing that he couldn't bear the thought of discussing her internal organs. 'I wouldn't want to bore you with the details, but I can't help thinking of them now the appointment's so near.'

'Of course not, honey. Well, good luck. Hope they don't – well, anyway, good luck. Oh, there's another taxi, I might just catch him. Great to have seen you again.'

And he didn't even kiss me, she grinned to herself in the darkness as she was being whirled along Piccadilly. Though after all that Stilton, I'm thankful!

Back home the answering machine was blinking madly. Most of the messages were for Elena, mainly friends who'd been abroad and didn't have her new telephone number. One was from Elena herself, to hope all went well in the morning, and then there was the final one, a voice Dodie didn't recognize.

'Hello, darling,' the deep, attractive voice said, and Dodie could almost imagine she was in the same room as the caller.

'Hey,' she said to herself, 'this fellow could

seduce a girl with his voice alone!' Then she snapped to attention.

'Marcus here, calling from Seattle to say how desperately I miss you, my love. I just thought I'd let you know I've got the funding for that software development. We should be able to tie it up within ten days to a fortnight, then I'll be home, and hoping against hope you'll give me the answer I want so that the other part of my life can be tied up too. Together with you, for ever, but I promised I wouldn't push you too hard. All my love, sweetheart.'

And that was it. It had been obvious from the sexy tone more than the words what he wanted from Elena. And if he'd got funding for whatever it was, he didn't need Elena's money. She hoped. He sounded delicious, and she'd have to watch herself. It wouldn't do to be flirting with her daughter's boyfriend. Or even, Dodie hoped, longing for Elena to find a satisfactory and enduring love, her husband.

She went to bed and dreamt of a deep velvety voice, but it was all tangled up with the sound of a rushing river, and police and ambulance sirens, and she woke at dawn, sweating profusely. The sirens were still sounding, but as she lay there trying to work out what was wrong, they faded away, and she realized she was back in the metropolis with all the sounds of civilization about her.

She knew she wouldn't go back to sleep, so she showered, made tea, fished a couple of frozen slices of bread from the freezer and stuck them in the toaster. Thank goodness, she thought, the tests didn't require her to starve beforehand.

It was still far too early to set out, so she began to make another list of the people who might have killed Rick.

Anna must be considered, for various reasons including artistic jealousy, or some quarrel as yet undiscovered, and because she was first to find the body, which was apparently always a significant pointer of guilt. Frank had had every opportunity, and might expect to be Rick's heir, though according to Anna they quarrelled frequently. Elizabeth might be jealous, or Serena. Gerard had lost money. And so might a hundred other people be jealous, have lost money, or have completely different motives.

Dodie threw down the pad in despair. She wondered how Hercule Poirot did it with his little grey cells. Surely it was better to have an incontrovertible fingerprint or strands of hair, which could be matched to one person and thus prove guilt?

She glanced at her watch and leapt up in dismay. If she didn't hurry she'd be late. Fortunately she'd packed her few necessities, and the bag was in the hall. Swiftly she made sure all the doors and windows were locked, set the security alarms, and decided it would be quicker to rely on picking up a cab in the street than phoning her usual firm.

She was fortunate, an empty cab had just dropped a passenger a few doors away. The traffic was unusually light, and she reached Harley Street five minutes before her appointment, with time to announce herself, climb the stairs to the second floor in order to lose a few grams, and collapse into a huge armchair in the waiting room just as the doctor came in to greet her.

Six

With the promise that the results of her tests would be available within a week, Dodie left the consulting rooms and walked down to Oxford Street. She had an hour to do some shopping before she met her mother for an early lunch in Selfridges, and then she could catch the afternoon train.

Aware that her mother would demand to see any purchases contained in large dress bags, Dodie bought herself a large new handbag, and pushed the expensive and large phial of perfume to the bottom, along with the delicate rope of pearls, both gifts for Elena's next birthday. She'd just put away er credit card when her mother appeared at her elbow.

Dodie kissed her on the cheek. She was fond of the old devil, she thought. Things hadn't been easy for her, and until Dodie had become established she'd supported her unreservedly. She couldn't, however, cope with her daughter's success either on the stage or with men, and had to show this by constant criticism. Dodie supposed it was a sense of insecurity.

Mrs Jackson was glancing sideways at a display of gaudy brooches. Dodie grinned.

'They have some lovely pearl necklaces,' she said bracingly. 'Just the thing to knock 'em all down at the Over-sixties.'

'I don't approve of using oysters that way,' Mrs Jackson said, sniffing. 'Oysters are for eating, not incubating beads you can hardly see.'

'They'd be an investment,' Dodie tried to cajole, but Mrs Jackson shook her head firmly.

'And don't try and persuade me to buy diamonds, neither. They've no colour either.'

Dodie twisted her hands, on which she wore two large diamond rings. 'Look how they catch all the colours,' she said, but her mother shook her head firmly.

'No, my girl. I don't mind men with more money than sense giving diamonds away, but I won't have you wasting your money on me. You may think you have a lot, but one day you might need it. If you want to give me a present, a nice piece of colourful costume jewellery would be very nice.'

Dodie had known it would be useless. Despite many efforts, she'd never managed to persuade her mother to accept a present of what she called 'real' jewels. They spent half an hour with Mrs Jackson happily comparing the merits of an enamelled representation of some imaginary bird unknown to nature, and a spray of metal flowers large enough to be mistaken for a bridal bouquet. In the end, feeling hungry, Dodie overrode her mother's objections and ordered the weary salesgirl to wrap them both. Then, ignoring the protests, she led the way to the restaurant.

It took time and patience, but eventually she convinced her mother that Markenlea was not a den of vice, nor Chicago in the twenties, nor a civil war zone.

As they left the store and Dodie flagged down a taxi Mrs Jackson had the last word. 'You never could abide any opinion but your own, my gal. I don't know where you get it from. Your father's side, I'm sure.'

She was still talking as the taxi driver, obedient to Dodie's signals and the proffered notes, drew away. Dodie grinned, breathed a sigh of relief, darted back into the store to raid the dress department for a consolation dress she'd spotted earlier, and just made it to Paddington to catch her train.

She was back in the village in time to join Elena in the garden, where she drank a large glass of iced lemonade, before reporting on her visit.

'When we have the results, we can start some action,' she said. 'At least it looks as though it's possible to treat with pills.'

'That's a relief. How did Gran take it?'

'I managed not to mention why I was up in Town. She was too busy worrying about lawlessness down here.'

Elena grinned. 'Poor Gran. Do you think she's missing the excitement? Shall I invite her to come and stay?'

'Not if you want a quiet life – apart from murders almost in your back garden. There were several calls for you on the answering machine,' she added casually. 'Have you checked them from here?'

'I did,' Elena replied, and then, averting her eyes, she stood up and announced that she was going to fetch some more lemonade. She took an inordinate length of time, and as she emerged from the kitchen and spoke, her words were mixed with the sound of high heels tapping along the terrace. They both turned to see Rachel, in a cool cotton skirt and long-sleeved shirt, coming towards them.

'Hello, hope you don't mind my coming straight round. I guessed you'd be enjoying the sun.'

'Come and sit down. I was just getting some more fruit juice. Or would you prefer tea?'

'Neither, thanks, I can't stop. I have a clinic in a few minutes. I just thought you'd like to know what they found at the post-mortem.'

'They've done it already?'

'For once they didn't have a queue. And the inquest is tomorrow, by the way, two o'clock.'

'Well, was it drowning, as you thought?' Dodie asked.

Rachel nodded. 'Yes, in the pool. And he'd been knocked unconscious beforehand, perhaps the old blunt instrument, or he may have hit his head as he fell, but they can't say what yet. It was easy for whoever did it to hold him under. No struggling, no traces of skin under his nails, and it happened an hour or two before you found him. I expect the police will be round again, asking us all where we were at the relevant time, whether we saw anyone, all the usual.'

'I think we're clear, we were both about the house all morning,' Dodie said thoughtfully, 'though of course they probably treat family alibis with suspicion. How about you?'

'Me?' Rachel looked offended for a

moment, then nodded. 'Of course. Everyone has to be checked. You'll have to believe me that I have no motive. And if I did kill anyone I'd make damn sure it was seen as an accident.'

She would too, Dodie thought. She was decisive, determined, and had an edge of hardness which showed in her sometimes brittle voice. Perhaps it all came from the squires, who, centuries ago, had held the power of life or death over their serfs.

'That's the most puzzling feature,' Dodie said. 'Why spoil that possibility?'

Rachel shrugged. 'Who knows? Anyway, I was on my own, unfortunately. No alibi. Charlotte went riding all morning.'

'We saw her,' Elena confirmed. 'How does she get round to the field where her pony is? It must be three miles by road and across the bridge.'

'She and Emily often cycle, if none of us can take them and be sure to pick them up. We put a shed in the field to store the tack, and they can lock their cycles in there. Gerard had gone for a quick round of golf, so he'll have people to vouch for him. I was pottering in the garden, and we're not overlooked. The church clock struck, but I'm so used to it I don't know if it was the hour or half or quarter. I know they were ringing the bells for the service when I first went out, and I saw Chloe Walls-Farmer being chauffeured there in that ancient Rolls her father has. All I can be sure of is that it was some time before I went in to change for Rick's party.'

'Tell me, Gerard is accounted for, so even the money he lost through that health club investment won't be thought a motive,' Dodie said. 'What about other people who invested in Rick's schemes?'

Rachel looked sharply at her. 'I know Rick was persuasive, and quite a few people in the village were induced to put up smallish sums of money for various of his projects. Rick never tried to ask for more than they could afford to lose, but until recently they usually paid off handsomely. Gerard made a killing a few years ago, when some land Rick had bought with him was sold at vast profit.'

'People tend to forget the good times, and feel resentful of the bad, I suppose,' Dodie said.

'What about other women?' Elena asked slowly. 'We really do have to consider everyone. You can bet the police will. He seems to have been the local Lothario.'

Rachel grinned. 'Don't pay too much attention to that. Yes, he liked women, but between them Elizabeth and Serena soon saw off any competition. He and Serena have known one another all their lives, and they've had an on-off relationship since they were both sixteen. When it was off with

Serena it was on with Elizabeth. I think they are both resigned to sharing. Or were. It just happened to be Elizabeth who was in favour when Rick decided it was time to get married. Anna is the only woman to have broken the pattern and moved in openly.'

'So even though the field seems wide open with local women and investors, and maybe from others elsewhere that we don't know about, there's no obvious suspect.'

'Where does our mermaid fit in?' Elena asked. 'I'm beginning to think she wasn't a coincidence.'

'Mermaid?' Rachel was amused. 'What's all this?'

'Didn't we tell you?' Elena explained.

Rachel looked thoughtful. 'Have you told the police? It could be important. Even if she had nothing to do with it, she was on the river and might have seen something.'

'Unfortunately, we haven't a clue about her. She gave us no name or any hint of where she came from.'

'She was determined not to,' Dodie said. 'Elena, where are the local boatyards? I think a trip to them is called for.'

Rachel laughed. 'To play detectives? Surely the police can follow that up?'

'Probably, but often people don't tell the police every small detail. I want to find out which one's lost a boat, and ask whether they know anything about whoever hired it.'

'Then I'll leave you to it. I must go, anyway. Happy sleuthing!'

Anna was due to go to the police station for her interview on the following day. Dodie again gave her a lift to the station, did a little shopping, and then drove back towards the river bridge, near which some boatyards were situated. It didn't take long to find the boatyard from where the mermaid had rented her abandoned boat. At the first one Dodie tried, which looked scruffy and untidy, a young, pimply man wearing nothing but skimpy shorts and numerous faintly indecent tattoos was in charge. He was uninterested, hadn't lost any boats, and once he confirmed that Dodie had no intention of hiring one, turned his back on her and switched on the small television in the office, which was little more than a lean-to shed clinging rather desperately to the wall which surrounded the site.

She had more luck at the next, with both information and attention. This yard was under the supervision of a man in his fifties, good-looking and still athletic. He turned out to be the owner, Harry Keeton, he explained, pointing proudly to the well-polished brass plate set into the brick pillar beside the gate. It was better cared for than most she'd seen in Harley Street, Dodie thought with an inward grin. When she explained what she wanted and fluttered her eyelids at him, he said that he well recalled the boat, it was an odd do altogether. He put away the paint-brushes he'd been using on an upturned boat and suggested a cup of tea.

'Have that chair, it's the only good one,' he gestured as he plugged in the kettle. This office was purpose-built, neat, newly decorated, and well furnished. The armchair was solid but comfortable, and he made tea with proper tea leaves in a squat brown pot, and laid a tray with china cups and saucers and a plate of both chocolate digestive and shortbread biscuits. Dodie was impressed and told him so.

'Was it difficult getting this boat back?' Dodie asked, helping herself to a chocolate biscuit. She had to forget her waistline in the interests of detection.

'No, it wasn't far off, and someone else who'd been that way told me where. It was just stuck in the reeds. Easy to tow in. Not submerged like some of them are.'

'Do you often lose boats?' Dodie asked. She'd never before thought of the effect on the boatyards when boats capsized. The more obvious effect of suddenly wet and cold sailors had been of more immediate concern.

'Not as often as you might think, seeing how incompetent some of the fellows are. They think they'll show off to their girls, and instead turn them over. But they usually come here and confess, and tell me what's happened. Otherwise they don't get any of their deposit back.'

'You ask for a deposit then? Is it a big one?'

He shook his head. 'Just a few quid. Enough to compensate for my trouble collecting the boats and drying them out, maybe replacing oars or cushions. If they have an accident I send them the balance later, what's left after I've costed that.'

'Do you have an address for this girl? It was a girl who hired the boat, wasn't it?'

'Yes, skinny chit. I prefer a few curves on a woman,' he added, with a friendly grin, and an admiring glance at her still slim ankles and shapely calves.

Dodie grinned back. 'Her address?'

'Somewhere in London. Let's see, it must be somewhere here.' He pulled a big ledger towards him and riffled through the pages. 'Yes, here it is. Sounds like a block of flats. Ealing.'

He pushed over the ledger and a sheet of his notepaper. Dodie copied down the address. She couldn't believe it had been so easy. 'There's no name. How did she pay?'

'Cash. New tens, they crackled, I remember, and she still had them in a band from the bank.'

So what happened to the rest of them?

The girl had not been flaunting wads of tenners after her ducking. Dodie was intrigued, recalling how unconcerned the girl had been at her lost purse which, she claimed, had only a couple of pounds in it. She hadn't looked the sort of girl to be so casual about losing a roll of notes.

Harry Keeton was speaking again. 'Now, I've answered your questions. What's your interest? Could it by any chance be anything to do with that murder?'

'I doubt it,' Dodie replied. 'It was so odd, and she seemed rather shocked, not quite sure of what she was doing. I thought I ought to try and find out if she was OK.'

'Well, I'm hardly surprised she capsized. She didn't have much clue about rowing. Went round in circles as soon as she was out in the river, nearly collided with one of the racing eights. But I was busy that morning, and couldn't stop to watch. She must have got going in the end, she wasn't in sight next time I looked. I do remember thinking it was odd her boyfriend didn't go with her.'

'Boyfriend?' Dodie sat up eagerly. 'Did you see him? How do you know she was with someone?'

'It may not have been a boyfriend. Someone, a man, dropped her off at the gates. I just happened to be watching someone leaving, my son Dave, as a matter of fact. This stinking great car stopped just outside the gates, blocked his way out of the yard while the girl got out. Dave might be able to describe him or the car. I only caught a glimpse of it, to see it was big and sleek.'

'Can I have a word with Dave? The girl was wearing an engagement ring, but she didn't seem to want to say anything about a fiancé. And she went home by taxi. She mentioned a friend with a car, but for some reason didn't want to call him.'

'If it was the chap who dropped her off, and she was soaking wet, she wouldn't want to mess up his upholstery. And it wasn't the sort of car a young man could afford. Not unless he was rich, and she didn't strike me as a girl to move in those circles. Though you never know these days, the way some of them dress.'

'Does Dave work with you?' she asked, willing him to get back to the point.

'No, and he's away for a few days, till the weekend. Can I get him to phone when he gets home?'

Dodie swallowed her disappointment. She hated waiting. But she had the address, and they could follow that up. She refused another cup of tea, and said she ought to be getting back. He escorted her solicitously to where she'd parked the car, held the door for her, and stood watching as she drove out of the yard.

Seven

Elena was busy on her new assignment, and had several phone calls to make, so she declined to attend the inquest. Dodie was curious to see who turned up, and went into town after lunch. Frank was there, looking rather frightened, sitting with a tall, grim-faced man in the back row. Later he introduced him to Dodie as Daniel North, Serena's husband. Anna was late, and looked flustered. There was no chance to ask her how she'd got on at the police station. No other of Rick's women appeared. As was expected, the formalities were brief, and the inquest was adjourned pending further police enquiries. Feeling deflated, though it was only what she had expected, Dodie paid a visit to a hairdresser Elena had recommended, and then drove home.

It was by then too late to drive to Ealing that afternoon – she'd only get snarled up in the rush hour traffic. But the girl wouldn't be at home during the day anyway. She and Elena could go that evening. Would Rachel be at home? Dodie thought it unlikely: it wasn't four yet. Serena and her husband would be at their office, which left Elizabeth, and Frank. She'd prefer to tackle Elizabeth on some more casual meeting, which Elena ought to be able to arrange. She'd pay a visit to Frank.

Dodie turned into the drive, thankful to see that all the police cars and vans had departed, as had the press. She had no desire to alert Detective Inspector Morton to her activities. He, with his suspicious mind, would resent her curiosity. As she approached the front door it opened, and Frank stood on the step waiting for her.

'Hello. How are you today?' she asked.

He stepped back for her to enter. 'Kind of you to ask. The rest of the village seem to have convicted me already,' he muttered.

'Cold-shouldering you?' Dodie asked sympathetically.

'I went to the shop this morning, for some stamps. Ricky had a lot of friends who live abroad. I'm not going to phone all of them. For all I know, I'd be charged for the calls by the executors. Sure to be if it's that snooty solicitor who has the last say,' he added.

'What happened in the shop?'

'There were half a dozen women in there, nattering like a flock of starlings, then when they saw it was me, they went dead silent. The queue for the post office just melted away, they were all suddenly looking for something else. No one spoke to me, and Ma Weaver, behind the counter, couldn't get rid of me fast enough.'

'I expect she was just embarrassed,' Dodie said soothingly. 'How are you managing here? What happens now?'

'I wish I knew. Here, want a drink?'

'It's a bit early, isn't it?' Dodie said quickly. Frank seemed rather loquacious, and she suspected he'd been drinking already. Not that she blamed him, but she didn't want to encourage him. 'I'd love a cuppa,' she lied, thinking that she'd be awash with tea soon, as she'd had some at the hairdresser's salon which hadn't been a patch on Harry Keeton's.

He nodded, and Dodie followed him towards the kitchen. She wanted to see more of this house, discover more about the people who had lived there. It was a large room – state of the art appliances, a big Aga on one side, and a centre table which would have seated a dozen people at a pinch. The big window overlooked the drive, and anyone here would be able to see people who arrived by car.

Frank filled the kettle, and got out a carton of teabags and two thick mugs.

'Do you know if the police have discovered anything else?' Dodie asked.

'No, they finished here this morning. They told me to stay here. Not as though I have anywhere else to go,' Frank said, sighing.

Dodie sat down to one side of the table,

and he took the chair opposite. 'But surely Rick will have left you something in his will? After all, you're his only relative.'

'He promised, but it all seemed so unlikely! I didn't imagine he'd die for years, I might easily have died first. I am a few years older. Now I expect that woman will get it all!' he added venomously.

'Anna? But Rick hardly knew her,' Dodie said. 'She'd only been here a few weeks.'

'But he met her getting on for a year and a half ago,' Frank said as he sloshed water into the mugs. 'He once told me, he first met her just after his book was accepted. She lived not far away, and she heard about the contract. It was in a lot of the local papers, how much he'd been paid, and she went to see him. Said she belonged to a local writers' group and wanted him to join, or go and speak to them.' He pulled a bottle of whisky from a cupboard and held it up to Dodie. 'Like some in the tea?'

She shook her head. 'No thanks. Did he join?'

'He said he went a couple of times, but it wasn't his scene. Most of them were women, and they all wanted to write poetry, or short stories for women's magazines.'

'You know, I've not read his book. I really feel I ought to. I've been out of the country, hadn't heard about it until I came to stay with Elena. What's it about?'

For a moment she thought Frank was about to burst into some tirade, but he took a deep breath and shrugged. 'It's clever, but not my sort of reading. It's about a chap who works for a big developer. A clerk, just an office worker. Rick put in a lot about the scams that go on in big building sites. I think it was that that people liked. They enjoy reading about sleaze and men who break the law and get away with it.'

'I wonder if there's a spare copy I could borrow? Elena's lent hers to a friend,' Dodie hastily invented.

'Might be some in the study.'

Frank went out, and Dodie again followed him. The study was a large, pleasant room. Two walls were covered with elegant fitted bookshelves, but surprisingly few books. A large Regency-style desk, empty apart from a pen stand, was in the centre of the room. A computer stood on a corner table, with a couple of printers and a fax and telephone nearby. A large photocopier was on another table, and a four-drawer filing cabinet stood behind the door. French windows opposite the door led into a conservatory.

'Wasn't your conservatory damaged on Saturday night?' Dodie asked, moving across the room to look through at the lush foliage.

'What? Oh, yes. Elizabeth. She came round here in one of her snits, and threw the usual tantrum. Ricky was furious, threatened to stop her alimony.'

He seemed to think that explained everything. But it could have given Elizabeth a motive. 'Didn't she throw bricks? We heard it. And wouldn't it have messed about with the temperature controls, destroyed all Rick's orchids?'

'Probably chucked a few of his plant pots at them. I didn't look. I never went in there. But now he's gone, what does it matter? Here's a copy of the book.'

He'd picked one up from a small pile stacked on a lower bookshelf. Dodie looked at the cover picture. It was dark and stylistic, but she could make out a few scaffolding poles, a large unfinished building in the shadows behind, with what appeared to be an ambulance standing in front of it, lights flashing. Hung on the scaffolding, but so vaguely outlined that it wasn't clear what they were meant to represent, were what looked like beer cans, and Dodie couldn't decide whether they were intended as an illustration of building site rubbish or there to make some kind of symbolic statement.

'Thanks. I'll bring it back when I can. I suppose you'll stay here for some time? They won't be able to get probate and start selling the house for a while, will they? When do you think we'll know about his will? Has his solicitor been in touch?'

Her questions didn't appear to upset

Frank. That one flash of anger was all the emotion he'd displayed, apart from a general air of misery, and what seemed like a constant animosity towards Anna.

'He phoned, asked me to stay here to look after things for the time being. And said he'd be in touch.'

They walked back towards the kitchen. 'You must have been in here on Sunday morning. When did Ricky go out to swim?'

'He had breakfast at nine, as usual. Then he worked in the study. He said he'd had an idea he wanted to get down. He was making some phone calls, too. I heard him, about half past ten, opening the French windows on to the terrace. After that I never heard nor saw him again.'

Dodie sipped the tea, which was by now lukewarm. She suppressed a grimace and heroically took another sip. 'You were here all the time. You'd have heard any cars coming, I imagine. It was a hot day, I expect the windows were open too.'

Frank sat opposite her and cradled his mug between his hands. 'I don't hear everything. I didn't hear Serena. Anna said she came back with her, but I didn't hear the car.'

'We saw her drive out of the gateway, when we were arriving. Did you hear us walking up the drive? That gravel sounded noisy to me.'

'I might have been in the cloakroom,' Frank grudgingly admitted. 'It's by the front door. Or I could have been making the beds. No, that was earlier.'

'Do the rooms look out over the pool? Might you have seen anything from those windows?'

He shrugged. 'The police have been over this again and again. I can't say the time exactly. I did look out of the window for a moment, but all I saw was an empty pool. You can't see the near end, the terrace hides it, but I don't think I saw any ripples. There would have been some if Rick had been swimming. He used up a lot of energy, made waves.' He suddenly bent his head, and passed a hand across his eyes. 'Who hated him that much? I'd have thought everyone stood to gain more with him alive!' he cried, and sniffed loudly.

Before Dodie could utter any words of comfort the doorbell shrilled, making them both jump.

'Shall I go?' Dodie asked, but Frank shook his head, and scrubbed at his eyes, which were moist.

'No. If it's those damned reporters I swear I'll throw them out on to the road and hope a heavy lorry's coming!'

'I ought to be going, anyway, but first I'd better pay a visit, if you don't mind,' Dodie murmured discreetly, and they went towards the front door together.

Frank flung it open, and for a moment, as she stood in the cloakroom with the door almost closed, Dodie couldn't remember who it was standing there. Then she recognized the tall, suave publisher just as he began to enter the hall, and she applied her eye to the crack in the door.

'Frank, old chap, how are you?' Piers Walls-Farmer asked. 'Have the plods gone?'

'The police have left,' Frank replied, emphasizing the word. 'What do you want?' he added, his tone ungracious.

'I happened to be down here, visiting my ailing mother-in-law yet again, and I called on Serena too. She suggested I might call in and collect the typescript of Rick's book,' Piers said, a little less affably. 'You may be more willing to give it to me. I know it seems insensitive, but we want to keep his name in the public eye. After all, the royalties will all go to his heirs, so if you're one of them it's in your interest to cooperate with us. I need to look at it as soon as possible to see what we can do, whether it needs much polishing.'

'You're all like vultures! The poor man's not buried yet!'

'Frank, I know it seems like that, but Rick had immense talent, we have to remind people of that. It's especially important now there'll only be two books. The reading public's so fickle, they forget so soon.'

'And publishers stand to lose money!' Frank sneered.

'If you've inherited anything it could be your money too!' Piers said sharply. 'Now, are you going to give it to me?'

'I don't know where it is.'

'In his study, I imagine. Rick was a methodical sort of chap. It will be in a folder, no doubt labelled with the title, and there'll also be a copy on the computer.'

'You're not going to ransack Rick's study!'

'Frank, be reasonable, just let me have a look. You needn't worry about my right to it. Rick was already under contract for the book, I'm entitled to have it. In fact the first draft was due three months ago.'

Frank hesitated, then turned away towards the study. Dodie watched as they went past, neither man noticing her. Thoughtfully she let herself out of the front door. Piers Walls-Farmer had parked his Jaguar behind Elena's more modest car, and Dodie was thankful there was plenty of room as she manoeuvred to turn and drive away. Would he ask whose car it was, she wondered, or assume it belonged to the housekeeper or a tradesman?

Anna had not yet returned when she arrived home, so she was able to report her discoveries to Elena.

'I want to go and ask the mermaid some

questions,' she said as she helped prepare vegetables for dinner. 'I suspect she may have seen something, and that may have caused her odd behaviour. I thought we could drive up after dinner. It's not all that far.'

'Anna hasn't got a key. I forgot to give her one. If she's not back we can't go,' Elena said.

'I can go on my own if necessary. Oh, that might be her now. I'll go and let her in.'

But it wasn't Anna on the doorstep. Piers Walls-Farmer stood there, a slight frown on his handsome face.

'Excuse me, but I believe Anna is staying with you? Could I possibly speak to her for a minute?'

'Come in,' Dodie invited. She wanted a chance to ask him some questions. 'Anna should be back soon. You can wait for her if you like.'

He glanced at his watch. 'Thank you, but I don't think I'll have time. I've a long drive for a dinner engagement. Do you know if she has Rick's latest typescript here? I know she did a lot of the secretarial work, and she might have been checking it. I need it as soon as possible. Deadlines, you know.'

'She didn't bring it, I'm pretty sure,' Dodie replied. 'She didn't bring much at all.'

She was puzzled. Hadn't he found it in Rick's study? Wasn't it even on the computer? Perhaps Anna had another computer to work on, or the script had been left in her own room, and Frank had not allowed him to search there.

He looked annoyed. 'I can't wait, but please will you ask her to send it to me as soon as possible? It's very important.'

Without waiting for a reply he turned away, and strode down the drive to where he'd left his car outside the gates. Dodie watched him roar off towards London, and was about to close the door when she saw a movement in one of the rhododendron bushes bordering the fence. Anna, looking cautiously round her, emerged, and sped towards the door.

'Whew, he almost caught me. Close the door quickly, please, in case he comes back.'

Dodie did so, and eyed the girl with some amusement. 'You're covered in dust,' she observed. 'Why didn't you want to see him? You were terrified of him on Sunday when he arrived.'

'Oh, I was terrified of everyone on Sunday! I – well, I thought he might be annoyed about that, as a matter of fact. I was too embarrassed to meet him. What was he doing here?'

'He's looking for Rick's new book. I was next door with Frank when he appeared, but Frank didn't know where it was, and they couldn't find it. He thought you might have it here, or know where it is.'

'I've no idea. Oh, something smells good! I haven't eaten all day, and I'm starving.'

Elena had come out of the kitchen. 'Good, you're back. Ready in ten minutes.'

It was almost nine when Elena brought the car to a halt outside a modern block of flats a short distance from Ealing Common.

'Do you think this is it?'

Dodie nodded. 'Yes, she could live here. They don't seem to be much more than studio flats, judging by how many small bathroom windows there are. Let's go and catch the mermaid.'

The flat they wanted was on the third floor, and there was an entryphone. When a man's voice answered, Dodie hesitated. Was it the wrong flat? Or was this the mysterious boyfriend?

'Sony to disturb you, but could I come up for a moment?' she asked. 'I'm looking for someone who's supposed to live here.'

The buzzer sounded, and she and Elena went in and climbed up two flights of bare concrete stairs. At least the walls were free of the sort of graffiti Dodie had seen in unprotected blocks of flats, and the stairs were relatively clean, but it was obviously a cheaply built and scantily maintained block. At the top a man in jeans and a T-shirt waited beside an open door. He was in his mid-twenties, had a shock of ginger hair, and wore heavy black-rimmed spectacles.

Dodie tried not to breathe too heavily. She must try to take more exercise. She smiled at the young man.

'Was it me you were looking for?'

'No, it's a girl. I'm afraid I don't know her name, but she's younger than you are, long black hair, and last weekend she had a ducking in the Thames when her boat overturned.'

He looked blank. 'I'm sorry, but you must have the wrong address. I live here on my own. And I haven't been near the river for ages, let alone fallen in.'

Dodie was beginning to suspect they had failed, but she clung to a faint shred of hope. 'Perhaps we have the wrong number, or it was written down wrongly. How many apartments are there in this building?'

'Just a dozen, and I know everyone here. There isn't a girl like the one you describe, and I've never seen one visiting here either. I'm sorry, but I can't help you.'

Eight

Dodie had just finished breakfast on the following day, alone because Anna had gone out and Elena had left a note saying she was going to the shop for more milk, when the doorbell rang. She went to open it, and found Frank, looking disgruntled.

'Well?' he demanded. 'What is it?'

'What's what?' Dodie asked.

He glared at her. 'Young Anna. She came over just now, said she needed some clothes, and you wanted to talk to me right away, it was something urgent.'

Dodie shook her head. 'Sorry, Frank, I didn't send any such message. Are you sure you understood her?'

'I'm not deaf!'

'Then she must have been–'

She stopped. Frank, with an oath, had spun round and was racing down the drive. He almost collided with Elena but didn't stop, swerving round her and vanishing behind the hedge.

'What was that for?' Elena asked as she came in and dropped her carriers of shopping. 'Why, when I go for one item, do I always come home with two laden bags?'

Dodie absentmindedly picked up an orange and began to peel it. 'He came here because Anna told him I wanted to speak to him urgently. Needless to say, I hadn't said anything of the kind. Now what is she up to?'

'She said she needed clothes from next door. I offered to go with her, because earlier she'd been terrified of meeting Frank, but she said she'd be OK.'

'So she wanted some time in the house by herself, and got rid of Frank. He obviously suspected her. Perhaps she wanted to look for something, or to retrieve something hidden.'

Elena was filling the kettle. 'We'll ask her when she gets back. I've invited Elizabeth and Serena to come over for a coffee.'

'Both? Isn't that asking for war to break out?' Dodie asked, licking juice from her fingers.

'They were in a huddle together outside the shop. I don't think they've spoken for at least a couple of years, perhaps longer, but they seem to have become buddies overnight.'

'Sharing out the spoils?'

'I suspect it's something to do with who will have control over the book. Serena may suspect Elizabeth will inherit, and she'll be frantic in case she goes to another agency. There's a lot of cash involved.'

'But if Serena negotiated this contract, surely she'll be entitled to her cut in any case?'

'I'm no expert, but there may be other rights, film rights and so on, up for grabs.'

Dodie rinsed her hands while Elena put away her shopping. 'It doesn't seem real. And you hope they'll tell us?'

'Or at least explain the sudden friendliness. I hope Anna doesn't come back to upset them.'

'We can sit in the garden. It's going to be another warm day. She might see us and keep out of the way. I imagine she's rather sensitive herself at the moment about tangling with Elizabeth.'

Elena began to collect mugs and a plate of chocolate biscuits on a tray. While she was carrying it out to the garden, the doorbell rang again, and Dodie went to open it. It was Anna, flushed and looking furious, clutching a large case. She had clearly packed in haste, since the odd edges of material were protruding from under the lid. Over her shoulder she had a duffle bag, and several well-filled manila folders poked out of the top.

'Bloody man!' she exclaimed. 'He's no right to try and stop me getting my own stuff!'

'Did he try to stop you with force?' Dodie asked. When Frank had departed in such a rush he'd looked angry enough not to care about charges of assault.

Anna shook her head. 'He came barging into my room, yelling at me that I hadn't any right to be there, but luckily Daniel turned up, and I was able to get away.'

The agency was clearly having to do without either partner this morning, Dodie reflected as Anna heaved her case inside. 'What did he want?' she asked.

'I didn't stop to ask!'

'Serena and Elizabeth are coming over in a few minutes for coffee,' Dodie warned her.

'Together?' Anna was incredulous.

'They are apparently the best of friends.'

Anna snorted. 'That'll last for about five minutes! If you're lucky. I'm going out for a walk. A long walk, so please tell Elena not to expect me for lunch.'

She turned as two virtually identical open-topped Mercedes swept into the drive. 'Rick was so unimaginative!' she said with a sigh, and dragged her case upstairs.

Dodie was suppressing a grin as she waited for the two women. Was this Rick's normal goodbye present to discarded mistresses and jealous wives? In which case Anna seemed to have lost out in that respect too by being in situ when he died.

It was the first time she'd had a close look at either woman out of their cars. Both were tall and thin, but there the resemblance stopped.

Serena's features were sharp, her nose and prominent chin pointed and her eyes a pale blue. Her gingery hair was cut short in a style which was comfortable and easy rather than fashionable. She had lip gloss, badly applied, and her only adornment was a huge gold ring set with what looked like genuine, and very expensive diamonds. She wore jeans and a skimpy top, and her bare feet were thrust into open-toed sandals.

Elizabeth, in contrast, looked the epitome of the grieving widow in her tailored black suit, dark stockings and high-heeled court shoes. She even wore a small hat with a wispy veil perched on top of her sculptured upswept hair, which was almost as black as her hat. She had full, voluptuous lips and widely spaced, large dark eyes, and her make-up was perfect. Dodie caught a whiff of Joy as Elizabeth approached. A particularly insensitive perfume for today, she decided.

'We thought it would be more pleasant out in the garden. Do come through.'

They smiled, in unison, and Dodie had a wild vision of a chorus line of all Rick's women advancing up the drive. She swung round hurriedly in case her amusement showed, and led the way through the house and on to the terrace. Elena had just carried out the coffee pot, and turned to smile at them and arrange seats close to the table.

'Have you heard anything more?' Dodie asked when they had all been supplied with coffee.

Elizabeth shook her head. 'The police seem to have done nothing, have no leads. Though it seems perfectly obvious, from what Rachel Dean told me, that it must have been Anna or Frank.'

'Anna didn't have time, I gave her a lift myself,' Serena interrupted. 'If it was Frank, then he must have expected something in Rick's will. Did Rick leave him anything, Elizabeth?'

She shrugged. 'I haven't any idea. The solicitor won't tell me. But before Anna came on the scene Rick told me he'd left me well provided for. Though his interpretation of that and mine differed considerably in the past, and I don't expect he'd have changed.'

Serena shrugged impatiently. 'You had a percentage of his income, but that won't carry on unless we find that typescript.'

'You mean the next book?' Elena asked. 'What's happened?'

'I only wish we knew,' Serena replied. 'Frank doesn't know where it is, or at least he says he doesn't. He couldn't find it for Piers yesterday. Daniel's gone there this morning to see if he can find it. There isn't even a copy on the computer, and that's the first time I've known an author wipe out all traces of an unpublished novel. It doesn't make sense.'

'Could Frank have wiped it, and perhaps have hidden the typescript, or made copies on a floppy disk?' Elizabeth wondered. 'He may be thinking of holding us to ransom until we offer him cash for it.'

'Anna must know! She was supposed to be working on it with him, doing some research,' Serena said, frustration evident in her voice and the way she was tapping her fingers on her knee.

'You didn't believe that, did you? It was a cover. The idiot girl might have thought that made it respectable. No woman whose name was ever linked to Ricky came out of it with any shred of claim to respectability,' Elizabeth said, and Dodie grinned to herself. These two might have a truce while their interests coincided, but it wouldn't take much to restart the war.

'No one cares these days,' Serena snapped. 'Isn't Anna here? I have to ask her if she knows where it is.'

'She's gone out,' Dodie said. 'I don't think she'll be back until much later. She said she was going for a long walk.'

Serena put down her mug. 'Then there's not much more we can do here. Might as well go to the office and see what calamities have hit us there. Thanks for coffee, Elena.' She stood up. 'And Elizabeth, do get on to that fool solicitor again. We have to know who has authority to sign the contracts. We can't wait on his piffling convenience. There's an option deal I have to see to this week.'

'But if there's no copy of the next book, doesn't that make it rather tricky?' Dodie asked gently.

Serena looked at her blankly. 'Oh, it'll turn up. Don't bother to see me out.'

'I ought to be going too,' Elizabeth said, but she made no move to do so. 'Elena, you live nearest to Rick. And Anna's come to you, she must trust you. I heard–'

She stopped, and began pleating the material of her skirt nervously. Elena glanced at Dodie with slightly raised eyebrows. Elizabeth looked up at them, and sighed.

'What is it?' Elena asked gently. 'I haven't been here all that long, you know, and actually I didn't know either of them very well. I may be next door, but the houses are a long way apart, and there are hedges and shrubberies in between.'

Elizabeth took a deep breath. 'It may be no more than a silly rumour, and,' she added with a suddenly venomous tone, 'I wouldn't put it past that little slut to have started it herself!'

'What rumour?' Dodie asked.

'That Rick was planning to marry her. Look, I'm fully aware he's had lots of women. I was used to it when we were married, but I clung on for years in the hope that one day he'd change. But he's never had anyone living with him before. It could have been serious.'

Elena assured her that she had no inside knowledge, that neither Anna nor Rick had confided in her, and that in her opinion she wouldn't have considered it likely. Elizabeth looked slightly happier, and finally took herself off.

'And what was all that about?' Dodie asked as they collected the mugs. 'Serena was only concerned to get hold of the type-script, and why should it matter to Elizabeth now what Rick might have planned to do? He didn't marry Anna in secret, I suppose?'

'It may become clearer when we know what was in the will. I confess I'm beginning to get curious myself.'

Dodie established herself on her favourite garden lounger after lunch. Elena had an appointment with the hairdresser, and Dodie decided it was time to recreate the list she'd started when in London, but had left there, and add to it. She thought for a while, and sighed impatiently. So far as she could see everyone she'd met had an opportunity and most of them had motives. She made columns on a large pad of paper, and began to write.

Anna could have come along the river bank, and then gone back and pretended she'd come on a later train. Did she stand to inherit some of Rick's fortune? Or might it have been a lovers' quarrel?

Frank had ample opportunity before anyone came for the party. Did he have expectations, or had Rick, perhaps, asked him to leave? He'd lose his home by killing Rick unless he knew he'd inherit money. But he might have killed him in a blind fury after some quarrel. Had Frank some dubious secret which Rick might have exposed? That would have been motive enough, perhaps. She must try to investigate Frank's background. Anna's too, come to that. She wondered where the girl had come from, how they had met. She'd ask her that evening.

Elizabeth could have walked along the bank. Yet surely, unless Rick could change the terms of her divorce settlement, she'd be better off with him alive and earning. The same argument about being better off with a live author than a dead one applied to Serena and Daniel.

Rachel might have had an affair with him, or be suffering from jealousy or unrequited love. So might most of the other women in the area, from all Elena said. Gerard and others had lost money through unwise investments, but these had been small amounts they could afford to lose, not life or death amounts that would ruin them. But

Gerard, according to Rachel, had been playing golf. She ought to check. Yet no one enjoyed losing money. But this argument could apply to anyone else, which seemed to include many of the villagers who'd invested in Rick's schemes.

And there was the mysterious mermaid who'd given the boatman a false address. She might have been nothing at all to do with it, but that false address was highly suspicious.

Dodie threw down her pencil in disgust. There were no clues here. She was concentrating on the people she'd met, simply because she had met them. The police had far greater resources to investigate the villagers, the women and the unfortunate investors. She had the very slight advantage of knowing some of Rick's closest circle, being in contact with them. And most murders, she'd heard, were domestic.

Another idea entered her mind. Did this arise out of the book? Might there be some clues there? She ought to start reading it, but it was warm and she was comfortable, and the book was in her bedroom. The bees investigating the flowers of the wisteria that covered the back wall of the house were droning monotonously. She closed her eyes and slept.

An hour later Elena returned and woke her

as she put down a tray with iced lemonade.

'Resting your eyes again?' she asked sweetly.

'Thinking,' Dodie replied. 'And making notes. Wasn't it Hercule Poirot who said it was better to exercise the little grey cells than rush round collecting fingerprints and scraps of fabric caught up in shoe buckles?'

'He might have done. Have you solved the mystery with your little grey cells?'

'Not yet, but I haven't given up hope! I mean to read that book, and see what all the fuss is about. In fact, I was just about to go and fetch it when you came back.'

'Fibber,' Elena said affectionately. 'I came back half an hour ago and you haven't moved a muscle all this time. Shall I fetch the book for you? To save your aged legs?'

'My aged legs can manage a few steps quite well, thank you. Has Anna come back yet?'

'No sign of her. I looked into her room, but she isn't there, and hadn't unpacked her case.'

Dodie went to collect the book, splashed her face with cold water to banish the last traces of sleepiness, applied more make-up, and returned to the garden. She read the blurb on the inside front cover, and groaned slightly. It wasn't the sort of book she'd have chosen. It seemed far too gloomy and angst-ridden, and she didn't think she'd have a great deal in common with a small-time clerk working in a building magnate's office. When she came to his terminally ill wife, his own descent into unemployment, depression and alcoholism, she almost gave up before starting. She liked an exciting thriller or mystery, where good triumphed and the wicked finished up where they deserved to be.

To put off the moment when she'd have to turn to page one, she read the profile of the author on the back of the cover. She studied the photograph of Rick. She'd only seen his dead body, and you could hardly judge character from that.

He was better looking than she remembered, despite the beard, and probably had the sort of animal magnetism that attracted women, even without the allure of his wealth. He looked intelligent, and she could believe he'd made a fortune. It helped that he also had an air of hardness, of inflexibility, lurking behind the practised smile for the camera. The details of his life were sparse, not mentioning marriage or family. He'd been born in the Home Counties, made a fortune in business, and retired early to devote himself to his new career as a writer.

Elena came and stood behind her. 'What do you think? It's an unusually accurate photo.'

'I'm still surprised he could pull women so easily. But small men often have something to prove. And he did make a fortune. But they are very careful not to specify it was made in property development. That's not admirable. It's politically incorrect. You know, I'd have expected him to go in for politics, not writing fiction. He'd have been a great success there. Have you read the book? All through?'

'Of course. I didn't dare not.' Elena laughed. 'You'll have to do the same, no excuses. It will be good for your soul, or something. I'm going in to start dinner. Don't go to sleep again.'

Dodie succeeded in staying awake, but it was a struggle. She found the first dozen or so pages exceedingly heavy going, but knew she had to persevere. It got better, she was relieved to see, when the details of the various scams which were operated on the building site were introduced. This one site, on the outskirts of London, was the background for the first part of the book, and Dodie assumed it was one in which Rick had been involved, there was so much convincing detail.

When Elena called her in for dinner, she took the book with her.

'Is Anna back?'

'No, and I don't propose to wait for her. If she hasn't the decency to let me know she'll be late she can have it dried up. I'll leave it in the slow oven. How far have you got with the wonder book?'

'A couple of chapters. I'm a little surprised that he should have been so open about all the scams on the building sites. You'd have thought he'd want to keep quiet about them, even though he'd sold out by then.'

'Yes, but I suppose it's a sort of kiss and tell, blowing the whistle exercise. It had more impact when there was all that publicity about an insider making revelations.'

'He comes across, in his main character's viewpoint, as very honest and concerned about them,' Dodie said thoughtfully. 'If he really was so concerned, I wonder if he made any effort to prevent these things happening while he had some influence?'

Before Elena could reply, the telephone rang. By the time she came back to the table with a message from an old friend they had both had enough of the subject, and spent the rest of the evening watching a video. It was after eleven when it finished, and Elena looked at her watch in some surprise.

'Where on earth is Anna?' she asked. 'Surely she ought to be back by now? Do you think I should contact the police?'

Nine

Dodie sent Elena to bed at three in the morning. 'I, as you are fond of pointing out, can sleep in the daytime,' she said, 'and you've got to go to London tomorrow, for that private view your friend is organizing.'

'Bettina will understand,' Elena said. 'I can phone her and explain in the morning.'

'It isn't every day a young artist has her own exhibition. And you were her best friend at school. You have to go. Why should the antics of a silly little girl who just happens to be your neighbour for a few months spoil your normal life?'

Elena eventually gave way, after making Dodie swear she'd wake her if Anna returned or the police telephoned.

Neither happened. Mrs Burns arrived, full of speculations, but cheerfully set to cleaning the kitchen when Dodie explained why Elena needed to sleep. Dodie busied herself unnecessarily rearranging the cutlery drawer, and encouraged Mrs Burns to talk.

'That young Anna, now, she seemed shy,' she commented. 'She kept out of my way, said she was working, but I don't really call writing stories working. I didn't often see her and Mr Wilbraham together. They were supposed to have separate rooms, too, but it was only a pretence. Stands to reason, pretty young girl and a man that's lonely, together in a great big house like that.'

The doorbell rang soon afterwards, and Detective Inspector Morton arrived and wanted to talk to Dodie and Elena urgently, he said. Elena appeared, rosy-cheeked with sleep, her hair tousled, and wearing a very fetching silk kimono.

'I didn't drop off until the birds were in full flood,' she muttered. 'Can we sit in the kitchen and have some really strong coffee?' She led the way from the hall, through the double-aspect dining room, and into the kitchen beyond. Detective Inspector Morton ducked his head to avoid the low beams and lintels.

'She's either guilty and frightened, and has run away, or someone is afraid she can implicate them and they've attacked her,' he said gloomily when they were seated at the kitchen table, each with a steaming mug of coffee. Mrs Burns, avid with curiosity, had been banished to clean the bedrooms. 'Do you favour one scenario more than the other?'

'I don't think she's guilty,' Dodie said slowly. 'Not of murder, anyway. I suppose she might have seen something when she first found his body, but she seemed truly shocked. If she suspected something she would surely have told you then? I don't think she was in a state to be calculating.'

'She made plenty of accusations, though she was singularly short of facts to back them up. But about yesterday. She said she was going for a walk. You've no idea where?'

'No, she didn't say.'

'And you didn't see which way she went?'

'No,' Elena said, sighing. 'I wish I had. But she hadn't anything with her, no bag for spare clothes, so I don't think she can have been planning to run away. That's what makes me so scared for her.'

'We've made enquiries at the railway station, but she could have slipped in without being seen. No one we've spoken to in the village admits to seeing her. It's rather soon to mount a full-scale search. Will you let us know at once if she returns or contacts you?'

'Of course,' Dodie said, and yawned widely. 'Sorry, I haven't had any sleep.'

The policeman gave her an unexpectedly attractive grin. In fact, when you looked at him as a man, Dodie suddenly realized, waking up slightly, he was quite a dish. 'Go to bed now. I'll not trouble you again for a few hours unless it's good news.'

He left, and Dodie, instead of going to bed, went into the sitting room on the far side of the hall to fetch Rick's book.

Elena eyed it dubiously. 'I can't imagine that was much of a help to staying awake last night,' she commented. 'You're surely not going to read it now?'

'I'm taking it upstairs with me, in case I can't sleep. A few more pages of it will do the trick. What time are you leaving?'

'I'm going on the four-thirty train. Sure you'll be OK tonight if I stay in London with Bettina?'

'I'll double lock all the doors and windows, and barricade my door. Wake me before you go.'

'I'll leave the car in case you need it. I'll order a taxi.'

'Try and get the fellow who took the mermaid. He might remember something. We never did ask his firm where he took her, the murder confused everything.'

Elena left, in due course. There had been no more news from the police, but people were beginning to hear that Anna had vanished. During the day Elena had taken half a dozen phone calls, and shortly after she had departed, followed by Mrs Burns on her bicycle, Dodie had a call from Rachel.

'I understand you're alone tonight. Would you like to come and sleep here? Gerard could fetch you in an hour or two.'

'Thanks, that's kind of you, but no. I feel obliged to stay here in case she comes back. It would be too awful if she came and found the house empty.'

'If you change your mind, just call me. You could tell the police, and they could leave someone watching the house. I imagine there is someone there in any case, looking out for the wretched girl. It's too bad of her to treat you like this when you've been so kind to her.'

'You don't think she can have come to any harm, then?'

'I suppose anything's possible, but I have the strong impression that girl can take care of herself. Oh, I know she was having hysterics when she found the body, that's different, a sudden shock. In general she seemed to be totally in control, aware of what she was doing, and – I don't know, she sometimes had a secretive, almost gloating expression in her eyes, especially when she was looking at Rick and thought no one was watching her.'

Dodie put down the phone thoughtfully. Was Rachel's observation accurate? It was hard to say. They'd spent so little time with Anna, and she was naturally shocked, but perhaps she hadn't been as devastated as she ought to have been to lose a lover in such grim circumstances.

Suddenly Dodie nodded, and went briskly upstairs. The police hadn't suggested looking at Anna's belongings. Perhaps they had searched her room next door, or perhaps they simply hadn't the manpower to cover everything, when it could have been a false alarm and Anna, not caring for the worry she might cause, might simply have taken it into her head to visit a friend and stay the night.

The suitcase contained only clothes, but they were of good quality, mostly new, with several designer labels amongst them. Anna had taken out a toilet bag and put a few items of make-up on the dressing table, but had unpacked no further. Her duffle bag was on the small armchair under the window, and she didn't appear to have unpacked that either. The folders Dodie had noticed were still there, exactly the same as far as she could tell.

Carefully, Dodie lifted them out. Underneath were a few computer disks, a couple of reporters' notebooks, and a wallet which held a few pounds, a single credit card, a library ticket, and a membership card for the Scribblers' Writer's Circle in Upper Markenlea. Right at the bottom, rather crumpled and dirty, was a leaflet giving details of a week's residential writing course at a specialist education centre.

It was dated almost three years before. Why had Anna kept this? She didn't appear to hoard the usual assortment of receipts and old letters and empty envelopes and shopping lists most people did.

There was nothing else, so Dodie turned her attention to the folders. There were three, two bulky ones full of loose pages, held together with thick rubber bands, and a slim one containing a few loose sheets of different sizes. After a cursory glance, Dodie concluded that the latter were notes for the novel Anna was writing. Some were typed, others handwritten, some in what looked like shorthand. None of them made a lot of sense, so Dodie turned her attention to the bulky ones.

The top sheet of the first she opened was labelled Chapter Ten, and Dodie put it aside and opened the other. This one started at Chapter One, but there was no title, nothing to show what it was, and no name of an author. Dodie began to read.

Another night went past with no news of Anna. Dodie slept late, for she had not gone to bed until after midnight. She had just finished a leisurely breakfast and was wondering what she ought to do when she heard the sound of a diesel engine outside. By the time she got to the front door Elena was fitting her key into the lock.

'You're back early,' Dodie said, as they kissed.

'Bettina had to get up at the crack of dawn for a TV interview,' Elena said. 'And I had some interesting news. But I'm dying for coffee. Bettina's a lovely girl, but she's gone in for health foods in a big way, and herb tea doesn't do anything at all for me first thing in the morning. I crave caffeine.'

Dodie had to wait until the coffee had worked its magic, but then Elena gave her a wide smile.

'Well?'

'The taxi, first of all. He took her to the far side of the river, just across the bridge, and dropped her in the car park there. A man arrived and paid the fare, and then they disappeared.'

'Could he describe the man?'

'No, apart from tall and he thinks he was wearing jeans and a long-sleeved shirt. Helpful.'

'But the mermaid knew he'd be there. Interesting. But that isn't all, or you wouldn't look like a satisfied cat.'

'No. I was at the back of the train, and when we got to the next station I looked out and saw Elizabeth and a man getting on. She had discarded her widow's weeds, so to speak, and was wearing a cream silk suit and coffee-brown bag and shoes. She had a hat on that would have done for Ascot. And his suit wasn't off the peg, either. When we got to Paddington I followed them, managed to get into the taxi queue right behind them, and heard him ask for Holland Park.'

'You shouldn't have got so close,' Dodie

protested, alarmed, but Elena laughed.

'They were so absorbed in one another they hadn't any eyes for anyone else. I'll bet you the fair Elizabeth has matrimony in mind, and that could have messed up her settlement from Rick. He surely wouldn't have gone on paying her a good proportion of his income if she married someone else. So that gives her a motive. And him, the unknown swain, come to that.'

Dodie considered this. 'It's possible, I think, but not a very strong motive. If he lived in Holland Park, which is what you're implying, he can't be strapped for cash. I've come across a much stronger motive, though at the moment I can't see how it all fits in.'

Before she could say more the doorbell rang, and Dodie sighed.

'Not the police again! I wonder if they've discovered anything by now?'

It was not the police. When Elena opened the door Anna stood facing them. She was muddy, her clothes were torn, and through a hole in her shirt they could see some long ugly scratches on her shoulder.

'Oh, I didn't think I'd make it!' she gasped, her voice hoarse, and took a wavering step forward.

'Anna, child, where on earth have you been?' Dodie exclaimed, while Elena took Anna's arm to help her.

‘I don’t know.’ She staggered. ‘I must sit down. I’m sorry, but I feel so muzzy!’

They helped her up to her room, and Dodie insisted she undressed and got straight into bed.

‘Don’t try to explain. Later will do. Are you hungry?’

Anna, lying back on the pillows, nodded. ‘And terribly thirsty,’ she said.

‘I’ll get some tea and toast,’ Elena said, and vanished.

Dodie fetched a glass of water from the bathroom, and Anna drank thirstily, then closed her eyes. A single tear slid down her cheek, and she was trying to suppress sobs. Dodie sat in silence, holding Anna’s hand. There were so many questions she wanted to ask, but the girl was in no state to answer yet. She had acquired several large bruises, and chafing on her wrists seemed to indicate she’d been tied up at one time. Her clothes were torn and filthy, her shoes muddy, and when Dodie bent down to feel them, they were wet inside.

Anna revived slightly when Elena reappeared with the tea, and gave them a faint smile.

‘Thank you,’ she whispered as she sipped greedily. ‘Gosh, I needed that.’

She ate the toast, thickly spread with marmalade, and then with a sigh slid down under the duvet and was asleep within seconds.

‘Do you think she’s all right? Ought we to ask a doctor to come and see her?’ Elena asked worriedly, staring down at Anna.

Dodie shook her head. ‘I think it’s sheer exhaustion. Yes, she has bruises and scratches, but nothing that won’t wait until she has a bit more energy to cope.’

They left the room, leaving the light on and the door ajar.

‘What about the police? Surely we must tell them, and they’ll want to question her.’

‘I think they’ll be reasonable. They can come and look at her, but they must realize they’ll get no sense out of her as she is.’

It was a young, uniformed woman police constable who came in response to their call. She looked at Anna, held her pulse, shook her slightly to try and wake her, inspected her head, and lifted the duvet to look at the bruises.

‘It can wait,’ she decided. ‘She doesn’t seem concussed or anything, no lumps on her head. But please call us the moment she wakes, and please don’t let her get away again.’

‘Cheeky kid!’ Dodie said, laughing when the WPC had gone. ‘I think I’ll send the Detective Inspector a bill for gaoler’s fees. There’s nothing we can do until she wakes up.’

‘Well, actually, there is, if you want to. I met Daniel near the station. I went to do some shopping before I got a taxi home, and he was in the chemist.'

'Not at the office?'

'He said he was working at home today, and he said Serena had gone off and told him to make his own lunch because their daily woman was away on holiday. He was highly disgruntled. I don't think he ever has to look after himself.'

'Then about time he did,' Dodie said virtuously.

'Maybe, but I thought it too good an opportunity to get him on his own. He's a bit reclusive, doesn't mix like Serena does, so I invited him to lunch. I couldn't carry anything more from town, I was laden with my case and my own shopping. So would you be a dear and get me some stuff from the shop, while I get started? I can keep an eye on Anna, and you look as if a breath of fresh air would do you good.'

'Go on, say it. I'm looking a hag, my age, a fright, and all the rest.'

'You'd still be a credit to the chorus line. It's only a few bits and pieces. And I suggest we don't tell anyone Anna's back.'

'Are you afraid Daniel will try to bash her on the head or kidnap her?'

Elena smiled, and Dodie, with another theatrical sniff, made a list of things her daughter wanted. She was, she discovered, thankful to be outside. The air was warm, the sun bright, and a gentle breeze made walking across the village green pleasant. Several men in whites were preparing the cricket pitch, and the pavilion was open. Dodie assumed there was to be a match later. She admired the red phone box outside the shop. At least they hadn't replaced that with the modern uninteresting plastic hood.

In the shop Mrs Weaver eyed her avidly.

'Oh, Mrs Fanshaw, we heard about Anna! What's happened? Has she been kidnapped, do you think? Or could she have drowned? Perhaps she felt she couldn't go on any longer and she's committed suicide!'

'Why should she do that?' Dodie asked, intrigued.

'Well, after so many tragedies, she must feel her life is doomed.'

'What tragedies? What do you mean?'

'Well, her other boyfriend. Don't you know about him?'

'Actually I don't. What other boyfriend? When was this? And how do you know about it?'

Mrs Weaver shrugged. 'I hear all sorts of things in the shop. But your daughter wasn't here then. It was a couple or more years ago. He was killed. It was an accident on the building site. I think he was a carpenter or a bricklayer or something – quite unsuitable for a girl like Anna, who'd had a good education. Whatever she's done, she once came from a good family.'

Dodie stared at her in disbelief. She hadn't heard anyone talk like this for years. Mrs Weaver was only in her thirties, but she suddenly seemed a generation older than Dodie.

'What was his name?' she asked. 'Do you know?'

'He was Irish, I think. Kevin, or Keiran O'Mara. He was ever so good-looking, tall and dark, and the most vivid blue eyes. Any girl might fall for him, but he was unsuitable, a rough diamond, as they used to say,' she added, giggling.

'How did you know him?'

'He used to play for the village cricket team. Anna came with him to most matches. I didn't know her well then, of course, she'd just come in for sweets or a drink. We didn't meet properly until she took up with Rick.'

Dodie nodded, abstracted. This could explain a lot. Then the church clock struck and she remembered the shopping. 'That's interesting. Have you any sour cream?'

Ten

Dodie arrived at the front door just as Daniel's car turned into the drive. This, she was intrigued to see, was a mid-range Ford, several years old, and not in the best condition. He wasn't in competition with Serena, with her Mercedes. Then she recalled that Serena's car was rumoured to have been given to her by Rick Wilbraham. Was the agency doing less well than she'd supposed, was Daniel parsimonious, or was he making a statement about his wife and her past indiscretions? Looking at his dour face, she suspected the latter.

'Come in. I'll just take this shopping to Elena. Do you prefer the garden or inside?'

'Too hot for outside,' he grunted, and Dodie nodded. He was in a tetchy mood. Most of the people they'd met during the recent spell of hot weather had revelled in the opportunity, rare in England, of being out of doors as much as possible.

'There's the sitting room. Make yourself at home, and I'll come back in a minute with some ice.'

She provided him with Scotch, noted with amusement that he declined the ice, and sat opposite him, on the far side of the fireplace where Elena had displayed her flower-arranging talents with a huge arrangement of greenery and yellow flowers which toned with the upholstery and curtains.

'You must be busy to work on Saturday. Do you work at home very often? It must be tedious travelling to London every day.'

'Always busy. I'd prefer to move the office down here, make life simpler, but Serena likes the buzz of London. Can't think why – we can write letters and make phone calls just as well from here.'

'Don't you have to entertain authors and editors? Take them out to lunch? And go to launch parties and things?' Dodie asked. She knew very little of the workings of the publishing world.

Daniel laughed, but he was not amused. 'We could go up for them. We don't need to do half as many, but Serena likes them, and as she's bringing in the big money at the moment, she has to have her way. I wonder what Piers will do for Rick's paperback now he isn't here? He'd planned a big splash next week. Rick was booked for dozens of radio and TV interviews, a couple of chat shows, everything you could think of.'

'Do you have any other partners?'

'No, just the two of us. Serena came to work for me as a secretary, you know.'

'Really? No, I didn't know that. Is that

how people become agents? Get into the business in any position and work their way up, so to speak?' Dodie winced inwardly. She could have phrased that better. But Daniel didn't appear to have noticed. She hurried on. 'I only know theatrical agents, but it was probably different in my days on the stage.'

He was gazing into his drink, and then he looked up at her, shrugged, and tossed it off in one swallow. 'She was bright, I grant you that. Full of ideas on how to attract the really big authors. Rick was her first big success. After she pulled off that deal I had to let her have her way more. But now he's gone, perhaps she'll come round to my view that it pays better in the long run to have a stable of regular, reliable authors rather than flash-in-the-pan sensations. And to deal with the big publishers. More dependable.'

Elena came in, apologizing for not being ready, and suggested they went straight into lunch. 'I know you have a lot of work, we don't want to take up too much of your time,' she said.

Daniel, with an attempt at a smile, rose to his feet. He looked slightly unsteady, and Dodie suspected the whisky he'd had wasn't his first that morning. But he walked firmly enough across the room, following Elena into the dining room, where a circular pedestal table in the Regency style had been set for three. Elena served bowls of soup, and fresh, warm rolls. For a moment there was silence, as Daniel ate hungrily.

'Were you saying, just now, that Rick's book was a flash in the pan?' Dodie asked, and Elena gave her a surprised glance.

'Oh, good enough, I suppose,' Daniel said hastily. 'But Serena hasn't discovered anyone else yet of nearly comparable marketability.'

'Did you need anyone else when you had Rick? Wouldn't his success, which would surely have been big with all the publicity he was getting, have been enough? Along with the other authors you have built up,' she added.

'It might have been, but now it won't. And what I was meaning, Mrs Fanshaw, was that very often second novels don't live up to the promise of the first.'

'I'm reading the first one now. Have you read the second? Is that as good?'

Daniel glanced swiftly at her. 'What do you think of the first one? Do you like it? I told her only men and literary types, and young hopefuls, would buy it.'

'Well, I'm none of those, thank goodness, and I found it interesting. What's the second one about? Surely it can't be set in the building industry again, can it?'

'I haven't read the new one.'

Elena's eyebrows rose slightly at his

brusque tone. 'I'll just get the salad,' she murmured, and collected the soup bowls.

Daniel shook himself slightly. 'That was good, my dear. Far better than I get at home.'

'Have you any theories about Rick's death?' Dodie asked.

He suddenly lifted his head and stared at her. 'Why should I?'

'Most other people have. Nearly everyone I meet has a different one, and I can't see how the police will ever be able to prove anything unless they get more evidence. It could have been almost anyone, most of his friends – or so-called friends, I doubt if the murderer could be described that way – had been on their own that morning, and had the opportunity.'

'I'm not sure I want to know. My God, if it turned out to be Elizabeth, or either of the Deans, or even Anna or Frank, what a scandal it would make! The press would chew it over for months, and then the trial!' He shuddered. 'Better all round to leave it a mystery, and let the interest die away when the next big story comes along.'

'Don't you want the murderer caught? And punished? Help yourself to the salad,' Elena added.

'You know, I don't think I do. There's probably hundreds of undetected murderers going about their normal lives, doing no harm, after the one killing. They might have had good reasons.'

'Don't you believe the theory that the second murder gets easier?' Dodie said. 'Or that if anyone suspected, the murderer would kill them for his own safety?'

Daniel considered it. 'No, I don't think I do. They're not all serial killers. Once they've achieved their objective, and so long as there's no real proof, why should they have to kill again?'

They ate in silence for a while, and then, when Elena rose to fetch cheese, Daniel looked at his watch and exclaimed in dismay.

'My dear, that was delicious, but I must go. Sorry, but I'm expecting a phone call. From America. I mustn't miss it. Thank you so much for coming to my rescue. You must both come round for drinks one day.'

Elena barely had time to reach the door into the hall before he was opening the front door. With repeated farewells he almost ran for his car, flung himself in, and drove off without bothering to fasten his seatbelt.

'Let's take our coffee into the garden,' Dodie suggested. 'I don't think I'll have any cheese, either.'

'What was all that about?' Elena demanded as they carried the remnants of the salad out into the kitchen and put the food away in the fridge. 'He's remarkably busy for a Saturday.'

'Undercurrents,' Dodie said slowly. 'He

and Serena seem to have quite a lot to disagree about. How long have they been married? Was her affair with Rick before or after the marriage?'

'Just before, I think. Elizabeth put it around that she accepted Daniel on the rebound, when she didn't persuade Rick to marry her, but I'm not so sure. Serena's determined to be a big noise in publishing, and it's my belief she thought Daniel would be a stepping stone.'

'It doesn't appear to be working out for her,' Dodie said slowly. 'Is the coffee ready? Then let's take it down the garden. I don't want Anna to hear us, and her room's too close to the terrace.'

They walked through the steeply sloping garden, splendid with riotously exuberant buddleia, ceanothus, lilac and paeonies in the borders, and a magnificent pink magnolia at the end of the upper lawn. When they came to the narrow patch of grass which ended in a steep slope towards the river, Dodie sank on to the grass and kicked off her shoes.

'OK, what have you found out?' Elena asked, flopping down beside her. 'You're being horribly mysterious.'

'Mrs Weaver told me Anna used to have a boyfriend, a rough diamond, she called him, who worked for Rick. The chap died in an accident on one of the building sites, and her theory about Anna's disappearance was that she'd found it too hard to cope with so many tragedies, and killed herself.'

'She has a lurid imagination. But I wonder if it's true, about the boyfriend?'

'And whether she met Rick through that connection with Rick's development projects?'

'We can ask her. But what did Daniel say before I came in? Do you think he suspects that Serena could have killed Rick?'

'He might. He sounded all confused,' Dodie said thoughtfully. 'And if what I suspect is true, he might think she had cause.'

'Cause? To kill the golden goose? That's crazy!'

'Ah, but you see, Rick may turn out to be the ugly duckling,' Dodie said, and told her what she had discovered.

'Then we'd better ask Anna as soon as she's capable of talking,' Elena decided, and stood up. 'This gives us a completely new angle. Let's go back to the house. I don't want to risk her vanishing again.'

They were not to see Anna immediately, however. As they came on to the terrace Elizabeth walked round the corner of the house. She wore a skimpy sleeveless dress, her hair was windblown, and she carried a large sun hat.

'Hello, there. I was expecting to see you at

the cricket match. Whew, it's hot today.'

'The day I get my mother to watch cricket will be when she's in a wheelchair and can't resist,' Elena said. 'It was certainly hot in London last night,' she added, and Elizabeth gave her a sharp glance.

'You saw me, I suppose? You were on the same train. I looked back when I was in the taxi and saw you in the queue.'

'Yes, I was surprised. I didn't see you get on at our station.'

'I left the car further up the line, at the next station. More of the late trains stop there coming back.'

'I stayed with a friend, so I didn't have to think about that,' Elena said smoothly. 'You looked very glamorous, as though you were off to the theatre or some elegant party.'

Elizabeth frowned. 'Oh, no. Well, I suppose it was a party of sorts. I went to dinner with some friends. A girlfriend just got engaged. It was actually her brother I was with. We decided to travel up together as we live on the same line.'

'He looked very attractive. Very handsome.'

'Is he?' Elizabeth fiddled with her hat. 'I suppose most women would think so. But I've known him since we were kids, and somehow men you've known as scruffy hooligans can never be taken seriously when they grow up, can they?' She put her hat on, and the wide brim shaded her eyes. 'I'll get sunstroke if I'm not careful, but it's so difficult to keep a hat on when I have the roof of the car down, and it's a sin not to in this weather.'

'Would you like a cool drink?' Elena offered. 'Come and sit in the shade.'

'No thanks. I mustn't stop. I'm helping with the cricket teas. I just popped over to ask if you've heard any more? I saw Rachel and she said Anna had vanished. Have you heard anything else? Do you think she's run away?'

'Anna's back, quite safe,' Dodie said.

'Back? Thank goodness. Where on earth was she? How thoughtless of her to just go off like that and not let anyone know!'

Elena was about to reply when Dodie spoke. 'Well, we have no authority over her,' she said quickly, forestalling Elena, who looked at her in surprise and then shut her mouth with a slight snap. 'She's free to do as she wishes.'

'Yes, I suppose so. Well, I'm glad nothing happened to her.'

'Why should it?'

Elizabeth shrugged. 'You never know. After all, there's a murderer still on the loose, and Anna might possibly know something. I'd better go. Be seeing you.'

'That was terribly unconvincing,' Elena said, laughing, when the sound of Elizabeth's car had died away. 'A friend's kid brother, my eye! And she doesn't care a toss about Anna, it was just an excuse to come and explain herself away.'

'If this is serious, it could strengthen her motive for killing Rick. If she was planning to get married again, what difference would it have made to her alimony?'

'Surely she'd have lost it? Better, you think, to kill him and hope to benefit from the will?'

'It's a possibility. But there's the difficulty about Anna,' Dodie said slowly. 'I'm getting impatient. I wish she'd wake soon.'

It was dinner time before Anna, looking pale and with dark circles under her eyes, surfaced. Dodie was laying the table when she heard the sound of the shower. Conscious of her instructions from the police, she rang the station and was told someone would visit them shortly. Five minutes later Anna, wearing a towelling robe and with a towel wrapped round her head, came downstairs. By common consent Dodie and Elena said nothing of what was on their minds until after the girl had eaten, and taken a glass of wine with the meal. They moved into the sitting room afterwards, but when Anna said she didn't want any coffee, and was still very tired and really would prefer to go straight back to bed, Dodie shook her head.

'No, Anna, you've been asleep all day. The police need to talk to you. You can spare us half an hour now. There are a lot of questions that need answering, and I think you can help us.'

'I didn't kill Rick!' she cried, looking frightened. 'I thought you believed me!'

'That wasn't what I meant. Anna, child, what happened to you? Where were you? Had you been abducted?'

Anna heaved a deep sigh. 'I suppose so. I don't know who it was, though. I was walking along a lane, a narrow one, and a van came along behind me. I stepped up on to the verge to let it go past, it was getting dark, but it stopped just behind me.' She shivered. 'I looked to see why it had stopped, and a man in a hood – I suppose it was a stocking mask, got out. Before I could run he'd caught me.'

'Just one man?' Dodie asked.

'Yes, I think so. I only saw one. But he was tall, and looked big. He must have hit me and I passed out. Next thing I knew I was tied up, and blindfolded, in the back of the van, and it was bouncing me all over the place. It was still on a narrow twisty lane, I thought, because it seemed to be hitting potholes a lot.'

'Do you have any idea how far he took you? How long you were travelling in this van?'

'No. I don't know how long I was out. But I think I passed out again – I was rolling all over the back of the van, you see, and I think I hit my head again.' She paused, and rubbed her eyes.

'And then?'

'When I came to, I was in some sort of shed, and it was daylight. I must have been asleep all night. It took ages, all day, before I managed to get my hands free. The shed door had a padlock on the outside, but the hinges weren't very strong, and in the end I managed to lever them off with a screwdriver that was in the shed. It was in a field, and the moon was up, so I could see quite well. I got to a road, and after a mile or two came to a crossroads and a signpost. I recognized it. It was about ten miles from here.'

'And you walked home? No wonder you're tired. But you could show the police where it was?'

'I think so. I know that crossroads, and there was a stream, before I got to the first road, because I almost fell into it. My shoes got wet, but not my clothes, luckily. I wasn't dressed for midnight strolls,' she added, attempting to laugh. 'But do I have to go to the police? They still think I killed poor Rick.'

'They know you're back, in fact they'll be here shortly, and this might help them to catch the real murderer. It must be connected in some way,' Dodie said.

On cue, two detective police constables they hadn't seen before arrived, heard Anna's story repeated, and said they'd be in touch the following morning.

When they'd left, Anna rose and said she was going to bed.

Dodie shook her head. 'First, Anna, tell us about your friend Kevin O'Mara.'

For a moment she looked horrified, then she gasped, and took a deep breath.

'Kevin? How do you know about him?'

'Mrs Weaver knew him, from the cricket. She said he was a boyfriend. Was he?'

Anna nodded, and her eyes filled with tears. 'He died,' she whispered. 'Did she tell you how?'

'Just that it was an accident on a building site. What happened?' Dodie asked gently.

'He was a carpenter. He was good, he carved beautiful animals, but he said he could earn more doing ordinary work for the developers. He was working on a house, a whole row of terraced houses in London that were being renovated, converted into flats. There was an explosion. A gas pipe had been broken somehow, they said. Anyway, he was at the top of the house and the blast threw him out of the window. He died on the way to the hospital.'

Dodie held her close as she sobbed, and gradually Anna grew calm again.

'Was it one of Rick's developments?'

'Yes. He worked regularly for Rick, all over the place, round here and often on London houses. If these big ones were converted into three or four flats, each one would fetch almost as much as the original house. Kevin had plans, when he'd made enough money, to buy up a house and do it up, sell off the other flats, and we could live in one of them. But he never got the chance.'

After a brief silence Anna looked up at them. 'Can I go to bed now, please? I really don't see what this has to do with Rick being killed, or my being abducted. And I can't tell you any more.'

'Yes, you can, Anna. Who really wrote Rick's novel?'

Eleven

Anna stared at Dodie. She was even paler than before. 'I don't know what you mean! Rick wrote the book, of course. If you mean who typed it, I don't know. I wasn't here then. I've done some of the typing on his second one.'

Dodie sighed. 'Anna, it's no use. I went through your things, to try and find some clue of where you might be, when you went missing.'

'You did what!' Anna's face grew red with fury and she leaped to her feet. 'How dare you! I thought I could trust you, and this is what you do when – when I'm not here, when I'm being bounced around in an old van, tied up, imprisoned, in fear of my life!'

'Calm down, child. We didn't know whether you'd just run away. That wouldn't have impressed the police, since you're technically still a suspect for Rick's murder. I wanted to find you before they did, persuade you to come back before they drew the wrong conclusions. I needed an address, family or friend.'

'Yeah, well. I suppose so. It still wasn't very nice,' Anna said sulkily, and slowly sat down again.

'I'm sorry, but I felt obliged to do it.'

Anna still sounded wary. 'OK, I understand. But it's a shock to hear your things have been searched.'

Dodie smiled at her. 'Good girl. But there's something else. I found what seemed like a different version of Rick's novel. His hero was a building worker, though, not a clerk. And the spelling wasn't very good, and the grammar was a bit off in places.'

'I haven't seen it but it doesn't sound like Rick's work,' Elena observed.

Anna chewed her lip, and then shook her head. 'All writers make changes,' she said. 'This was just a first draft, and Rick must have changed his mind. Changed the character, I mean. I've done that sometimes, too. You start off, and then find reasons why the first character isn't right, or something. That's what must have happened.'

'Did Rick tell you that?'

'Well, not in a lot of detail, but he sort of implied it. When we were talking about writing, sometimes.'

Dodie sighed. 'I can accept that. But what about the spelling and grammar? Rick was educated, he wrote correctly. Why are there so many mistakes in this copy?'

'When you do a first draft, and especially if you're not a proper typist, you make a lot of silly mistakes,' Anna said, her manner determinedly patient. 'I still do, when I'm in a hurry to get it all down before I lose the thought or the thread of a story. And I'm used to typing. This must have been a first draft, and Rick would have tidied it up later on.'

'Why did you bring it away from the house?'

'Are you accusing me of stealing it?' Anna demanded, flushing again and gripping the edges of the chair with both hands.

'No, just asking a question. Though I suppose strictly speaking any papers belong to Rick's estate and you shouldn't have removed them,' Dodie said calmly. 'There's a market for authors' manuscripts, isn't there? This could be valuable.'

'But that's why I took them! Oh, don't look so startled, I wasn't stealing them. If you want to know the truth, I suspected what it was, and I was afraid Frank might destroy them. Or that snake Piers might pinch them and claim they belonged to him, if Rick had ever handed over that draft.'

'He couldn't do that, could he?' Elena asked.

'I don't know! But I wanted to make absolutely sure they were safe, and the only way I could do that was to keep them myself.'

Dodie sighed. She wasn't satisfied. 'What about the folder of notes?' she asked.

'The notes?' Anna frowned. 'God, were you grubbing about in those too?'

Dodie frowned at her. 'They seemed to me to be ideas for Rick's next novel. There were details about building sites again, and what looked like extracts from accounts, and a list of characters, and some of these had the same names as people in the first book.'

'It just happened to be with the others when I picked them up,' Anna said. 'I don't know what they are in detail.'

'Where did you pick them up from? The study? Is that why you sent Frank over here while you were supposed to be packing, so that he wouldn't be able to stop you going in there?'

'No!' Anna almost shouted as she jumped to her feet and began pacing up and down. 'Rick had given them to me, those two folders, to look at. I was interested in how he worked, I asked to see it. They were all in my room. The other must have been caught up with them, between them or something, and neither of us had noticed.'

'I thought you were helping Rick with his second novel, doing research for him and so on. Where are those notes? And where is the typescript of this second novel?'

Anna looked hunted. 'I don't know! When I did anything I gave it straight back to him, and he put it away.'

Dodie shook her head. 'When I began to read, I thought these chapters were for the second novel, and then I realized that although some details had altered, names and so on, it was the same book. His second one has disappeared. There's no trace of it in his study, it's not on the computer, and neither his agent nor his publisher has it. Anna, you are the most likely person to know what happened to it, why the computer was wiped clean. You haven't hidden it somewhere, have you?'

'No.'

It was a blank denial, and though Dodie felt for a few moments that she'd like to try some form of third degree, she reluctantly concluded that she could not give way to her inclinations. Why didn't the silly chit see that they were trying to help her?

'You had some computer disks in your bag,' she tried another tack. 'What are they?'

'My own novel!' Anna snapped. 'And if you try to find out what's on them, I'll – well, there are some laws about privacy!'

She stood up and stalked towards the door. 'I'm leaving. I know when I'm not welcome.'

'Don't be foolish!' Elena snapped. 'It's after ten, how can you find anywhere else tonight? You're welcome to leave in the morning, unless you've calmed down. Frankly, I'll be glad not to have to feel responsible for you any more.'

'I'll go to The Plough,' Anna said. 'First thing in the morning. They sometimes take in paying guests.'

She flung herself out of the room and Dodie and Elena looked at one another and sighed in unison.

'Did you believe her?' Elena asked.

'Not really. It was a plausible story, but people who normally write correctly don't make the sort of errors I saw.'

'Is it possible he could have dictated it, and an incompetent typist transcribed it?'

'There may be some sort of explanation, but whatever it is, it doesn't help to find the new typescript, or discover the murderer.'

Anna apologized stiffly the next morning, but insisted that she preferred to leave.

'I didn't sleep much, so I went out before you got up, and they can let me have a room at The Plough,' she said. 'Thank you for all you've done, and I'm sorry to have been a nuisance. And before you ask, I've told the police where I'll be.'

'Do you need a lift with your luggage?' Elena asked coolly.

'No thanks. I'm all packed, so I'll go now.'

'Without any breakfast?' Dodie asked. The girl looked as though she hadn't slept at all, she was flushed, the black smudges were under her eyes again, and her bruises were much more visible. She had the makings of a majestic black eye.

'I had some coffee when I went across to the pub. And I can manage my case, thanks. You know there isn't much in it!'

Elena was so incensed by this that she ignored Anna, leaving Dodie to let the girl out of the front door and wish her goodbye.

'The ungrateful little tyke!' she exploded when Dodie returned to the kitchen. 'Well, if the police do charge her after all I won't be wasting my time being sorry for her!'

'She was frightened,' Dodie said thoughtfully. 'Obviously she's scared of whoever abducted her, but I think she was scared we'd find out more. She wasn't telling much of the truth last night.'

'I suppose it could have been someone who thought she might have this wretched second book. Serena, and possibly Daniel, and that publisher fellow are the obvious suspects,' Elena said as she prepared breakfast. 'They all want it because it's money for them.'

'But Elizabeth or Frank might feel, if they have inherited anything under Rick's will, that it belonged to them, and they could try to sell it for a higher price. I don't know how these deals work,' she added fretfully.

'You'll have to write your memoirs and find out!' Elena said, her good temper restored. 'Didn't Serena say she'd sold two books? If they were already sold, that deal would surely stand?'

'But Frank and Elizabeth might know as little about that as I do. Now who's that at the door? The post's come already, and it's too early for callers hoping to cadge a cup of coffee.'

'You don't know this village,' Elena said, grinning as she passed her mother and went into the hall.

Dodie reached for some toast and put two more slices in the toaster. She could hear voices in the hall, and then Elena laughed. A moment later she ushered the visitor into the kitchen.

'Look who's here.'

It was a young man, ginger haired and

wearing dark-rimmed spectacles. For a moment Dodie's mind went blank, and then she recognized him.

'Good grief! The man in the flat in Ealing. The one who isn't our mermaid. How did you find us?'

He looked startled. 'I didn't know it was you,' he said, shaking his head. 'My boss sent me here, to speak to Anna Terry. I thought she was staying with you.'

'She was. You've just missed her,' Dodie said. 'But this needs explaining. Come and have some coffee. You must have started out early to get here at this time. On a Sunday, too.'

'I did,' he said ruefully. 'Thanks, I'd love some. We're so busy at the office it's the only chance I've had to come.'

When he was supplied with coffee and toast Dodie spoke. 'We ought to introduce ourselves. I'm Dodie Fanshaw, and this is my daughter, Elena da Rocha.'

'Paul Maitland. But how did you come to be at my flat the other evening?'

'We'd been given your address. By a mermaid.'

He looked startled, then laughed. 'I wish I knew one,' he murmured. 'It would be amusing.'

'Well, I am embroidering,' Dodie said, grinning at him. 'She fell into the river and came up the garden for help. She left in a taxi, and didn't give us her name or her address. We got that from the boatyard where she'd hired the boat she capsized. That was your address.'

'How peculiar. What did she look like?'

'Wet or dry? She had long black hair, was slim, pretty, and pretty indistinguishable from hundreds of other twenty-somethings. Not a lot of help. Oh, and blue eyes.'

'As you say, not much to go on. She may live somewhere near me, I suppose, and gave that address for some reason. How very odd.'

'Unsolved mystery, Mr Maitland. But you wanted to speak with Anna, didn't you? You're not from the police?'

'Police?' He looked horrified. 'Of course not. What have the police got to do with it?'

'Anna's – boss, boyfriend, whatever we call him – was killed on Sunday.'

'Yes, Rick Wilbraham, I know. That's why I'm here, in a way. She worked for him, and my boss sent me to talk to her. For some reason she won't speak to him.'

'Who is your boss?' Dodie asked sharply. She had a horrible suspicion she could guess.

'I work for Wallaby Publishing. I'm in the publicity department. Well, I am the publicity department at the moment. The other two left and haven't been replaced. Mr Walls-Farmer sent me.'

'And you want to know where the typescript of the next Rick Wilbraham masterpiece is,' Dodie nodded. 'So does everyone else. People seem to be more concerned with that than with trying to find out who murdered him.'

'I'm sorry,' Paul Maitland began, but Dodie waved her hand at him and smiled.

'Not your fault. I want to know who murdered him, but since everyone in the entire village and beyond seems to have had the opportunity, we have to find out why first, and then we might begin to know who.'

'Anna went to stay at the pub,' Elena put in. 'It's on the far side of the green. I wish you better luck than the rest of us have had. The wretched typescript has vanished.'

'That would be terrible!' Paul exclaimed. 'It's bad enough we'll only have two books, but if this can't be found and we only have one, what a waste of talent! Thanks for the breakfast. I feel much better now, but I mustn't take up your time. I'll go and find Anna Terry.'

'Before you go,' Dodie said, catching at his jacket sleeve as he rose to leave, 'did you have anything to do with the first book?'

'Marketing it, yes.'

'Did you see it as a typescript? Before it had been printed, I mean?'

'No, I don't have anything to do with editorial. The sales people would probably have seen a copy, but we're given the blurb and author information, and take it from there. Why?'

'I'd like to know who edited it – speak to them. Just a hunch, that's all,' Dodie said almost to herself.

'Girl called Janice. I don't know who copy-edited, but I could find out. We use a lot of freelancers for that.'

'Copy-editing? What's the difference?'

'The editor makes major changes, rewrites, and keeps track of production schedules. Copy-editors go through and make sure of spellings and punctuation, continuity, house style and so on, the nitty gritty.'

'That's the person I want! Could you be a dear and telephone details to me when you get back to the office?'

'Sure. Now I'd better go and see Anna, but from what you say it won't be much good. I wonder what has happened to it?'

He'd hardly gone before Detective Inspector Morton was on the doorstep.

'I've been to The Plough to see the young lady,' he explained.

'Is Anna better now? And do you have any new leads?' Dodie asked.

'If I had, I couldn't tell you,' he said. 'She's fit enough. We want her to come with us and try and show us where she was imprisoned, if she can find it again.'

‘From what she said it can’t have been too far from that signpost, and she knew where that was.’

‘Has she any relatives living nearby, do you know?’

‘I think she has family in Brighton, but she hasn’t mentioned any others,’ Dodie said. She’d found no hint of anything like an address book in Anna’s belongings, but of course she could have left some things behind at Rick’s house.

‘I’d prefer to have an older woman, not a policewoman, with her. She struck me as being rather hysterical.’

‘I don’t think she’d want me,’ Dodie said hurriedly, suspecting what was coming.

‘Why not? You befriended her.’

She’d better confess. ‘I looked through her things when she went missing, to try and find something like this, an address book, or letters, and she objected pretty strongly. There wasn’t anything. But she resented what she saw as invasion of her privacy. That’s mainly why she moved out. Couldn’t you get Dr Dean, perhaps? They’ve known one another longer. I met her for the first time on Sunday – just a week ago, though it seems much longer.’

‘I understand. But she’s asked for you. We’re going this afternoon. Will you come?’

Twelve

Elena had invited several of the villagers to a barbecue supper on Sunday evening, and planned to spend the afternoon preparing dips and salads. A couple of girls she often employed to help were coming in, and by the time Dodie's police escort arrived she was deep in preparations.

Anna was subdued. She arrived in an unmarked police car driven by a young, plain-clothes woman introduced as WPC Crossley. The Detective Inspector sat in the front, and Dodie got into the back beside Anna.

'Sorry,' she muttered, and Dodie squeezed her hand. She was longing to know what had happened between Anna and the young man Paul, but didn't want to ask questions in front of the two policemen.

'Are you feeling a bit better now?' she asked instead. Anna looked pale still, and kept rubbing her temples.

Anna grimaced. 'Not much. I'm still aching, but I slept again this morning, and I feel less exhausted now. You know that beastly publisher sent someone else to try and get that wretched typescript from me?'

'Yes. You mean the young man Paul? You

saw him?'

'I did eventually convince him I didn't have it. I'm beginning to wonder if Rick didn't destroy it himself.'

'Destroy it? But why?'

'He wasn't happy with it. He was talking about starting a completely new one. But I don't know if he destroyed the other one, maybe that night I was away. That could account for it not being on the computer. The only other solution is that for some reason Frank did.'

'You haven't mentioned before that he was unhappy with it.'

'Well, no. It seemed disloyal. And actually I didn't think it was too bad.'

'Surely it would have been to Frank's advantage, assuming he inherits some part of Rick's money, to have it published?'

'He's a bit crazy. He doesn't think like other people. And he was jealous of Rick. Maybe Frank went mad, destroyed it, and that was what the row was about, and Frank could have pushed him in the pool, and when he saw Rick was dead he panicked and tried to disguise it with that stupid stabbing.'

Dodie glanced at the Detective Inspector. She could have sworn his ears were red, burning with curiosity as he listened. Did Anna honestly believe this theory, or was she being devious, trying to deflect suspicion on to Frank?

Anna seemed to have said all she wanted to, and lapsed into a gloomy silence. Dodie tried to work this new factor into her deductions. If the new book had been destroyed, by Rick himself, quite a few people would be furious with him. That included Serena and Daniel, and Piers Walls-Farmer. It might include Elizabeth who would lose some of his income, assuming he didn't produce an alternative book swiftly. If he had planned to abandon authorship altogether it could possibly have affected Frank's position. That would depend on whether Rick stayed in the house. And it could affect Anna even more, if she was there purely or mainly as a secretary and research assistant. She didn't appear to have seen the implications, or surely she wouldn't have made the suggestion.

The big car swiftly covered the ten miles which Anna had so painfully walked, in the dark, bruised and frightened. At the signpost she roused herself to direct the driver down the lane, and after another mile or so called out to her to stop.

'I think that's the stream I fell into,' she said, pointing to the middle of a field of pasture. 'And beyond it, the ground rises a little. I remember that now, I had to go up a slope, and then I was coming down.'

'So the shed could be over the hill.'

The driver was consulting a large-scale map. 'There's a track a bit further on. The man who took you there wouldn't have wanted to carry you this way. We'll go and see.'

A mile further the track veered off to the right, and they followed it slowly. It was rough, badly rutted, and the car bounced alarmingly, but it was just passable, though Dodie almost thought she'd rather have walked. After a few hundred yards they came to a wider clearing, and a shed outside which stood a tractor, the engine gently turning over.

The door of the shed was propped up against the wall, quite detached from the frame, and Detective Inspector Morton swore softly. 'There goes all chance of finding evidence,' he said. 'It'll have been ruined by now. Let's talk to the farmer, anyway.'

The farmer was a thin, wiry man in his seventies. His totally bald head was covered by a greasy old cap, which he doffed when he saw Dodie. He listened silently as the policeman explained what they wanted to see, and then shrugged and spat.

'Please yerself. I keeps this old tractor in here. When I came up yesterday the door'd fallen off its hinges, but that dain't surprise me. Wood was rotten, anyroad.'

Detective Inspector Morton looked inside the shed, and the others crowded round.

The wood round the hinges showed signs of being gouged, and there were rusty tools and bits of metal lying around, any of which could have caused the damage. On the floor were numerous short strands of rope and twine, and he exclaimed in frustration.

'You could have had a dozen people tied up here, and never find any of the rope responsible! I'll send a team up, but the chances of finding anything significant are pretty remote. There might be the odd fingerprint we can match up later, if we ever get hold of a suspect. And there's no direct link. Your abduction might have been quite unconnected with the murder.'

'That seems unlikely,' Dodie said quietly.

'I agree, but it's remotely possible. I'll phone in and then we can be getting back.'

The three women retreated to the car, but it was too hot to want to sit inside. Anna sat on the ground, hugging her knees, and the others leant against the car. The young policewoman smiled down at Anna.

'Are you OK?' she asked.

'Sure, I'm fine,' Anna said curtly, sighed deeply, and lowered her head on to her knees.

'Haven't I seen you at the Scribblers?' WPC Crossley persisted. 'You used to come a year or so back, but you don't now.'

'Yes. You're a writer too?' Anna asked, with a spark of animation in her voice as she glanced up. 'I didn't recognize you with your hair tied back. Mandy, isn't it?'

'Yes. I'm surprised you remembered me. I wasn't able to go that often, with shift work and overtime. I'm not very good.'

'You wrote a brilliant short story once, I remember. About a child who'd run away from home. Is the group still going strong?'

'We could do with some more members. And as I said, I'm often working late and don't make it. Why don't you come back? We could do with some talented people. We meet every Tuesday, at the Library.'

'Maybe I will,' Anna said. 'But not until this is over.'

When they arrived back in Markenlea Elena abandoned her cooking and came to the front door. The Detective Inspector had opened the car door for Dodie and was gallantly escorting her to the steps.

'I've made some iced coffee, would you all like to come in and have some?' Elena invited.

Detective Inspector Morton hesitated, then glanced back at the WPC and Anna. 'Thank you, but I think we should get back to the station. We need Anna to make a statement.'

Anna heard and groaned. 'Do I have to? I'm still very tired, and all I want to do is sleep.'

'It won't take long, I promise. Then we'll take you back to The Plough and you can sleep as long as you like.'

They departed, and Elena asked how it had been. 'Did you find the shed?'

'Yes, but no clues left. Where's that iced coffee?'

'Go into the garden and I'll bring it out.'

'Everything done ready for this evening?' Dodie asked as she sank into a garden chair.

'Enough to allow a break,' Elena said as she put the tray down.

'I must go to this writing group in Upper Markenlea,' Dodie said thoughtfully.

'You? A writer?'

'I'm thinking of writing my memoirs. They should be quite fascinating, I'd have thought. Brought up in an East End slum, picked out for the chorus line, then a film starlet. And no fewer than four marriages.'

'And what's behind all this?' Elena queried. 'You have problems writing a letter. If there were no telephones in the world I'd never know where you were.'

'Ah, but this would be different. I'll go and see Piers. I'm sure he'd be interested, and he might even give me a huge advance.'

'But you don't need the money! You're rolling in the stuff!' Elena began to pour out the coffee.

'So was Rick Wilbraham. This will be a two-pronged attack – approach a likely publisher, and get help with the actual writing from this group Anna used to belong to.'

'Well, just make sure you don't get spiked on Morton's fork!' Elena said as she handed her mother a plate of cakes.

'No, thanks, darling. I have a sufficiency of curves. Your Morton's fork sounds intriguing. Wasn't the real one something to do with a taxation squeeze? Just like these days, if they don't get it off you one way they'll try others.'

'By the way, talking of your attractions, that boatman phoned half an hour ago. Harry Keeton, he said he was. Your admirer.'

'I don't suppose he said that. You mean the mermaid's boatman.'

'He'd rather be yours. He was so disappointed when I said you'd gone out with a handsome policeman. He wanted to take you out on the river, he said. I believe he said in a punt. I think he fancied displaying his muscles as you lay on cushions and admired him.'

'I've no desire to be tipped out of a punt by some macho geriatric. Or have to fight off an amorous swain under the willows. It was bad enough in my young days, when one didn't bother so much with comfort.'

'Spoilsport! He had another inducement, too. His son will be at the yard later this afternoon, around five. He thought you might like to speak to him.'

Dodie looked at her watch. It was half past four. 'Mm, yes. I ought to go along. But perhaps I should send you. It was only an off chance that he might have a description of the car or the man who delivered the mermaid to the boatyard.'

'But that trail's gone cold by now. She will be for ever a mystery.'

'My going to that writing group will be more profitable, I know. Elena, be a darling and remind me to ring the library tomorrow. I must find out where they meet, and whether they admit simple beginners such as I am.'

Dodie, having been told once more that she was superfluous to requirements in the kitchen, took herself down to the boatyard. She might as well see Dave. There she contrived to refuse the father's invitations with excuses that she had to get back to help her frantically busy daughter, and interview Dave, who turned out to be a beefy and not too bright young giant.

'Yeah, I saw the car Dad asked me about,' he confirmed. 'Did she kill old man Wilbraham? Had it coming to him, I reckon. Lots of fellers on the buildings had it in for him.'

'You knew some of his workers?' Dodie asked, surprised.

'My Dave used to do specialist carpentry work,' his father put in proudly. 'He's a real craftsman, wasted here, but at least he's got a job to tide him over while trade's bad.'

'Did you by any chance know Kevin O'Mara?' Dodie asked, wondering if this might be her lucky day after all.

'Kev? Yeah. Poor devil. He oughtn't to have been working in that block. Old man Wilbraham didn't always see that all the safety checks were made. He was in too much of a hurry to get finished and rake in his profits.'

'Are you saying he might have been liable for that explosion? The one when Kevin was killed?'

'Here, don't you go putting words like that into Dave's mouth, lady, that's libel,' Dave's father put in, and his pugnacious glance towards Dodie contained anything but admiration. She was more thankful than ever she hadn't accepted an invitation to go out in a punt with him.

'If there'd been any doubts, it would have come out then,' she said easily. 'And Kevin's family could have claimed compensation, I suppose. Did he have anyone? Was he married?'

'Had a live-in girlfriend, I think. I saw her a couple of times when we were working round here.'

'Was her name Anna?'

'Something like that. Ann or Annie, or Anna. Could have been any of 'em. Why?

How come you know about him?'

'Oh, something I heard,' Dodie said vaguely. 'Well, I don't suppose that was the girl I came to ask about?'

'No, nothing like.'

'And the man? And the car? Did you see them?'

'Didn't see the feller, he stayed in the car. It was a Jag. Latest model, too. I'd have thought anyone with one o' them would have had his own boat, not have to hire out a rowboat.'

'Perhaps she was just a neighbour or something, and he was dropping her off as a favour.'

'You don't go kissing your neighbour – not for a good minute,' Dave said, giving a dirty laugh. 'I had a right good view. They only split when I tooted the horn, and I wouldn't have done that if I hadn't seen one of our regulars coming up the road opposite. He'd be wanting to get in, and none too pleased if his way was blocked.'

Dodie thanked them and escaped. Somehow it didn't fit. The mermaid had been alone, but someone had been waiting for her in a car on the far side of the bridge. Her ring had been small, not an expensive one, and yet she was involved with an apparently rich man. Why on earth had she hired a boat she couldn't handle and gone out on the river all on her own?

She drove back to Elena's, more puzzled than ever. Back on her garden lounger she read some more of Rick's novel, until Elena appeared, bringing with her a furiously angry Serena.

'I could kill that little wretch!' Serena was saying. 'She was supposed to be helping Rick, and now she seems to have made off with his new typescript, and she denies it and won't tell me where it is.'

'Why is it suddenly so urgent?' Dodie asked.

'It's overdue, and Piers is breathing down my neck every few hours. I wish his wife would go back home! Her people are loaded and have staff to run that enormous house. They don't need Chloe as well, just for a broken arm, but she's their one ewe lamb. It's bad enough when he keeps phoning, but when he comes down here he's taken to calling on me too!'

'Odd,' Dodie commented, and Serena snorted.

'I'm no longer surprised by publishers. Have you any ideas? Is it at all likely she hid it somewhere in your house while she was staying here? I tell you, I'm desperate, clutching at straws!'

'It's unlikely,' Elena said. 'After she departed in such a huff I stripped her bed and I'm positive there was nothing in the spare room she used. She wouldn't have dared leave it anywhere else in case we found it. Assuming she had it at all, but I don't think she had.'

'What will happen if you don't find it?' Dodie asked.

'In the worst case there'll be no book to publish, and we'll have to give back that part of the advance. Piers doesn't let people hang on to money they haven't earned. And if people know there's no second book he's not likely to make as much as he hoped on the first. He might even make a loss. And he was depending on Rick to make up for some other poor sellers.'

'Have you ever seen this script?' Dodie asked bluntly.

'No, just a very brief outline. Rick was always secretive. He didn't even let me know he was writing the first book until it was finished, and I have to say it was good, needed very little editing.'

'No spelling corrections? Not even a little changing of the grammar to make it correct?'

Serena stared at her in astonishment. 'Rick? Not likely! He was fanatical about things like that. I've been with him when he's pointed out to fruit stall owners that they had apostrophes in plurals. More than once he had rotten tomatoes – without the apostrophe – thrown at him.'

'Then I'm definitely going to that group!'

'What do you mean?'

'Oh, nothing important. Just a plan to keep me occupied and out of Elena's way for a few hours. Tell me, Serena, does anyone know what's in Rick's will yet?'

Her anger, which had been subsiding, erupted again. 'Don't get me started on that! The solicitor phoned Elizabeth yesterday afternoon. She gets a tenth, so does Frank, and that bloody Anna gets the rest!'

'Anna? But – everyone thought – I mean, did Rick change his will as often as he changed his women?' Dodie exclaimed.

Serena glared at her. 'It's not funny. She's also his literary executor. That should have been me! It means she can dictate to me what happens, and without me Rick would have been nowhere!'

'Well, well,' Dodie murmured as Serena, with a brusque remark that she had things to see to, took her leave.

Elena had decided it would be more tactful not to invite Frank or Anna. The combination of either of them and Serena or Elizabeth could produce fireworks. For now the two former rivals were on amicable terms, and Elena prayed they would remain so at least until after her party. The Deans and the Baxters were among the guests. Serena and Daniel appeared, and Elizabeth, and a dozen more people from the village. Dodie had seen some of them around, and they were soon spread out on the lawns, eating delicious food and gossiping, mainly about the murder and the lack of progress the police were making.

Dodie was moving across the lawn when she heard Serena's voice. She sounded furiously angry, hissing her words. Dodie looked round, and caught a glimpse of Serena's bright-blue dress behind a beech hedge which screened the greenhouse. Then Daniel's voice interrupted, and Dodie halted, pretending to be absorbed in the last pink and gold rays of sunset.

'It's all your fault,' Daniel was saying angrily. 'If you hadn't made such a fuss about the wretched book we wouldn't be in this pickle now!'

'You were glad enough to spend our percentage of the advance,' Serena hissed back.

'And now we'll have to give a lot back! I warned you, he was a flash in the pan. You shouldn't have made it a two-book deal until you were sure he could produce another. So many of these over-hyped authors can't live up to expectations.'

'Until we find the damned thing we can't know what it's like. You might help, rather than sit there smugly and do nothing.'

'You got us into this mess–'

'So you keep saying! But the agency is

ours, and it's your name at stake as well as mine!'

'The people who matter know the truth. Just because he was an old flame of yours, you had to prove to him you could do this wonderful deal. What were you hoping for? That he'd come back to you? A best-selling author would be better than a steady agent as a husband? Well, don't try it again for the latest man in your life!'

There was the sound of a hand connecting with a cheek, and Dodie winced. Then she moved swiftly away as she heard the bushes rustle, and with difficulty refrained from watching to see husband and wife emerge from their seclusion.

It was growing dark, a long soft twilight, very warm and still. Dodie had just claimed a chair near to the group with Elizabeth when she pricked up her ears again. A shrill voice, one she recognized from the meeting in The Plough on the day of Rick's death, was speaking.

'I hear you've been cut out of his will, Elizabeth? Is it true that so-called secretary scooped the lot?'

'Hardly worth your staying single, was it?' another voice put in. 'You could have married that fancy man you're always going to see, and enjoyed wedded bliss again.'

'I don't know how these vicious rumours get spread,' Elizabeth said with a calm

Dodie had to admire. 'It must be through nasty malicious gossipmongering.'

Attagirl! Dodie silently applauded her. The rumours were probably largely true, but in her time Dodie had been subjected to many catty remarks, and she had learned to defend herself. She enjoyed hearing other women giving back as good as they received.

Their reply was lost in the sound of another commotion, and the guests turned to stare at the wild figure who was rushing towards them. He was thrusting his way through the boundary hedge round Rick Wilbraham's garden. As he broke free he brought with him leaves and broken branches stuck to his trousers which were soaked, clinging to his legs as he ran.

'Frank! What the devil's the matter, man?' Gerard Dean demanded, and Frank swung towards him clutching his arm.

He was sobbing, and could hardly speak. Rachel grabbed a glass and hastily filled it with whisky and took it towards him. 'Here, drink this. It's all right, Frank. Now just tell us calmly what's happened.'

He gulped the whisky, took a few steadying breaths, and managed to speak.

'It's a girl. Down by Rick's boathouse. Caught in the weeds. I think she's dead!'

Thirteen

While Rachel went back with Frank just in case he was wrong and the girl was still alive, Gerard phoned for the police, and then waited for them at the end of the drive. The guests divided into those eager to remain and savour the excitement, and others anxious to distance themselves from this tainted vicinity. The latter soon departed, in some haste. The former, aware that the food had all been eaten, sufficient alcohol drunk to make it wise to walk home, and night was approaching, eventually drifted away with various insincere injunctions to Elena to let them know if there was anything, anything at all, they could do to help her.

While Elena was occupied with speeding the others on their way, Dodie began collecting plates and glasses and taking them into the kitchen. She had everything cleared away by the time Elena came back in.

'Whew, I thought some of them would never go,' she exclaimed, switching on the coffee machine before sinking into one of the kitchen chairs. 'Do you think it's Anna?' Elena was frowning as she worked through the possibilities. 'Anna could have been killed at any time this afternoon, I suppose. I wonder when she came back from that visit to the police station? I half expected Detective Inspector Morton to come and ask you more questions when they brought her back.'

'We don't know it's Anna,' Dodie said with a sigh, 'though it's most probably her.'

'Frank didn't say so, and Rachel is still down there with the police, I imagine. They came while I was seeing people off, and Gerard took them down.'

'If she killed Rick is it credible that we have two murderers in the village? Unless,' Dodie said, 'one of them killed Rick in a fit of rage, or frustration, and tried to pin it on to Anna.'

'Then they'd want her alive, to take the blame. Killing her makes her innocent, or at least shows there is another murderer about.'

'Unless it's an accident, or suicide.'

Elena groaned. 'More doubts. And more suspicions flying around. I don't think I want to stay in this village.'

The front doorbell pealed, and they looked at one another. Elena drew her shoulders back. 'Well, it looks as though we'll soon know. That's probably the police.'

It was WPC Crossley. Elena brought her into the kitchen and she looked wearily at Dodie.

'You work long days,' Dodie said, concerned. The girl, and she was no more than her early twenties, looked pale and drawn. 'You look as though you could do with a coffee. There's some in the pot.'

The policewoman smiled and shook her head. 'I'm OK, thanks. We're used to long hours when there's a murder inquiry. I can't spare the time. Detective Inspector Morton asked me to come and ask you if you'd both mind coming down to see the body.'

'Us? Why?'

'He didn't tell me. I've only just arrived, got the message before I'd even got out of the car, told to come straight here and fetch you. They'd been here for some time. Please?'

Dodie snatched up a jacket from the hall as she went. It was getting colder now darkness had fallen. They followed WPC Crossley who produced a powerful torch from her large handbag and shone it to guide them. Once more they walked along the road, scrunched across the gravelled drive, past the swimming pool, and on to the lawn above the boathouse. The scene was gruesomely familiar. A body lay face-down on the grass, and a man, Dodie assumed a police surgeon, was examining it. Rachel and Gerard stood to one side, and several policemen were searching the slope and the bank below, where a photographer had set up a battery of lights and was busy filming.

Detective Inspector Morton came to meet them as they halted a few yards away. 'Don't worry, you won't be destroying evidence. Mr Rogerson hauled her up here and tried to revive her before he went for help. We'd be grateful if you'd have a look at her.'

Elena grasped Dodie's hand as they stepped forward. The harsh floodlights illuminated the scene, and they saw the girl's slim body, her limbs outlined with the flimsy, wet material of her long skirt. It was of some flowered material, Dodie noted. She didn't want to look at the face. She had liked Anna, despite the girl's often unpredictable behaviour and occasional hostility. But she had to look. The doctor bending over the body glanced up, smiled briefly, and rolled it over so that they could see. Dodie swallowed, and then her eyes widened, and she glanced at Elena by her side, who was looking equally shocked.

'That isn't Anna,' she said in relief.

'Do you know who it is?' Detective Inspector Morton asked.

They were back in Elena's kitchen, drinking coffee. WPC Crossley sat at one end of the table taking notes, while the others warmed their hands on the mugs.

'Not her name,' Dodie said again. 'Nor do we know where she comes from. I called her the mermaid.'

She explained how the girl had appeared the morning Rick died, saying her boat had capsized. He wanted every detail, and looked sceptical when they told him about the false address she had given.

'And you say you discovered later that the young man who lived there worked for Mr Wilbraham's publisher. How does she come into it? There must be some connection.'

There must, but Dodie couldn't think what. Besides, it was now after midnight, and she was too sleepy to concentrate. Eventually the police decided they could discover no more, and left, and Dodie and Elena were free to go to bed.

Dodie dreamed of seaweed which caught unwary mermaids and strangled them, dragging them down in their clammy embrace into watery graves. 'But mermaids live in the water, they can't drown there,' she muttered, as she woke to find Elena, dark rings round her eyes, standing beside the bed with a large tray of tea and croissants.

Dodie sat up and rubbed her eyes. 'This is an unexpected treat. Or have I suddenly become an elderly invalid to be taken care of?'

Elena grinned at her and set down the tray. 'I couldn't sleep, and you were clearly having nightmares from the mutterings coming from here, so I thought I might as well get up and we could indulge. Croissants from the freezer, local honey, and your favourite jasmine tea.'

They ate and drank in silence for a while, then Elena sighed. 'Grandmother rang an hour ago. She'd heard the news on the radio late last night. I suppose we can be grateful she didn't ring at midnight.'

'Is she threatening to descend on us to keep us out of mischief? That would be the last straw.'

'I dissuaded her. Told her the police were arresting all strangers in the village on suspicion. You know how respectable she is, she'd never live down the shame of a night in a police cell.'

Dodie chuckled. 'You're a chip off the old block.'

'What do you make of it?' Elena asked. 'I can't make any sense of it at all. It's tough on the unknown girl, but I can't help be glad it wasn't Anna.'

'Have you heard anything? Has anyone phoned?'

'No, and it's after nine. I would have expected half a dozen phone calls by now from people who were here last night, thank you calls as normal, and nosy calls because of the excitement. Apart from anything else they'll all be agog to know the gory details.'

'Perhaps Frank is getting all the calls.'

'He isn't there, remember? Rachel insisted he went home with her and Gerard. He was in such a state, she said he couldn't be left alone.'

Dodie drank some more tea, then pushed away the tray. 'Right, I must shower and then there's things to do.'

'Mother, don't you think it's getting a bit – well, dangerous? Oughtn't we to keep our heads down?'

'And let whoever it is get away with it? I can't think who she was and what she had to do with it, but I'm convinced she was just caught up in the business somehow, and she has to be avenged!'

Elena laughed. 'How melodramatic! You sound like an avenging fury yourself!'

'Maybe. I suppose the police have more resources to find out who she was, but they don't know the people. Look, I've been thinking. There's some connection with Wallaby Publishing and that young man who lives in Ealing. Otherwise why should she give the boatman his address? Could it have been him she was with the first time? She had a cheap engagement ring, something a young man like that could afford. And someone was waiting for her afterwards.'

'And someone in a big car dropped her off. That doesn't sound like a young man on a lowish income.'

'That could have been incidental. He might have a wealthy father. Borrowed his car. Or suppose she was coming out here to meet her boyfriend? Someone gives her a lift, a neighbour, perhaps, and she gets here much earlier than she expects. How can she fill in the time?'

'She thinks she'll take out a boat,' Elena suggested.

'I wonder how long she hired it for? I didn't ask that. I remember they had a list of charges up, half and full day rates.'

'And how did she get there last night? Was she killed there, or her body brought there later, from somewhere else?'

'If it was after the party started someone might have seen her and whoever killed her, somewhere nearby.'

'And if it was her body brought from somewhere else there'd have been too many people milling around to risk carrying her through Rick's garden. Either way she must have been brought by boat.'

'Or she walked here herself, and met someone by accident or arrangement. She could have walked along the bank, or come by road earlier in the day,' Dodie mused. 'I wonder if the police will think of that?'

'I don't think they'll miss the possibility. But if she did, that implies someone local met her and killed her down on the bank.'

'Unless she fell in or jumped in by herself.

But I don't believe that. It would be too much of a coincidence.'

Elena nodded. 'Could she be one of Rick's other women? She killed him, and came here in a fit of remorse?'

'Or she was Anna's rival, or she killed Rick and Anna knew, and Anna killed her. But that brings us back to having two killers on the loose, and I don't believe it.'

Elena picked up the tray, and simultaneously the phone rang. 'Here it comes, the curiosity calls. Have your shower, and I'll see what the gossips want.'

Half an hour later, Dodie went downstairs.

'That was the police, amongst half a dozen other calls,' Elena told her. 'There was a break-in at one of the boatyards last night, after they'd closed. Not the same one, it sounds like the one with the uncooperative yobbo. One of the rowing boats was stolen. Well, it was taken, apparently, and returned. But they discovered that the knot was tied differently.'

'So she had been brought by boat, apparently. But would she go out in a stolen – or borrowed – boat like that?'

'Perhaps she thought it romantic!' Elena said scornfully. 'Some people do, they don't care about being a danger to themselves and others, not being able to see what they're doing.'

'But if it were an accident the boat wouldn't have been returned. If it was after the boatyard closed, it couldn't have been anyone already at the party.'

'Which leaves Anna, Frank, and outsiders,' Elena said, and exclaimed in annoyance as the phone went again.

'Frank wouldn't need to steal a boat. Not unless he was trying to be devious,' Dodie said when Elena came back. 'Why leave her on his own doorstep, and be the one to discover her?'

'If she knew Anna, she might have been willing to go with her.'

'But with the alternative theory, Elena, she could have been killed much earlier, somewhere else, and they only needed the boat to get her dead body from there. That would make much more sense than having to entice her into a boat in the dark.'

'It's far too complicated for me. Let's wait and see whether the police identify her and find some other motive. That call was for you.'

'Why didn't you say? Or did you think I didn't want to talk?'

'It was just a message. WPC Crossley had passed on your name to the secretary of the writing circle, and that was to say you'd be very welcome to join them for their next meeting. It's tomorrow evening.'

Dodie grinned. 'She is eager, when she's

so busy at work. Yes, I suspect that's an angle the police won't have got on to. Did you actually finish Rick's book?'

Elena nodded. 'Well, at least I skipped through it. It was all too turgid with illness and alcoholism and total despair.'

'And close to home. Isn't that very similar to Frank's own story? Didn't he have an invalid mother, have to give up his job to look after her, and then have a breakdown, unspecified?'

Fourteen

'Is Frank still at Rachel's?'

Elena shook her head. 'No, Rachel rang, said he insisted on going back home, afraid someone would break in.'

'Come on then, let's go and see him.'

'Hang on. Won't the police be there?'

'They won't be in the house,' Dodie said, feeling energetic now there was something for her to do. 'And if they are we can come away again.' She looked out of the window. 'It looks like the end of the good weather. I'm going to get a coat, I don't like the look of those clouds.'

'I've been wondering about moving somewhere that's warm all the time,' Elena said as they went along the road. 'I've taken against this place. Who knows what will happen next, where the next corpse will turn up, and whose it will be?'

'Most of your friends are here,' Dodie said. 'You'd miss them.'

'They are mainly school friends, because I was at school in England. It wouldn't be impossible to make new ones elsewhere. I've a yen for California or Florida.'

'Not Seattle?' Dodie suggested, and Elena gave her a hard look.

'That's always wet and damp,' she said dismissively.

Dodie sighed. It obviously wasn't the time to talk about Marcus. 'Wait and see,' she advised. 'You may feel differently when we've sorted this out.'

There were a couple of unmarked vans in the drive, but no police activity near the house. Frank came to open the door, looking suspicious until he saw who it was.

'Come in. I thought you were the press,' he said, casting anxious looks beyond them.

'Have you been pestered?' Dodie asked sympathetically. She'd had her own problems at times with the media.

'Not yet. I don't think the police have released any details, but you never know who will let on. Any of your guests last night could have tipped them off,' he added to Elena.

'I wanted a few words,' Dodie said. 'Could we sit down somewhere for a moment?'

Frank suddenly became aware that he was keeping them standing in the hall. 'Come into the drawing room,' he said, and led the way towards the back of the house.

Dodie went to look out of the windows. There was a strong breeze blowing, and the water in the swimming pool was slopping gently over one side. The trees beside the river were bowing and dipping before the wind, the branches of the willow horizontal ribbons. 'It'll rain soon,' she commented, turning back and sinking into one of the squashy white leather sofas.

'How are you feeling now?' Elena asked. 'It must have been a terrific shock to you, finding another body. Did you think it was Anna at first? They did have some similarity, they were – are – the same build, and both have dark hair,' she added, giving up the complication of tenses.

'I thought it might be at first, but as soon as I pulled her free of the weeds I saw it was a stranger.'

'Did you get her up that bank all on your own?' Dodie asked, with what she hoped was a voice full of admiration for his strength.

'She wasn't heavy. And there's no room down there right on the bank to lay her out, try artificial respiration. The police reckon I ought to have left her there, but I couldn't be sure she was dead, could I? Not without a good look at her.'

'Of course not,' Dodie said soothingly. 'And they could hardly hope to find fingerprints on the weeds and grass. But that wasn't what I wanted to talk about. I've read all of Rick's book now, and there was something that puzzled me.'

'Oh. Did you bring the copy back? I'll have the executors shouting at me, no doubt, saying I hadn't the right to lend it out.'

'I forgot it,' Dodie apologized insincerely. She had no intention of letting that copy out of her hands when it might still provide a clue. 'I'll bring it round soon. But I wondered, you didn't know Rick before the book was published, did you?'

'I met him some months before.'

'I thought I recalled you said you wrote when you read about the big advance he was getting?'

'That was a year or so before the book was published, but I didn't write straight away. I wrote a few months later.'

'Of course, that was why I was confused. I was interested, you see, that Rick had used a story about a man giving up his job to look after a sick wife. It was so similar to your own life.'

Frank looked at her as if she had suddenly sprouted horns. 'It was my mother, not at all the same. And he – the character – then went dotty and nearly drank himself to death. That wasn't me!'

'Of course not. But I did wonder if Rick had borrowed the basics from your own life. I believe writers take one fact and then change it so that the origins are unrecognizable.'

'Rick didn't know about me before I contacted him,' Frank insisted. 'Now, if that was all, I have a lot to do. The executors have asked me to make an inventory, and there's a lot of things in a house this size, even without police all over the place.'

'Well, well, he was touchy,' Elena said as they went back towards home. 'Do you think he was telling the truth?'

'I think the best person to know that would be Elizabeth. Was Rick writing the book while they were still together?'

'I don't think I've ever heard anyone say. Let's see, the book's been out for six months, Serena made the deal a year before, it probably took him at least a year to write. We're going back two and a half years, and I wasn't living here then. Neither was he, come to that.'

'But he could have been thinking about it long before. Let's phone her,' Dodie said.

Elena resolutely declined to make the call. 'You would explain such a peculiar question far better than I would, mother dear. I'd better go and start lunch.'

'Let's go to the pub. I suspect I'll have some more questions for Anna, and I still need to reassure myself she's OK. I know it's irrational, but I need to see her.'

Ten minutes later she joined Elena in the sitting room, where Elena was catching up with the news on TV. 'Is there anything on there yet?'

'No, unless it's made the local news. What did Elizabeth have to say?'

'She finally left Rick in February, almost two and a half years ago. And they got divorced eighteen months later. At that time, when she left him, so far as she knew, Rick had no notion of writing anything, let alone a novel.'

Elena raised her eyebrows. 'So he must have developed the idea, and written it, pretty quickly. What about Frank?'

'Also as far as she knows, though she was at pains to point out that by then they were living pretty separate lives, he didn't have any idea Frank even existed.'

Once more they encountered curious stares when they entered The Plough, but with the weather so much cooler, and it being Monday, it wasn't crowded with visitors out for the day beside the river. They asked for Anna, only to be told she'd gone to London for the day. At least this reassured

Dodie that she was safe. Having eaten, they were about to pay the bill when Dodie's admirer, the boatyard proprietor, came in. Harry Keeton saw them at once and came across to their table.

'What's all this I hear about another murder?' he asked, pulling up another chair and sitting down. 'The police were round asking if I'd had any signs of a break-in, or an attempt. I told them I locked up securely at night, not like that ramshackle outfit further down.'

'Did you hear much more?' Dodie asked him.

'You're the one in the know. It's you the police confide in. But they did hint. Was it that lass you were asking me about the other day? It sounded like her from the description. They wanted to know if I knew anything, had seen her again.'

Dodie saw no harm in telling him. The news would be out soon enough.

'Yes, it was her.'

'Strewth! What do you make of that?'

'Not a lot, at the moment,' Dodie confessed. 'One thing I forgot to ask you before, did she book the boat for the whole day?'

'Yes, though from the looks of her I didn't think she could get more than a few yards.'

Dodie was thinking furiously. That destroyed her theory of the girl just occupying her time while waiting for her boyfriend.

Perhaps she'd been planning to meet the man who paid for her taxi on the river somewhere, the other side, perhaps. There was a convenient, anonymous car park there if they hadn't wanted to be seen together. Otherwise, how could he have been waiting for her so very opportunely? Maybe he'd seen her capsize. But why had she been so reluctant to admit his existence?

They had no answers, and much to Elena's barely suppressed amusement, Dodie had some difficulty in evading Harry Keeton's pressing invitations to try out some of his boats, for there were some very interesting places to go to, places most casual river users didn't know about, he said earnestly.

He left with them, without even buying a drink, and they refused his offer to drive them home, pointing out that it was only a hundred yards away. Reluctantly he parted from them, and waved energetically as he roared past driving an ancient Land Rover, with an empty trailer hooked on and bouncing around so much they feared the two might come adrift.

Elena collapsed into giggles. 'No wonder he prefers his boats. That wouldn't make a very convincing love wagon,' she gurgled. 'But perhaps he carries a mattress in the trailer!'

Dodie tried to look disapproving. 'I'm shocked at you!' she said. 'I hoped I'd brought my daughter up without such vulgar notions! Love wagon, indeed! Where on earth did you hear that phrase? Mind you,' she added, 'I don't think I'd prefer a punt. Far too narrow, at least for my present dimensions. He'd roll off into the water!'

They dissolved into further giggles, and hurried home, hoping none of the villagers would misinterpret their hilarity.

On the following evening, Tuesday, Dodie presented herself at the meeting of the Scribblers, and found half a dozen diverse people in the allocated room, sitting round in a rather dispirited circle.

A tall, thin woman with shingled hair leapt up to greet her. 'Mrs Fanshaw? Do come and join our happy little band. Mandy told us you'd be coming, and apologizes that she can't be here herself. She has important police work on hand, you know.'

It sounds like anti-terrorist activities, rather than acting as secretary and chauffeur in a rather sordid murder investigation, Dodie thought, while smiling benignly round the circle.

'What do you do?' an elderly man asked rather wheezily.

'Do? Oh, what do I write?' Dodie said. 'Well, nothing much as yet,' she said cautiously. If she admitted to thinking about memoirs they might get too interested in her past life, and that she wanted to avoid. 'I really came to see whether you could give me some ideas,' she added, smiling hopefully at the others.

They seemed to have cheered up a little. 'You'll find plenty of advice here,' the thin woman predicted. 'We're all very experienced. Most of us have some publications to our credit.'

'Really? What do you all do?' Dodie asked.

It turned out that Miss Thin, as Dodie christened her, wrote sweet little inspirational poems for a children's magazine the local town parishes supported. Mr Wheeze wrote a gardening column for a small local freebie newspaper. Dodie wondered if he'd be able to lift a weed, let alone a spade. Of the others, two women admitted to writing stories for women's magazines, 'Though none have yet recognized our talent,' the larger of the two said sadly. The remaining couple, both older women, wrote poetry, and had been successful in a local competition. 'Both achieved commended,' Miss Thin said proudly.

'Do you have any members who write novels?' Dodie asked, and they sighed, like a Greek chorus, deeply and in unison.

'There was that fellow,' the large woman said. 'The one who was so tragically killed.'

'Killed? Oh, dear, how sad. How did that happen? A road accident?' Dodie asked, trying to sound concerned at the same time as being casual.

Miss Thin took charge. 'No, no. Nothing so ordinary. He was blown up. An explosion, would you believe.'

'Good heavens! Was it terrorists?'

'No, a gas leak. So tragic, he had a great deal of talent.'

'I thought his girlfriend was better,' Mr Wheeze opined, 'even though she only came a couple of times.' The poets disagreed strongly, and there was a spark of animation as they debated the point.

'Does she come here now?'

'No. Now, that's enough gossip, ladies and gentlemen. We must move on to the business of the meeting. We have a short formal meeting first, then those who wish to can read out what they have brought,' Miss Thin explained to Dodie. 'Did you bring a contribution?'

Dodie was about to fish out her purse when she realized what the woman meant. 'Oh, no, I felt far too diffident, my first time,' she replied. 'I thought I'd better see what you did first. See whether I could match your standards.'

'Don't worry, you'll soon learn,' a poet said rather smugly.

Miss Thin frowned at her. 'Order, order. Now, has anyone any sales to report this week? No? Oh dear, we must pull our socks up, mustn't we? How many of us have sent out submissions?' Every hand went up. 'Good, good. Were they new pieces, or old ones?' It appeared they were old ones, being sent out hopefully to new markets. 'Can we all make a resolution to do something new this coming week? Good. That's the spirit. Now has anyone any other news to share?'

One of the poets had brought along entry forms for a competition. Dodie took one, saw that each poem of not more than twenty lines had to be accompanied by an entry fee of three pounds, and wondered briefly if anyone ever made any money from poetry except the competition organizers.

Someone else had heard of a new publisher who wanted contributions to a new magazine for older people. Mr Wheeze, with smug satisfaction, told of the demise of another magazine which had, Dodie gathered, once short-sightedly rejected his work. Then they moved on, as Miss Thin explained kindly to Dodie, to the creative part of the evening.

Two incomprehensible poems were read and exhaustively dissected and discussed and lavishly praised. An article on the carrot fly and other revolting little grubs and insects, knowledge of which was deemed indispensable to serious gardeners, made Dodie thankful she'd had supper some time earlier, and then what she thought was a rather good short story was heard in silence, and greeted with perfunctory praise.

'You'd think some wretched editor would take it, wouldn't you?' Miss Thin demanded. 'Now we will break for tea and biscuits. I'll go and put the kettle on, I think it's my turn.'

She hesitated, but no one volunteered to take her place, and with a sigh she went into the adjoining kitchen and began to clatter cups and saucers about.

Dodie turned to the woman who'd just read the story, who happened to be sitting next to her. 'I thought that was good,' she said in a low voice. The others had begun to chat amongst themselves. 'Have you ever tried to write a novel?'

The woman shook her head. 'Oh, I couldn't. They are so long! I don't have the confidence of young people, like Anna and Kevin.'

'Was Kevin the boy who was killed? Did you like his story?'

'Well, it was good, no doubt about that. Some of the tricks they got up to on the building sites were amusing, in a way, but I didn't enjoy it when the man was looking after his sick wife, too gloomy.'

'Did Kevin read all of it out? It must have taken a long time.'

'Oh, no, just extracts. But he stopped coming towards the end. Before he was killed, I mean.'

'Why was that?'

The woman nodded towards the kitchen. 'She doesn't like anyone who's better than she is. Did you notice how she said hardly a word about my story except to pick on the place where I'd used "frightful" twice in one sentence? Kevin's grammar wasn't perfect. Well, what can you expect of a man who probably skived off school half the time? But I think he got discouraged. He told me once that he was going to ask his boss to correct it for him. He was helpful, he said.'

'Why not his girlfriend?'

'He told me she was too busy with her own work, and anyway, there was some other problem between them at the time, I suspect, and he couldn't ask her.'

Dodie drank the rather weak tea, and listened to the other contributions in silence. She was scarcely aware of what was said, she was thinking so hard. At the end she thanked Miss Thin, said she'd found the evening instructive, which was true, and that she would almost certainly come again, which was almost certainly false.

On the way out she managed to walk with the woman who'd been so helpful. 'Do you ever go for a drink afterwards?' she asked. 'There's a pub over there. Can I treat you to something stronger than tea?'

The woman, after a moment's hesitation, agreed. Her name, Dodie discovered, was

Moira Jenkins, and she lived near the town centre, a flat over a shoe shop which she managed, she said, so didn't have far to walk home.

As they sipped gin and tonics, Dodie directed the conversation round to her reading habits, and discovered that she didn't have a lot of time for reading what she described as heavy books, certainly not those which were entered for prizes like the Booker. She'd heard of Rick Wilbraham, wasn't it terrible the way he'd been killed, but she had never even looked at his book.

Fifteen

'So what are the motives now?' Elena asked.

She and Dodie were sitting having breakfast the following day. Outside, the summer weather had reverted to normal, for England, Dodie thought gloomily. It was wet, windy and cold. She demanded sun in summer, and at other times of year as well if possible. She would be glad when her tests were done, the results known, and possible treatment concluded. Then she could leave and go to somewhere more reliable, like the Sahara.

'If it's as I suspect, and Rick used Kevin's

book, changing it and tidying up the grammar, who knows? And why did he do it? Wasn't the risk of being found out too great?' Dodie asked.

'How did he get hold of it? It must have been Anna who gave it to him after Kevin's death.'

'Not necessarily. Kevin might have given him a copy for some reason, asking advice perhaps. I wonder if Rick had ever shown any interest in writing before?'

'Then Kevin died, and Rick stole the script and pretended it was his own?'

Dodie frowned. 'Let me think. Let's start with the writing. Kevin does this, and the people at the writing group know. I wonder if anyone else did? There was that leaflet for a residential writing course in Anna's bag. I wonder if she went to that, or if Kevin did?'

'Maybe they met there.' Elena stood and went to look out of the window at the lashing rain. She shivered. 'Can you remember where the course was, or who ran it?'

'Yes, it was an Arvon course. I remember thinking the name was like the cosmetics, Elizabeth Arden. It's possible they met there. I can ring them up. They might tell me who was there, or I'll find out some other way. Hand me that pad, I'd better make a list.'

Elena passed the pad to her, and stood warming her hands on the Aga. 'The police would have more authority to ask for this sort of information, wouldn't they?'

Dodie made a note, and sat for a while chewing the end of her pencil. 'But can you see them following up this idea? It's so tenuous, all supposition. OK, he writes the book and various people know about it. We need to try and find out who, and talk to them.'

'How did it get into Rick's hands? Presumably from Kevin, or possibly from Anna.'

'I think Anna knows all about it. That's what the typescript I saw in her bag was, Kevin's original.'

'What was she doing about it? Do you think she was blackmailing Rick, if she knew what he'd done? Does this explain why Rick made a will so much in her favour?'

'Not necessarily,' Dodie said, pushing her hands through her hair. 'She might have been in on it from the start, or at least since Kevin died. In either case she'd expect a big share of the profits.'

'If she was blackmailing him, is that why she was living with him? Was it literally that, no sex involved?'

Elena shook her head. 'Knowing Rick, that doesn't seem likely.'

'Then do you think he could have found out about the book, and deliberately seduced her to persuade her to cooperate?'

'All this must have happened after Kevin's death.'

'Which begs yet another question,' Dodie said with a sigh. 'Was he murdered?'

'You mean – the explosion was deliberate? Surely not! That would make Rick a murderer, just on the chance of making some money if the book was published.'

Dodie poured more coffee. 'If Rick had finished the changes, or even just done a few chapters and shown them to Serena, and she sold the book for such a huge advance, he'd be terribly tempted. His property business was in the doldrums. Elizabeth was taking a big slice of his income, and although she would get more with this deal, he'd have more too.'

'That's horrible!'

'Murder is.' She made another note. 'We need to know the precise dates when all these things happened. How can we find out without letting people know our suspicions?'

'We could ask someone.'

'Who can you trust? Elena, you know this village, is there anyone who cannot be involved, but who would know enough about it to answer some rather odd questions?'

After a moment Elena shook her head. 'I don't know people well enough. Even if someone like Gerard couldn't have killed Rick, this second murder could have been done at any time yesterday. I doubt if anyone has a good enough alibi to be cleared of that.'

'And from what I've seen, the fact that we were asking questions would be all over the village in minutes, and if the murderer was frightened, we'd be the next victims.'

'We could go and look in the newspaper archives,' Elena suggested. 'We could find out when Kevin died, and surely there would be some mention of Rick's advance in the local papers? We know the rough dates, and you could ask that Ms Jenkins, she might have a better idea.'

'That probably means a day in London. Elena, I have a bad feeling about this. If we don't find the murderer soon, they'll kill again. It might be quicker to ask Anna directly.'

'Let's try another way. Rick changed the main character, from a carpenter to a clerk. There must have been some other changes to fit this. Would Kevin have gone along with it?'

'I suppose if he thought Rick knew more about books he might. After all, I get the impression Kevin wasn't a scholar. He worked with his hands, and though he seemed to be a craftsman, even an artist with his carvings, he probably hated school when he was a boy. I was never too fond of it myself,' Dodie said with a sudden chuckle. She turned to another page. 'That would be a treat for my memoirs,' she said as she wrote. 'And no, I'm not telling you.'

Elena grinned. 'What makes you think I'm interested in your youthful indiscretions? Back to Kevin. That sort of man would almost certainly be willing to be swayed by someone he regarded as educated. If he wrote this book he had a flair for words, and he could tell a good story, but didn't Ms Jenkins say he wasn't good at spelling or grammar?'

'Yes. I suspect he might have been unsure of himself. He'd have accepted Rick's advice. So we need to know the timing. Were these changes made before or after Kevin died?'

'Or before or after Serena first saw the book. Rick might not have known whether it was any good before she said so.'

'There's no alternative. We'll have to ask Anna. She's the only one who might know.'

Elena sighed, and then agreed. 'OK. Shall I ring her and ask her to come here?'

Dodie considered. 'We'll go and find her, I think. She might refuse to come here. But let's wait a little and see if this rain clears.'

Dodie stacked the dishwasher while Elena prepared a marinade and placed chicken breasts in it. Then they went into the sitting room, and tried to read the papers while looking out of the windows every few minutes. The rain grew worse, and Dodie sighed in frustration.

'If what we think is true, it also explains

why there's no second book. The notes Anna had seemed like ideas for one, but perhaps they found they couldn't actually write it.'

'In which case Serena, and the publisher chap, would be hopping mad. That is, if they knew.'

'It would make them look fools and they might lose money.' Dodie made another note. 'At least Serena would have to give some back, and Daniel implied that Wallaby Publishing wasn't too successful.'

'How might they have discovered it? Is there anyone else who might have known?'

'Kevin may have had friends or family who knew. And those people at the writing group might have known, though I doubt it. Moira Jenkins hadn't made the connection, and I don't think any of the others were intellectual enough to be reading Booker contenders. And there's Frank. Is it possible he knew?'

'How? Would either of them have confided in him? Could they have trusted him enough?'

'Rick or Anna might have told him, I suppose. But I can't help thinking it's more likely he overheard something, or found some papers. That study was remarkably tidy, unlike any other study or office I've ever seen. I thought at the time he wasn't a great reader, and all the writers I've known – well, all two of them – had hundreds of reference books.'

'Shall we go to The Plough and ask Anna, then? Let's get it over. This rain's not going to stop, and at least she's unlikely to be going out in this weather.'

'Have you a wetsuit I can borrow?'

Elena laughed. 'Come on, you can only get wet. I have a huge golf umbrella, you can huddle under that. And spare wellies, good job we take the same size in shoes.'

Grumbling, Dodie wrapped herself up in a voluminous raincoat, slid a pair of wellington boots on, pulled a waterproof headsquare over her hair, and peered miserably out of the front door while Elena struggled to get the massive umbrella open.

There was no one else visible, a fact which Dodie pointed out to Elena with relish. 'No one else is daft enough to come out in this downpour,' she said with a self-righteous air.

'It was your idea originally, Mum, but we needn't go if you want to back out,' Elena said brightly. 'We don't have to play detectives. We could leave it to the police.'

'Humph! And not likely. Do you think they've got anywhere near this far?'

'Detective Inspector Morton seems very intelligent. I suppose we'll have to tell them soon. If Anna confirms it.'

'And even if she denies it. She hasn't told

the truth so far. Or to be accurate, she's avoided telling it, denying things, which amounts to the same thing.'

By this time they were at the front entrance of The Plough. Another door at the side opened into a passageway which led up to the few bedrooms. It wasn't spacious enough, or a large enough part of the business, to rate a reception desk, but just inside the door, in a small vestibule, there was a bell with a large notice attached, instructing visitors to ring and wait.

Dodie rang, and then tried the inner door, but it was locked. She took off the head-square, shaking off the rain.

'This rain must go upwards and sideways,' she muttered. 'Like guided missiles, it creeps under your umbrella.'

Elena had been shaking the umbrella out of the door, and now she furled it and stood it in a corner of the vestibule. As she began to reply the inner door was suddenly opened, and the publican's wife peered out.

'Good heavens, I didn't expect anyone in this weather. It's Miss da Rocha, isn't it? Come in, do. But can you please slip your wellies off, I've just hoovered the carpet.'

'We came to see Anna,' Elena explained.

'Oh dearie me, what a shame. She'll be so sorry to have missed you.'

Dodie sighed. 'Where is she, do you know, and when is she coming back?'

'Well, I don't rightly know. She was out all day Sunday, nearly midnight it was before she came in. Then off she went to London first thing Monday. She came back yesterday, round about teatime, and said she had to spend more time in London. She'd be staying with a friend, she said. She paid me for the room, and took her case with her. Had a taxi to the station, in ever such a hurry, she was.'

'See you back here at four,' Elena said as she locked the car. 'If you go down in those lifts it comes out in the shopping centre, and you won't get wet. The shop you want is to the left after you get there.'

Dodie nodded, and set off across the dingy car park. She'd spent a couple of hours on the phone when they'd returned from The Plough, but had only succeeded in discovering from a rather acidulous Miss Thin that Arvon courses were held frequently, and no, she didn't believe in them herself, and she didn't think anyone in the writing group had ever been to one. Dave was away again, and Dodie had found it necessary to invent a husband in order to escape importunate demands from his father that she go out with him and have a bit of fun. Moira Jenkins was her last hope of discovering something more about Kevin.

Moira was sitting beside the till in an otherwise empty shoe shop. There were noises from the room at the back indicative of boxes being rearranged, and the occasional subdued giggle. In response to the ping of the old-fashioned doorbell, a blonde head peered round the curtain which hid this storage area, but it soon disappeared when Moira sprang to her feet with a cry of welcome.

'Do come in, Dodie dear. There hasn't been a single customer all afternoon, and I was beginning to think we might as well pack up and go home early!'

'The weather is atrocious, isn't it,' Dodie said, and glanced at the displays of pastel-coloured shoes and racks of sandals. She hadn't meant to buy anything, but it would keep the woman talking if she scented a possible sale.

'It's not typical June weather, that's for sure. How may I help you?'

'I'm looking for some sandals,' she said, hastily changing her mind and not asking for weatherproof thigh boots. They wouldn't have any, and if they did the unpredictable weather would promptly revert to heatwave mode, she decided glumly. White sandals would always come in useful, she consoled herself. She glanced at the racks. Why were the styles she preferred never in fashion and the styles she loathed always just at the height of their popularity? Oh well, the less fashionable the better, they wouldn't look out of fashion quite so rapidly. And she could always donate them to Oxfam.

Moira entered into the business of deciding for her the style she would like and the price she would want to pay. She was a much more forceful personality here than at the writing circle, and Dodie fantasized that if Miss Thin departed, Moira would come into her own there.

In between praising Moira's selection of ghastly shoes, endlessly trying them on, and walking up and down to 'try the feel of them, dear', she managed to slip in a few questions.

'How long does it take to write a novel?'

Moira grimaced. 'Far too long for me. It would take me years, I like to get every word perfect before I go on to the next.'

'Do you know how long it took Kevin?'

Eventually Moira was persuaded to concentrate, and she thought he'd been working on it for two years. She couldn't be pinned down to anything more precise, but she did recall that he'd read out the final chapter at the meeting before Christmas.

'Not later, of course, because the poor boy died in January, not many weeks afterwards. I remember it because we had our Christmas party the same night. Not much of a party,' she sniffed. 'A mince pie she cooks, which is always burnt on the outside and the pastry soggy in the middle, and no more than a teaspoon of mincemeat, I swear. And a thimbleful of horridly sweet sherry that woman brings, and has the nerve to charge us all a pound for the privilege.'

Dodie hid her satisfaction at how easily she had obtained it, and how definite the information was, and returned to the task of finding reasons for rejecting the sandals Moira thought so suitable.

'Kevin's death must have been a great shock, as well as a loss to the group. Was the funeral held here? He did come from somewhere round here, didn't he?'

'He'd lived here a few years, but his family came from Ireland. The south, you know,' she added with a little disapproving shake of the head. 'Why, there was even a suspicion at first that he'd been carrying explosives himself, and had blown himself up.'

The IRA? Dodie shook herself. That was a complication she'd never envisaged and could do without. She dragged her attention back to Moira.

'Of course, it was the gas leak, and so they discovered,' Moira said. 'But some people didn't want to believe the truth. It was all jealousy, really, because Kevin had such a way with his writing. It was so convincing, somehow. You know what I mean?'

Dodie nodded mendaciously. 'I'll take those,' she decided, pointing to a pair she knew she'd never wear. She glanced at her watch. 'Goodness, is that the time? I'll be late.'

'Oh, I was hoping to persuade you to stay and have a cup of tea. It's been so pleasant talking to you.'

'Another time, perhaps,' Dodie said, handing over her credit card. She would take care to avoid this shop in future.

Outside, she briefly contemplated abandoning her purchase in one of the tasteful litter bins which decorated this shopping centre, but thought Elena might have a better idea for a suitable recipient. After all, some people might like the dreadful things.

She hurried to the library, and found Elena in the reference section, surrounded by reels of microfilms in front of a monster machine which, Dodie gathered, enlarged the pictures and showed them on the screen, and even printed out copies.

'He died in January last year,' Dodie told her.

'Yes, I found a brief mention in *The Times*, now I'm looking for more details in the locals.'

'I'll go and trawl the phone books, then.'

An hour later they left together and as they walked to the car park Elena reported her findings.

'No information on any family apart from an elderly grandfather in County Cork, who was bedridden and unable to come to the inquest,' Elena reported in some frustration. 'And the old man died a week later. I just happened to catch a mention of it. Verdict on Kevin was accidental death, but no information of how the gas could have leaked. It was assumed a broken pipe somewhere in the house, which was all unfit to live in. The site manager gave evidence that the Gas Board said they'd turn off the mains, but he assumed they'd forgotten. The Gas Board said they had done it. The coroner made caustic remarks about both of them, but he seemed prone to making caustic remarks, judging by a couple of other reports I read before I found the right one. What did you get?'

'Too much,' Dodie groaned. 'Dozens of Terrys in Brighton. Thank goodness I was able to photocopy the pages. Your phone bill is going to increase a lot tonight.'

They took it in turns, between five when they got home, until half past ten, to ring up all the Terrys. Then, having been abused in two successive calls for ringing at the dead of night and waking up decent folk who'd just managed to get to sleep, they abandoned the search until the morning. They'd come across no trace of Anna.

Then, at eleven, when they were thinking of retreating to bed, the phone rang.

'Mrs Fanshaw? Dad asked me to ring. It's Dave here, Dave Keeton. He said you wanted to know about Kev.'

Sixteen

Harley Street secretaries never showed their ruffled feelings, Dodie thought. When this one finally connected, she merely mentioned that she had been trying since early morning, but the line had always been engaged.

'And to no purpose,' Dodie said in frustration. They had once more been ringing up all the Brighton Terrys. 'We'll have to go there. There must be rates books, or street directories, or voters' lists.'

'That could take days,' Elena protested. 'Most of them wouldn't be in alphabetical order, and we have no idea which area Anna's parents live in. But that's not important. What did the consultant want?'

'It's aggravating. He wants me to take one of the tests again, apparently the result wasn't clear.'

Elena tried to hide her concern, but Dodie caught the flash of fear in her eyes. 'When?'

'On Tuesday. Which gives me time to meet Dave Keeton, and follow up one or two more ideas I had during the night. Thank heavens the heavens have closed up again. There couldn't have been any rain left. At least today it's only cold and windy, with no sun.'

'When are you meeting Dave?'

'He offered to buy both of us lunch, at the Stars and Garters in town. What on earth have stars to do with garters? I trust his father's not joining the party, and they don't hope to make it a cosy foursome. Young Dave was inspecting you pretty closely the other day. Looked as though he wanted to see your garters.'

'We'd better go, then.'

Half an hour later they were about to enter the newly refurbished, rather garish hostelry which had a hanging sign recalling the worst of Hollywood's notions of Merrie England. A pair of rustics in amazingly hygienic rags gambolled merrily in the hay, a coy garter held aloft by the bucolic swain, with a ring of tinsel stars looking benignly down on them.

'Ouch!' Dodie exclaimed as she stopped to inspect it, causing a slight eddy of pedestrians who, no doubt, were familiar with its excesses and wanted only to reach the food and the beer inside. 'It reminds me of the part I once had of Maid Marion. All I can say is that if the poor wench had to survive in this sort of weather in the middle of uncomfortable forests and dressed in half a bodice which kept falling down off her shoulders every time she moved, she deserved to snaffle Robin, if only to keep her warm occasionally.'

Dave and Harry were not there, so they found a table and sat down, sipping wine. Five minutes later Dave and Harry bustled in and joined them, smiling broadly.

'Now, then, the menu. They do a smashing steak and kidney pudding, topped with real suet,' Harry said. He licked his lips. 'I always treat myself to it when I come here. What will you ladies have?'

They chose the ploughman's, unable to face steak and kidney encased in suet, real or otherwise. Dodie managed to avoid sitting next to Harry, and while Elena kept him occupied, Dodie tried to discover what Dave knew about Kevin.

'We were mates, went for a beer together once or twice,' Dave said. 'When we were on the same site, that is. I didn't know him outside. He'd never come to the football with us.'

'I heard he went to the local writers' group occasionally,' Dodie said as casually as she could.

'Oh, yes. He said once he was trying to write a book. Daft sort of thing to do, I thought. Who'd publish something written by someone like us? We're just the workers, not schoolteachers and clever blokes like that. Besides, you have to be odd to spend your time writing about imaginary people when there's plenty of real ones about.'

It was a point of view, Dodie thought, amused. 'Did you know any other friends of his?'

'Met a girl he was with, once. Said he'd met her at some course. She was a writer too. More the type, I'd have thought. You know, posh accent, been to a private school.'

Dodie nodded. 'That was probably Anna. I think they all three met at the same course, and because Kevin worked for Rick, he felt a bit shy.'

'All three? Do you mean Rick too?'

'Yes. Do you know when that was?' Dodie asked. 'It must have been some time before Anna moved in with Rick.'

Dodie was making calculations. The three of them had met about three years ago, and a few months later Kevin had died. That left Rick less than a year before his book was accepted. That was time, presumably, for him to have made any changes he wanted. But Anna, possibly, had not come back to the area until after the book was published. That, she concluded, raised intriguing possibilities.

Dave had lost interest and Dodie allowed Harry to draw her into a discussion with Elena about the government's latest idiotic proposals. Evading his attempts to corner her, she said a swift goodbye and thanks, and almost dragged Elena outside.

'Sorry I let the cat out of the bag,' Elena laughed. 'I hadn't realized you'd pretended to be still married.'

'Serve me right. I should have found a more likely excuse.'

'Poor man, he's really smitten, and he was telling me how lonely he is since his wife died,' Elena said reprovingly. 'Thirty years, he'd been married, and he kept reassuring me he was the faithful type.'

'I hope you told him I wasn't!' Dodie said severely, and Elena gave a hoot of mirth. 'I think four husbands are enough for anyone. And can you see me presiding in the boatyard office, making bookings, and even launching rowing boats in the season? Ugh!'

'He was also eager to tell me he had a nice little nest egg, and he could afford a month on the Costa del Sol every winter, when business was slack and he could shut the yard.'

Dodie thought of her cruises, the winters in Bermuda, or the Bahamas, and one year in Cape Town. For the first time she felt a twinge of remorse. He was offering what to him, who had worked hard for every penny, seemed luxury, and it was unkind to mock. Harry had no idea she was a wealthy woman, though how he imagined Elena could afford an expensive riverside house at her age without family money, she didn't know.

When she voiced these thoughts as they drove home Elena grinned back at her. 'I have the impression he thinks I'm a pampered kept woman. He was fishing to see whether I knew any millionaires.'

'Do you think Marcus will be a millionaire one day if this business of his takes off?' she asked, trying to make her tone as casual as possible, but knowing she'd failed miserably when Elena's smile disappeared, and she took a couple of corners too fast.

'I've no idea, and I wish him luck,' Elena said curtly, and when they reached home vanished into her room for a couple of hours.

Dodie wished she could help with whatever it was about this man that bothered Elena. Well, he'd be back in England soon, and meanwhile she needed to think about what she'd learned that afternoon.

Ten minutes later she picked up the phone. If she had to go to London she might as well use the time there to advantage.

Failing Anna, who seemed to have gone to ground, Frank was the person closest to Rick. He might know more than he had so far admitted. If she let him know what she suspected, he might say something useful. She left a note for Elena propped up against the kettle, and let herself out of the house.

When Frank opened the door she moved

in past him before he could protest. He seemed slow this afternoon, and she wondered whether she'd woken him from a nap. But as she went past him she smelled the whisky fumes, and as he turned to face her he swayed slightly.

'I've got a couple of ideas,' she said briskly. 'Can you spare me a few minutes?'

'I'm busy, still doing that inventory,' he said, not offering to go into any of the rooms, and holding the front door open. She suspected he was hanging on to it in order to remain upright.

'This won't take long. I don't suppose you've found this second book everyone's so anxious about?'

'No. And what's more, I don't believe there ever was one.'

'Why do you say that?'

'Rick didn't spend much time in his study. Most of the time, if he was supposed to be in there, he was in the conservatory messing with his blessed plants.'

'What about Anna? Could he have been dictating to her, and she was typing it out?'

He shook his head and closed the door at last. 'Come into the kitchen. I had the kettle on.'

He took a slightly meandering path along the hallway, and Dodie followed, trying to walk in a straight line and not copy his weaving gait.

'Did Anna spend a lot of time with him?'

'Not a lot. She had another computer in her room, and she was up there for most of the time, damned leech!'

Anna had writing ambitions. Was it possible she was trying to write a second book, and pass it off, with Rick's help, as his? Dodie was beginning to believe that Rick had no writing talent. She'd heard nothing about him writing anything before this wonder book was produced, and surely most would-be writers tried their hands at other things before they produced a success? This meant Anna was implicated fully. Had she given Rick Kevin's book? Why hadn't she moved in with him then? It must have been a year or more before she actually reappeared on the scene.

Suddenly Dodie thought of an explanation. 'Has anyone looked on Anna's computer? Could she have a copy of the new book on that?'

Frank shook his head. He poured out a mug of tea, and offered Dodie a biscuit. The tea was stewed, and the biscuit limp. When he refilled his own mug he turned to a whisky bottle on the work counter and added a hefty slug.

'I don't know how to work the pesky machines, but Serena was up there the moment she was able to come back in the house. And she came down again in a worse temper than I've ever seen her. And I've seen some, believe me. She behaved more like a wife than Elizabeth did, shouting at Rick and abusing him for all sorts of things.'

'Nagging him to finish the book, you mean?'

'That, but also she'd go on at him about things like getting his hair cut, and buying a new suit, and paying bills on time. He was always a bit casual about that sort of thing.'

'He paid you wages, I suppose. I hope you're not out of pocket. Probate takes so long to sort out, and then I suppose the house will have to be sold before you can get your share of the estate.'

Frank stared at her, and for a moment Dodie thought he was furious, and going to order her out of the house. Then his expression relaxed. 'And little enough that is, after all he got from me,' he muttered resentfully. This time, when he topped up his mug, he didn't bother to dilute his whisky with tea.

'What do you mean?' she asked softly. 'What did he get from you?'

'You've read the damned book?'

'Yes.'

Frank hiccuped. 'Pardon. Well, it's obvious, isn't it? All that crap about the man looking after his sick wife. That was me, looking after my mother. That's where he got the idea from.'

'But – I thought you said that you hadn't

known him before you heard about the big advance he got?'

'That doesn't mean he didn't know about us,' he explained slowly, a gleam of triumph in his eyes. 'He did, or he couldn't have got so many details right.'

'I don't expect people will make the connection with you,' Dodie said soothingly. 'Lots of people have to give up their jobs to look after sick relatives.'

'Well, if that was all, perhaps. But you know I had, well, a little trouble with my nerves after Mother died?' Dodie nodded. 'He used that too, and had the cheek to turn me into an alcoholic. A drunkard! That's what he did to me, made me out to be a weak fool that couldn't hold his drink.'

Dodie was beginning to understand. Having heard of his famous cousin, and discovered somehow the storyline of his book, he'd managed to cash in. Rick, probably afraid of exposure, had taken the easy way out and paid Frank to keep quiet.

Frank leaned forward and winked at her. 'But he made up for it, I'll give him that. He paid me well. But I earned it. Until he left most of his money to that little slag!'

'You were here a long time before she was, weren't you?' Dodie asked, her voice, as she told Elena later, dripping with sympathy.

'She didn't turn up till after he'd published the book. I think she gatecrashed his party – the one you have, I forget the name.'

'A launch party,' Dodie offered.

'Thass it. You launch a book. Like a boat. Or a body. He brought her down here the next day.' He yawned widely, not bothering to cover his mouth.

'Was he working on the second book before she came?'

'He shaid he was, but he never spent much time in his shtudy. Too busy poncing about with the litererery set, enjoying all those shtupid little girls shaying how wonnerful he was.'

'Girls? Had you ever seen the one who was drowned before? Was she one of his hangers-on?' Dodie asked urgently.

'And the wretched man just put his head on his arms, on the kitchen table, and went to sleep!' she said indignantly to Elena over dinner.

Elena had become her normal cool self again. 'Will he be OK?'

'I let myself out, and found a spare key in a bowl in the hall. I was going to go round later and make sure he's OK.'

'We'll both go. You shouldn't have gone there on your own, you know. He could be the murderer, and if he thought you suspected him, you'd have gone in the river too!'

Dodie pooh-poohed the idea. 'Nonsense.

But the timetable's becoming clearer. Kevin writes the book, which Anna almost certainly knows about, dies, and soon afterwards Rick gets his advance. That's when Frank hears about his cousin and turns up on the doorstep, either begging or threatening. Then, with few signs of Rick producing best-seller number two, his first book is published, and Anna turns up. What's the betting she reads it, as she'd met Rick, and accuses him of stealing Kevin's book?'

'But if it's true she gatecrashed Rick's launch party, she wouldn't have had time to read it before then. That would have been the day the book was published, surely?'

'I'm sure there are ways,' Dodie said firmly. 'She knew people in publishing, she might have been able to get hold of an early copy, maybe one sent out to a reviewer. And bookshops have to have them in ready to put on the shelves. One might have been sold early. And Frank said she came down the next day. So he stayed up in London, she read enough of a copy she'd bought at or before the party to recognize Kevin's story, and contacted him before he came back here.'

'So the question remains, did she try to blackmail him, or were they working together in the hope of being able to write another book?'

'And,' Dodie said, and couldn't keep the

satisfaction out of her voice, 'they discovered it wasn't so simple. They must have thought, as they were both trying to write before, that it would be easy. And they may have thought the publishers would be able to sell whatever they produced on the reputation of the first book.'

'But they couldn't produce it. What shall we do? Get in touch with Detective Inspector Morton and give him the theory?'

'Maybe we'd better. Though I can see the wretched man's look of disbelief. It's not proof, just a theory.'

'I don't think he'd scoff,' Elena said thoughtfully. 'He's not so bad, for a policeman. The only others I've met before were a pompous little prat who pulled me in for doing a couple of miles above the speed limit on the M4 once, and a pair of incompetent wallies who came when I was burgled, when I had the flat in Hampstead.'

'We ought to go and check on Frank now, and we'll ring the not so bad Detective Inspector Morton in the morning. He'll be at home with his family by now, I imagine.'

Seventeen

The telephone rang three times before they finished breakfast.

'That was Harry,' Elena said, chuckling as she came back to the table after the first call.

Dodie groaned.

'He says that as it looks like being a fine day, would you like to go out in a new boat he's got.'

'Fine day?' Dodie glanced out of the kitchen window at the scudding grey clouds. 'I expect he thinks the Costa del Sol is equatorial weather. And why should one boat be any better than another? I don't want to be experimented on with a boat that might not be waterproof.'

'It's a small river cruiser. Has a very comfortable cabin. A double and two single berths. He says they are very comfortable. He tried it out for a couple of nights before he bought it,' Elena reported, trying to keep the smile off her face.

'What did you tell him?' Dodie asked, giving her daughter a suspicious look.

'Don't glare at me!' Elena laughed. 'I told him that you were still in bed. I said that older people needed to take life quietly, and at your time of life you didn't like too much excitement, and you'd had enough the past few days to last a lifetime.'

'Thanks, darling. I must remember that line. Any time I get importunate suitors offering me comfortable double berths I'll have to claim benefit of age, and say I'm resting before I have my next facelift.'

The second call was from Serena, who didn't bother to answer questions, just announced that she was coming round, and they weren't to go out before she'd seen them.

Elena managed to slip in a call to the police station, and the duty officer told her that Detective Inspector Morton was out, but he'd receive the message when he got back from his unspecified business.

'You could have told someone else,' Dodie said. 'Now we'll have to wait for him to call back, as well as Serena.'

'I don't expect him to believe us, so what hope would we have an underling would take us seriously?'

The next caller insisted on speaking to Dodie.

'Hello, it's Moira Jenkins here. I hope you don't mind my calling, but I saw a friend of mine last night, and she was on the course where Anna and Kevin met. Would you like to talk to her? Will you be coming to the next writing group meeting?'

'I – unfortunately I have to be in London that evening,' Dodie said, shuddering.

'Oh, well, I'll be sorry to miss you, but in some ways it would be better if we could chat on our own. Can you come round one evening to my flat for supper? My friend says any day will suit her. How about this evening, or is that too short notice for you?'

Dodie thought quickly. As long as she wasn't bombarded with horrible shoes she didn't want, she could bear it. Besides, she might find out something useful.

'This evening will be fine,' she agreed. 'But I have to be back early, I'm afraid, I have to be here for a telephone call from America,' she said, planning her escape.

She could feel Moira's avid curiosity coming along the wires. Bother, she'd have to invent something. They'd never be satisfied without a full explanation.

'We'll expect you, then. Great. Would seven be all right, as you won't be able to stay late?'

'Yes. The flat's above the shop?'

'Side door.' She gave Dodie extensive instructions on where best to park her car. 'See you then. Byee.'

Dodie began to clear away the dishes. 'I can't see how the mermaid is involved. That's the problem, one doesn't know all the possible suspects. How can anyone know all about someone else's life, know whether someone quite unconnected with their home, or work, or the usual crowd of friends and neighbours and acquaintances, that they may have met secretly, for any number of reasons, may want to kill them?'

'Perhaps it's as well most murders are committed by people close to the victims.'

'Let the police ask around. They'll be able to find out,' Elena said, but her tone was doubtful.

As she finished putting away the breakfast things the doorbell rang. It was Serena, looking a little more harassed than normal. She gave Elena a distracted look and went straight into the sitting room.

'Have you any idea where the damned thing is?' she demanded.

'You mean Rick's new book, the typescript of it?' Dodie asked.

'Yes, of course! What else would I be interested in?'

'No, we don't have a clue where it is. It's not likely we should, is it?' Elena said sharply.

Serena gave an apologetic smile. 'I'm sorry,' she said, and sighed. 'I thought that as Anna seemed to trust you, she might have dropped some hint. It's so important to me, to the agency. If I don't manage to deliver, Piers will never buy anything from me again. And Daniel's threatening to dissolve our partnership.'

'Surely they can't hold you responsible for Rick's failure to produce?' Dodie asked.

'You don't know either of them! Daniel and I are pretty well finished anyway, we never were suited, but I hoped we could carry on as business partners. I really love the buzz of it, the excitement of finding new authors and doing big deals!'

Dodie thought she'd only found one author and done one deal. 'Is Piers so unreasonable?'

'Him! He's ruthless where his own business is concerned. It's my opinion Chloe pushes him. She's a partner, you know, though she doesn't do any actual work. It was her money helped him set up on his own. But it's my reputation too! You see,' she said a little shamefacedly, 'I told Piers the book was coming on well. That was what Rick told me,' she added.

'Did you ever see any of it? A first chapter, or a plan of it?'

Serena shook her head. 'I believed him, but now I'm beginning to doubt if he ever started it.'

Dodie was too, but she didn't want to add to Serena's worry. 'Have you any idea where Anna's parents live?' she asked instead.

'Somewhere in Brighton, I think. Or near there. Do you think she's gone there?'

'She's gone somewhere. I think she has a sister too, but somewhere in London's a pretty big place to search, and we don't even know her sister's name.'

'You spoke to Frank last night. Do you think he knows?'

'How do you know what we did?'

'Daniel was coming past and saw you turn into the drive. He said he was tempted to follow you, but decided it would do no good.'

That was perhaps as well, Dodie reflected. If Daniel had discovered them assisting a drunken, still pretty comatose Frank to bed the previous night he might have been suspicious.

'This business will finish me with him, as well as Piers,' she added gloomily. 'He thought I was taking a risk with Rick's book anyway, and was furious when I pulled off the deal after he'd said I couldn't. He was convinced I took him on because of the past – well, you must know Rick and I were close at one time, before he married Elizabeth.'

'Was Daniel jealous?' Dodie asked bluntly.

'What he possesses he hangs on to,' Serena said, and Dodie could hear a small note of complacency in her voice. 'That applies to authors too. He wouldn't let me take on any of his existing clients when he made me a partner in the agency. He said I had to find my own, and Rick's been the only winner

I've found so far.'

'What will happen if the book isn't found?' Elena asked.

'Piers won't pay any of the royalties due, until the advance has been cleared. And I persuaded him into a bigger first payment on the first book than normal. He may only be able to clear that on sales from the second. Hell! He might even claim some back on the grounds that the deal was for two books, and we haven't delivered. I can't afford to let him take us to court.'

'But surely Rick's estate will have to pay that, not you?' Dodie said, frowning.

'Yes, and then demand some of the percentage we received. And which we don't still have. It's all been spent. God, I wish I knew where to look next!'

'Find Anna, I imagine. She's the one most likely to know.'

Serena nodded and rose to her feet. 'I'd better be off, I have an appointment in London. Good Lord, is that the time? I'll have to break all the speed limits.'

She almost ran out to her car, and drove wildly out of the gateway. A moment later a black car pulled in, and a frowning Detective Inspector Morton climbed out. He was alone.

'I'm glad I'm not in the traffic division,' he commented as he approached the front door. 'You wanted to see me?'

'Come in,' Elena said, and he took the seat recently vacated by Serena.

'Now, what did you want to tell me?'

Half an hour later they had moved to the kitchen and were drinking coffee. The Detective Inspector was making notes as Dodie went over their theories once more.

'It could explain a lot,' he admitted, 'but it's not proof, and we have to have that. Motive is simply a guide, a pointer to who might have committed a crime, not an accusation.'

'But it doesn't explain the other murder. We haven't thought of how she could be involved,' Dodie admitted. 'Have you discovered who she is? And are you allowed to tell us?'

'Yes, and I can tell you. An appeal is going out on the local radio tonight. Her name's Felicity Matthews, and she lived in Croydon.'

'How did you discover that?' Dodie asked. 'Had you got her fingerprints on record?'

He shook his head. 'No, it was a lot simpler. She had a wallet in her pocket, with a diary, and she'd been very efficient and filled in all the personal details. You can't think how many people don't bother, and what roundabout routes we have to go in order to track them down. More than once when lost property's been handed in we've rung phone numbers entered into diaries on some recent day and found only a prostitute on the other end.'

Dodie snorted. 'That's no surprise! So what do you know about her? Did she live with anyone, family, or share a flat?'

'She had a small flat on her own,' he said, and sighed. 'She clearly didn't have much money, and there were several final demands sitting on the desk. She was heavily overdrawn at the bank, and we also found a suicide note.'

'Suicide?' Dodie said incredulously. 'Why here? Does that mean she chucked herself into the river at the exact – well, almost exact – spot where she was shipwrecked a week or so earlier? It doesn't add up. She was odd, but I wouldn't have said suicidal, when we met her.'

'One can never tell. She said in the note, which was typed, by the way, that she was desolate because Rick Wilbraham had promised to help her, and now he was dead there was no point in struggling on. Almost her exact words.'

'Another of his women?' Elena said. 'How did he acquire so many? I didn't find him in the least attractive, that way.'

'Where did she work?'

'She didn't, apart from the occasional temping job. Apparently she'd been living on a small amount her mother left when she died a couple of years ago. There never was a father. Not a visible one, anyway. She was an aspiring writer, judging by the typescripts we found, and not a successful one, if the pile of rejection slips indicated anything.'

'Poor child. What a lonely existence,' Dodie said. 'But it must have been through her writing that she met Rick. Have you traced any other friends?'

'Not yet, hence the radio appeal tonight. That might bring in something useful.'

'Let's hope so. More coffee?' Elena asked.

He shook his head. 'Sorry, but I ought to be going. Incidentally, we're not releasing the note until the inquest, so please don't pass it on.'

'Of course we won't,' Elena said quickly.

'I need a stronger drink than coffee,' Dodie declared. 'It's almost time for an early lunch. How about a triple gin and tonic?'

'Brilliant. I'll make them, with all the trimmings. Go and sit in the other room.'

Dodie was huddled over her pages of notes when Elena thrust a tall, frosted glass into her hand. She took a gulp, coughed, and jabbed a finger at her pad.

'Do you know something, I have never put Daniel down on my lists of suspects. Why not?'

'Daniel? Killing Rick? Yes, I suppose so, if he's as jealous of Serena as she implied. But would he have done it if it harmed his agency? From his car either he's not doing very well, or he doesn't like spending money, so he'd not be likely to bump off an author who could become a goldmine.'

'Unless he discovered Rick didn't have another book. That would damage his reputation as much as it would Serena's. But why did I consider her and not him? I don't even know where he was that morning.'

'He's a very quiet man. He tends to get overlooked when Serena's around. And if he was jealous of Rick because of her, as well, I suppose it's possible.'

'Right. So where was he the first Sunday?'

'At home, presumably, while Serena was haring off to the office, being the busy executive.'

'She'd only just left home,' Dodie pointed out. 'Or so we assumed. Anna said she'd taken some big envelope down to the letter box by the station. Why couldn't she have posted it in London? Why go in the opposite direction? Especially if she was in a hurry.'

'We've always assumed she would have been able to walk along the river bank and kill Rick earlier. We never wondered whether Daniel might have missed her.'

'Or she him. Elena, you've known them as a couple. How do they seem to you?'

'Normal, so far as I could see. Not lovey-dovey, but not openly rowing or hostile.'

'So they might have been working together. I wonder if that's possible? We haven't ever considered a plot.'

Elena shook her head. 'I don't think a joint effort would work. They'd never be able to trust one another. It's far more likely they spend so much time apart neither of them would find it odd if the other vanished for half an hour or so.'

Dodie nodded. 'I suspect you're right. And another thing. You'd expect a couple who worked together, in the same office, to travel up to London in one car. But they seem to use both. I'd have thought a car journey the ideal time to discuss problems, or whatever. It was the only time I could be sure of having your father's undivided attention!'

'Daniel wouldn't have used the Mercedes, because Rick gave it to Serena. And she'd want to show her independence.'

'It looks as though they are not an ideal couple. So no plot, but add Daniel to the list, with the same opportunities as Serena.' Dodie yawned. 'This gin was a mistake, it's making me sleepy. What's for lunch?'

'Just soup and salad.'

'Let's have it now. I must go and have a nap afterwards if I'm going to stay awake at Moira's tonight.'

But when she went up to her room afterwards she didn't lie down. Instead she began to write, swiftly and fluently, on some new pages of the pad she'd brought up with her. If she was going to follow her plan when she went up to London she had to have something convincing to back up her story.

Eighteen

Dodie set off for her supper feeling despondent, and suspecting it would be a waste of time. She found Moira Jenkins cloying. In the evening, Moira had told her, she could park in a small lane which opened into the shopping precinct, and from there it was only a few yards to the shoe shop.

'You won't want to be in the multi-storey late at night,' she'd said with a shudder of horror. 'They have all sorts of weirdos roaming round once the shoppers and office workers have gone home.'

By the time Dodie had driven round the outside of the shopping precinct three times without locating the lane, she was beginning to prefer the weirdos to this concrete jungle. But on her fourth circuit, just as she was heading for the car-park ramp, and to hell with the weirdos, a small Mini in front of her suddenly swung left, and Dodie saw a narrow entrance she'd taken for the back yard of one of the shops. She edged Elena's car through the gap, and found it opened out into a reasonably wide though short street, blank walls of the shops and flats to either side, the only sign of commercial possibilities two huge but closed access bay gates.

The Mini was parked at the end, and a woman in flowing draperies to match Dodie's own preferred wear, emerged, locked the car, and strode off towards the precinct. Dodie, being cautious, and dreading the very idea of being blocked in, or having to manoeuvre in a limited space if other people knew of this spot, turned her car to face the way out.

She went towards the shops, found that the shoe shop was only a few yards from the entrance of the small lane, and saw the woman in draperies being admitted to a door at the side. Then Moira looked out, and waved eagerly.

'Oh, good, that's nice. Beryl has just arrived too. Mind the stairs, they're rather steep. Let me lead the way.'

Chattering all the time, she led Dodie up the stairs. Beryl was already in the small sitting room, standing as if mesmerized in front of the large television set, which was, to Dodie's relief, blank screened. She had little patience for hosts who couldn't do without background entertainment.

Dodie was introduced, Moira pressed her to accept a small sherry. 'Very dry, a lot better than we get at the Scribblers, isn't it, Beryl? Beryl's a member too, she writes wonderful poetry, and she's even started a novel.'

Beryl nodded agreement, but Dodie couldn't decide what she was agreeing to, Moira's estimate of her poetic genius or the quality of Miss Thin's sherry.

'Did you watch the local news earlier on TV?' she demanded as soon as Moira finished speaking.

'No, I was busy cooking. Why?'

'That girl!' Beryl paused, but neither of her listeners showed any comprehension. 'You know, the one who was drowned the other day. They showed a picture of her on the news. Had anyone seen her, and all that.'

Dodie almost said she'd thought it was to be on the radio, but stopped herself just in time. She didn't want it known she was associated with the police, to a degree in their confidence.

'And do you know who it was?' Beryl continued.

'Do you?' Dodie asked. 'If you do the police would want any information you have.'

'Well, I've met her. She was on that writing course you wanted to know about,' she said, smiling at Dodie.

'She was a writer?' Dodie managed to turn

it into a question. 'Then she'd have met Kevin and Anna on the course too.'

At last, she was gloating to herself. They had a connection between the mermaid – she really must stop calling her that now they knew her name – and Anna. Had she met Rick through Anna? Or had he been on the course as she'd assumed earlier? Had she met him then or later? And had she known about Rick stealing Kevin's book? It was beginning to seem as though it was her knowledge that had made her dangerous to the murderer.

Then another thought struck Dodie. Had the – no – her name was Felicity – had Felicity been trying to see Rick that first Sunday morning? Had she seen his dead body? Had she caused his dead body? Was that why she seemed so distrait when she'd come up from the river? And where did the man fit in with all this? Or men, Dodie amended. There could have been two, the one in the Jag who'd dropped her off, and the other in the car park who'd paid her taxi bill.

'What sort of course was it?' she asked Beryl, forcing her wandering thoughts back to the present. This woman could have some of the answers.

'For people writing novels. It's a fairly free course, you can go and work if that's all you want, or talk to the course tutor, get advice on your novels, and naturally, you are with other writers, so communion with other artists is very important.'

'Do you know if any of them, Kevin, Anna or this dead girl, had ever met before?'

'I'm positive they hadn't,' Beryl insisted.

'Was Rick Wilbraham there too?' Dodie asked.

'No, certainly not. I'd have remembered him. Most of the others were a lot older. The three of them were the youngest there, so naturally they gravitated together. I must say I thought Kevin was more taken with Felicity, but Anna didn't seem to mind playing gooseberry, and by the end of the week I wasn't sure which of them he preferred.'

So Felicity might have been jealous of Anna and Kevin? Had Anna introduced her to Rick, and perhaps even supplanted her in Kevin's affections? Or was Anna, for some reason, jealous of Felicity? Dodie groaned inwardly. There were too many possibilities. Dodie banished speculations to the back of her mind, to be looked at later, and while eating a surprisingly tasty meal of chicken, bacon and mushrooms in a delicious sauce, set out to discover all she could about the three young writers.

'Did you read out your work to each other?' she asked. 'Have you any idea which of them was the most talented?'

'Kevin, very definitely. Anna wasn't bad,

the bits I heard, but Felicity didn't have a clue. Her prose was terribly wooden, I wouldn't have thought she had the slightest chance of being published. She said she'd had a couple of articles published in some small journal. And quite honestly, that's all she was good for, I'd have thought. Oh dear, I shouldn't be talking like this when the poor girl's dead. I wonder what happened? Did she fall in, not able to swim? But she could swim,' she interrupted herself. 'They all went off to the local swimming pool one afternoon, and I remember Anna saying she was like a fish in the water.'

She'd said she wasn't a very good swimmer, Dodie recalled. Was that modesty, or had she been trying to conceal something? If so, what?

Rick had been a good swimmer, but he'd been drowned. She wondered whether it was possible for a good swimmer, within reach of a river bank, to be able to drown unless helped on their way.

She asked other questions, but Beryl didn't know a great deal more. Anna, she thought, had been writing a thriller or a crime novel, but from the small amount she'd heard it wasn't easy to guess. Felicity was writing a historical romance set in the middle ages. The only useful item of information, which confirmed her theory, was that Kevin's book had been about a man working on a building site who had lost his job when his mother grew sick, and later descended into alcoholism.

Dodie was thankful she'd prepared the ground for an early departure, when they settled down to discuss what they were all writing. Before they could ask her, for she was prepared to admit her current project to no one, she excused herself and said she'd have to hurry back for this phone call from a friend in America.

Stemming a flurry of questions and exclamations about their own desires to visit the States, she escaped, and drove home swiftly, her mind buzzing with new speculations.

Elena was talking on the phone when she let herself in. She was smiling, and Dodie went through into the kitchen to make herself a coffee. The food had been unexpectedly good, but Moira had made very poor coffee. Dodie suspected it was instant, half a spoonful per cup, and she needed caffeine.

A moment later Elena joined her. 'I'll have some too. That was Daniel. Anna rang him today at the office.'

'Anna? Thank goodness. I was beginning to think she'd disappeared for good. Did she say where from?'

'No, and 1471 didn't come up with the goods.'

'What did she want?'

'He said she wanted to talk to someone, but not him or Serena. In the end, apparently after he'd gone through almost the entire village, she agreed to meet Rachel. He's just been setting it up. Rachel's going up to London for some medical jamboree, it begins tomorrow, and she's staying over till Monday. She's agreed to meet Anna for lunch then, before she comes home.'

'And I'll be up in London that day. Do you know what train she's coming back on?'

'No, but I can find out. I know she doesn't like to leave her car at the station, so Gerard will give her a lift in. Now, what did you find out?'

As they sat drinking the coffee Dodie told her.

'It doesn't get easier.'

'No. Any more calls while I was out?' Dodie asked.

Elena chuckled. 'Harry phoned. He's getting familiar, began to call me his love and his dear. He wanted to know if you were feeling better. He was at pains to let me know he'd nursed his poor old mother through her last illness, as well as his wife, and knew what it was like to watch someone suffer.'

Dodie gazed at her in horror. 'What does he think he's up to? I thought it was a romp in the double berth at first, now it seems as though he wants me as a substitute mother! What did you say?'

'I thought I'd end your budding romance. Talk about role reversal! It was you who ended one or two budding unsuitable romances for me when I was sixteen!'

'Like that ski instructor? Or the gardener's boy at your too indulgent school? So how did you do it? Give him a stern warning?'

'I said we were planning to go to America in a couple of weeks, I was thinking of moving there and we'd be house-hunting for me. Then for good measure I said you were probably going to live with me. I didn't commit you. You can always change your mind if you get desperate for a bit of adoration.'

Dodie blinked. 'Are we going? Or rather, are you planning to go? Has Marcus–'

'Marcus has nothing to do with it,' Elena said sharply. 'He rang as well, as it happens, and I told him it was all off. I don't want to see him again.'

'That's your decision,' Dodie said, suddenly serious. 'I'm not quarrelling with it, but I wish I knew why. He seemed to have everything. He was kind, attentive, showed great promise with his own business, so he wasn't after your money to finance it, and very good-looking.'

Elena sighed. 'I know. I kept telling myself all that. He's perfectly amiable, attractive, ambitious. I didn't love him, and I just didn't know what else I wanted, but whatever it was Marcus couldn't provide it.'

'There are men somewhere out there you might be able to love,' Dodie said softly. She felt rather guilty, and she had to ask. 'Have my matrimonial tangles put you off marriage?'

'Not really. Very early on I discovered that love doesn't last, and whatever other compensations there might be, sometimes they are enough, other times not. I don't have rosy dreams of the one man in my life who's just out there waiting for me. But I won't go into marriage without feeling some kind of love, and I haven't felt that for Marcus.'

Their newspaper wasn't delivered the following morning, and Dodie walked across to the shop to collect it. She found Charlotte and Emily standing outside, arguing hotly. Both wore jeans and carried hard riding hats. They turned round and grinned at her.

'Hello, Mrs Fanshaw,' they chorused.

'Hello, girls. Just off riding?'

'Only for a measly hour,' Charlotte said with a pout. 'Then we're supposed to come back and revise. It's yearly exams next week.'

'Horrid, beastly exams,' Emily exclaimed. 'I don't see why we have to have those as well as all the tests they give us!'

'That's because you've got a rotten memory,' Charlotte told her. 'Mrs Fanshaw, look at this picture. It's that girl, you know, the one who drowned in the river.'

Dodie looked at the tabloid paper. Felicity's picture, not at all a bad likeness, was prominently displayed on the front page. The police must have found it in her flat, she thought. It definitely wasn't that of a dead, drowned girl.

'What about her?' she asked.

'I saw her, that Sunday Mr Wilbraham was killed. But Emily says I can't possibly remember someone I never saw before.'

Dodie had snapped to attention. 'Where was this?'

'Over on the other side of the river. We were giving the ponies some jumping practice. We're both entering for some gymkhanas later in the summer,' she added in excitement.

'Were you in the field where you keep the ponies?' Dodie tried to be patient, get her back on track.

'No, the next one. The farmer doesn't mind us going in there, honest, so long as we make sure the gate's closed. There are some fallen trees, just the right size for practising. I want Dad to put up some proper jumps in our field, but he never gets round to it.'

'He said one day soon,' Emily put in

gloomily. 'He said that months ago! And my dad can't do it, he's got problems with his back. Doesn't stop him playing golf though.'

'And all the poles and bits of wood are there. They'll go rotten before they get put up for us to actually use!'

'And you saw this girl?' Dodie prompted. 'Was she in the boat? Could you see the boats from the field?'

'No, she was on the bank, talking to a man.'

'A man? Did you recognize him? Was he anyone local?'

'It was too far away to see them properly,' Emily insisted. 'You're just imagining things to try and make yourself sound important.'

'No, I'm not! You need glasses, Emily Baxter! I saw her, I tell you, and I'd have recognized her again, like I did the next week! So there!'

'Hey, steady on,' Dodie said. 'Are you saying you saw her two Sundays running?'

'She wasn't running,' Emily muttered, and Charlotte cast her an impatient glance.

'The first week we were in the field, jumping our ponies, like I said. She and a man were talking on the bank. It seemed to me they were quarrelling about something. Then they both climbed down the bank, out of sight. I wanted to go and see what they were doing, but Emily made such a fuss I didn't.'

'Well, they might have been – you know,' Emily said, and blushed vividly.

'Oh pooh.' Charlotte, the doctor's daughter, brushed this off. 'Not right down there, where anyone out in a boat could see them. Anyway,' she added, turning back to Dodie, 'we saw them again a bit later, and they were both in a boat, and he was rowing it across the river.'

'Do you remember what time this was?'

Charlotte looked at Emily. 'Did you look at your watch? I didn't.'

'Nor me. But we left here, from your house, at half past nine. By the time we got to the field and had saddled up and had a trot round our own field, it must have been well after ten. Then we'd been jumping for quite a while. You kept turning round and coming back instead of taking it in turns like we said,' she added, and Dodie intervened to put an end to another threatened argument.

'Never mind. So it could have been half past ten. That was the day I saw you riding across the village green. How long did you stay there, and did you see any more?'

'About an hour. Then we came home, when you saw us, because we'd forgotten to take the new tin of saddle soap earlier. I watched them for a bit, because it seemed sort of odd they'd gone across the river, not along it,' Charlotte said. 'But the island hid them, and people do go through the channel behind it if they don't know any better. It's a lot shallower,' she explained.

'So you didn't see them coming back?'

'Not her. But as we were riding on the path next to the car park, on our way to the bridge, you know, I saw the man coming back across the field.'

'How long does it take you to ride round here?'

The girls looked at one another. 'Half an hour?' Emily suggested.

'Yes, maybe a bit longer,' Charlotte agreed.

'And then you saw the girl again the next Sunday? The day she was drowned?' Dodie asked.

Charlotte nodded. 'It was the same girl, Emily! I know she was further away, but I did recognize her. And it was the same man, too, even if I only saw his back. I'm sure it was the same.'

'When?'

'A bit later. Mum said I had to be back on time for lunch, we had some ghastly relations coming,' Emily said resentfully. 'She made Dad come and fetch us at one o'clock, and he was ratty just because we hadn't cleaned the tack. Made us go back and finish it the next day, after school.'

'So they were walking along the bank? Did they seem to be quarrelling then?'

'Do you mean he was the one who killed her?' Charlotte asked swiftly.

Dodie considered them. On the whole they seemed intelligent, sensible children. 'It's possible,' she said slowly. 'Listen. This is very important. Promise me that if you ever see him again you won't speak to him, or in any way let him think you might have recognized him.'

'In case he murders us?' Emily asked, and though her eyes widened, Dodie was thankful she didn't look unduly frightened.

'Yes,' she said bluntly. 'If you're alone, keep well clear of him. Don't go near any car he's in. Try to get to where there are other people as soon as possible. And if you see him and you're with your parents, or anyone you know, tell them and ask them to phone the police. I think you ought to tell the police anyway. Shall I come and talk to your parents?'

'Mine are both out. Mum's away at this conference, and Dad's playing golf,' Charlotte said. 'There's only Mrs Trueman at home. She's our daily,' she explained.

'Emily?'

'Dad's playing golf, too, and Mum's gone shopping, but she'll be in at lunchtime. Charlotte's coming back with me afterwards. You're not going to stop us going riding now, are you? Anyway, I couldn't say I'd be able to know them – him, again.'

'That doesn't matter, but they'll want to hear from both of you. You never know, being together you might think of something else. But if you talk about it make sure there's no one, absolutely no one about who can overhear what you're saying.'

They nodded, and to her relief she saw that they were treating it seriously. They weren't frightened, but neither did they think it was all a game.

'We promise, cross our hearts,' Charlotte said solemnly, and Emily nodded in agreement.

'Go and have your ride, and I'll come and talk to your mother, Emily, after lunch. Where do you live?'

'At the Manor. It's behind the church, up that long drive. Elena, I mean Miss da Rocha, knows.'

'Good, I'll be there, and I'll try to bring a detective with me. Enjoy your ride, now.'

They smiled, mounted their bicycles and rode off, waving. Dodie continued into the shop for the paper, hoping she had done the right thing, putting them on their guard without frightening them too much. She would be on tenterhooks until she saw them again, and could pass over their safety to their parents.

Nineteen

Dodie walked slowly back to Elena's house, trying to read the story below the picture of Felicity.

'You were a long time fetching the paper.' Elena took it and read the story.

Dodie told her what Charlotte had said. 'So now I must ring the police station yet again. Unless you'd like to do it?'

'You have all the information,' Elena said, rising and picking up the tray. 'They'll be paying you a special retainer soon.'

Dodie walked to the Manor House after lunch. On the green the village cricket team were in the middle of a match, against their keen rivals from the next village the opposite way along the river from Upper Markenlea.

'Local derby, Rachel says,' Elena explained. 'Instead of half a dozen people watching, most of the village turn out. I'll have to go across later if I want to be accepted as a proper resident!'

'Then perhaps I'll join you when I've finished.'

The driveway to the Manor curved gently between a walled vegetable garden on one side and a row of ancient oaks on the other, beyond which were neat small fields where sheep and cattle grazed. It was a perfect English scene, Dodie thought, not a gleam of harsh yellow rapeseed to be seen, just a field of what looked like barley in the distance beyond the pastures. The house itself was not large, but it was charming. Built of brick, with timber frames, and dating back to the sixteenth century, the small-paned leaded windows gleamed in the sun, and the weathered tiles undulated gently over a jumbled collection of roofs, the rooms apparently added totally haphazardly.

The Baxters greeted Dodie with rather strained smiles, both of them coming to the door when she rang the bell. They ushered her into a large, square and low-ceilinged hallway, then through into a large and cluttered sitting room overlooking the back garden. Dodie had no time to admire the colourful herbaceous beds before they urged her to sit down and began to voice their dismay.

'So good of you to come, Mrs Fanshaw. The girls have told us all about it, and we're terribly worried. Do you think we ought to send them away until this man is caught? He might be local, and we wouldn't have a moment's peace whenever the girls were out of our sight,' Jane Baxter said in a rush.

'Mother!' It was Emily, curled up in a

huge armchair with a spaniel draped across her lap. 'We can't go away! What about the gymkhanas?'

Charlotte, sitting on the floor and stroking a golden Labrador, nodded urgently, but didn't speak. Dodie tried to smile encouragingly.

'Let's hope the police catch him soon. And with what the girls have to say, this might make it easier. Have they contacted you? I telephoned the Detective Inspector as soon as I got home.'

'They are due in a few minutes.'

'Then they'd be the best people to advise you,' Dodie said, feeling guilty at letting down the girls by this evasion. 'The police don't reveal what they've discovered,' she said with an attempt at cheerfulness, 'so there's no reason this man could know what they saw. I expect the police will advise reasonable precautions, and you'd have to take those wherever the girls were if there was any chance of him knowing they'd seen him.'

'We could send them to America. My sister lives there,' Charles Baxter said, while his wife clutched her throat and breathed deeply as if to calm herself.

For a moment Emily looked eager, then she shook her head. 'They live in a big city, and I bet there are more gangsters there than in Markenlea. They all have guns, too,' she added confidently.

To Dodie's relief, for she didn't want any responsibility in adjudicating this particular argument, the police arrived. WPC Crossley did the questioning, gently and sympathetically, and afterwards Detective Inspector Morton reassured the parents that there was no need to send the girls away.

'We may need to see them again, but we came in an unmarked car, so even if the fellow we want is on the green now, he couldn't know the truth.'

'He may know the cars you use,' Jane said quickly.

'True, but we've made door-to-door enquiries in the village anyway, and have to go back to many of the houses. This would look like a routine visit. It's only in the unlikely event that he saw the girls, knows them, and knows that they saw him and put two and two together, that they'd be in any danger.'

Dodie departed, leaving the Baxters to discuss what precautions were needed. Back on the village green she saw Elena crossing towards a group of people sitting on benches and collapsible chairs outside the pavilion, and went to join her.

She had just seated herself when she was greeted by a cheerful voice from behind her.

'Mrs Fanshaw, or may I call you Dodie, how nice to see you're a fan of the best game ever invented.'

Before she could greet Harry Keeton, Dave butted in. 'Rubbish, Dad! Give me football any day.'

They joined the group, Harry taking one of the chairs, Dave flinging himself down on the grass.

After half an hour of fending off heavy-handed compliments, Dodie rose to her feet. 'Elena, I feel a migraine coming on. I must go home. No, don't bother to come with me. You know how they are, all I need is peace and a dark room and one of my pills. I'll see you later.'

Sunday was unusually quiet. There were no visitors, no phone calls, and it seemed very odd. Dodie decided to go up to London on Monday afternoon and stay the night again. As she stepped on to the train she was almost bowled over by a man who rushed on to the platform swinging an attaché case and leapt on behind her.

'Sorry,' he panted. It was Daniel North. 'Oh, Mrs Fanshaw, it's you. So sorry, but I thought I was going to miss it.'

They found seats opposite one another and Dodie looked at him with interest. Now she'd included him in the list of suspects, she paid him more attention than she ever had before. He'd always been overshadowed by Serena, who was a much more vibrant personality.

'Why are you using the train, and so late in the day?' she asked, intrigued. 'I thought you drove up to town?'

'I do normally, but the damn thing's got a burst radiator, and the garage can't get a replacement until tomorrow. I have to go to a launch party, one of my authors, and if I'd missed this train I'd have been unpardonably late. Sorting out the car took me all morning.'

'One of Wallaby's authors?'

'No, I don't do many deals with them. I prefer to go to the big boys, and if I choose my authors carefully, which I do, I know where I can sell them. You'd scarcely credit the rubbish I receive from people who think they can write but can't.'

'I imagine there's a lot of that,' Dodie said sympathetically.

'Serena's not experienced enough yet, I'm afraid. She struck lucky with Rick, but I've had to veto some of the people she wanted to take on. She even wanted us to represent that girl who was drowned last week.'

'Really? That was a coincidence, wasn't it? Or had she perhaps introduced her to Rick?' Dodie was thinking furiously. Did the police know this? Had Serena told them? It opened up all sorts of new possibilities.

'Just the sort of daft thing she would do. Girl couldn't write a decent letter. You can usually tell by that, you know, don't even have to read the script sometimes. Besides, there's enough authors already. We don't want to bother with more.'

'Really?' Dodie said faintly, her visions of publishers scouring material in search of brilliant new talent vanishing. She changed the subject hastily. 'So Piers Walls-Farmer is a small outfit? How could he afford such a big advance for Rick's book, then?'

'He's had one or two minor successes, but not enough. The days of the small houses are over. To survive today, and stay small, they have to be more specialist than he is. The houses like his, small and general, are very vulnerable to being taken over. I doubt if he'll survive for much longer on his own. He was hoping that Rick's book would help him promote a more literary list, and with it being tipped for the Booker he has attracted one or two authors. But now, who knows what will happen.'

'What else does he publish?' Dodie asked.

'Memoirs, foreign translations, some scientific books, mainly biological texts, country books, and a bit of fiction. It's quite a varied list, which may be an advantage, but it's not a very coherent one. If he sells, it might pay him to split into divisions and sell each separately.'

'We met Serena on her way up to London, that Sunday Rick was killed,' Dodie said. 'And now you are going to work in the evening. I hadn't appreciated that agents didn't work normal office hours.'

'Serena's a law to herself,' he said brusquely. 'She has no need to go to the office at the weekend!' He opened his case and drew out a folder. 'If you'll excuse me,' he said, 'I promised to read this script before tonight.'

Dodie spent the rest of the journey gazing from the window. She was thinking hard. So Wallaby Publishing wasn't doing very well, might even, if she understood Daniel's references, be in danger from a takeover bid. And maybe Serena hadn't been going to London that day. Perhaps that explained her need to post the large envelope in Upper Markenlea. Had she, by any chance, been going to meet a man? If so, it might provide her with an alibi and eliminate her from the list of suspects. She must mention it to Detective Inspector Morton. That's funny, she thought, she didn't know his first name. She began to speculate on names which would suit him, and whether, if he had a name like Andrew or Stephen, his friends called him Andy or Steve. No, they wouldn't dare, and neither name suited him, but she hadn't a clue what did.

They reached London and Dodie took a taxi to her house. She hadn't made any plans for the evening, apart from a phone call to her mother, then an hour recuperating by watching television and having a long soak in the bath. She'd open a tin of baked beans for supper, she decided. As a kid in London's East End she'd known these as the greatest possible treat. Good grief, she suddenly thought. Am I getting old, wanting to experience childish things again? Certain childish things, she amended.

Mrs Jackson was her usual complaining self, but Dodie, mendaciously assuring her that the police were on the verge of making an arrest, managed to dissuade her from descending on Markenlea to protect her family. Avoiding questions about her reasons for visiting London again so soon, for she was determined not to give her mother more cause for fussing before it was inevitable, she implied it was to see a man, which was perfectly correct, she thought, grinning, and briskly ended the call. Her mother had washed her hands of Dodie's matrimonial adventures, and for a wonder stuck to her resolution, and refused to discuss them.

Television was boring, supper was eaten, and she decided to ring Elena. To her irritation, which swiftly turned to anxiety, the answering machine was on. Even when she began to leave a message Elena didn't pick up the receiver. Maybe she was in the bath. Dodie told herself not to be so fanciful, and asked Elena to ring her in the morning. Then she went to have her bath. She tried Elena's number once more, with no success, and went to bed, tossing and turning for hours until she at last fell into a restless sleep.

When the telephone rang the next morning it took her a while to recall where she was.

'Hello, Mum, Elena here.'

Dodie breathed a sigh of relief, but knew better than to admit her fears to her daughter. 'Sorry, just woke up, not very bright-eyed yet.'

'What did you want last night?'

'Nothing in particular. Just a chat. I wondered if you'd heard any more about Charlotte? Did the police believe her?'

'How should I know? What time's your appointment?'

'Not till ten. I thought I'd stay up and do some more shopping,' she said. 'I'll catch the four o'clock train back, I expect, if that's all right. Can you meet me?'

'Sure. No problem. One small snippet of news, though. I hear Elizabeth is planning to contest the will. She's claiming undue influence by Anna.'

'Who told you that? And can it possibly succeed?'

'Frank telephoned, late yesterday afternoon. He's furious. He feels it will delay the settlement, and he'd rather get a small amount soon than wait for years and see it all vanish into the lawyers' pockets.'

'Perhaps he'll talk her out of it. I travelled up with Daniel.' She related her new suspicions. 'Have you heard that Serena has another man anywhere?'

'No, but I'll make some discreet enquiries. Someone who will know if there's anything in this.'

'Don't do anything silly!' Dodie said in sudden alarm.

Elena laughed. 'Don't worry, my potential informant won't let on to Serena that we're on to her.'

She rang off after wishing Dodie luck with her new tests, and Dodie went to shower. She'd been trying not to think of the consultant, but she couldn't put it off any longer. She sighed, and began to dress in a bright-scarlet dress scattered with huge black flowers. She felt like making a splash this morning. But not in a river, she amended, shivering, as she pulled out some scarlet shoes.

Twenty

Once more Dodie smiled at her consultant, submitted to the tests, and nodded when he said they would be able to tell her the result in a couple of days. He was so sorry the earlier ones had been inconclusive. But the signs from the others had been good, and he thought he would be able to prescribe a course of drugs for treatment. It was very unlikely surgery would be required.

Feeling slightly more cheerful, she took a taxi to Greek Street. Then she realized she'd be far too early for her lunch appointment, but Foyles was round the corner. She redirected the taxi. She could use the time to look at the latest books, inspect them and try to analyse what made them interesting or successful.

It was just one when she walked into the restaurant. The waiter took her straight over to a corner table, where a man was already sitting. He stood up and smiled.

'Mrs Fanshaw, how nice to see you.'

'Thank you. But do call me Dodie.'

'And I'm Piers. What will you have to drink? Champagne?'

What else, Dodie thought. 'That would be lovely,' she replied, and hoped she didn't sound too gushing. He was smooth, the sort of self-confident man who instantly raised her hackles. Perhaps publishers always had to exude this air of confidence. After all, theirs must sometimes be a chancy business, where bluff and confidence meant so much.

They ordered, and Dodie deliberately chose the most expensive items on an expensive menu. If he thought they were going to do a deal, then she wanted him to be fully aware that she was not going to be a pushover.

Over the first course they chatted about the weather, which both deplored, the state of English cricket, about which Dodie knew little and cared nothing, and the iniquities of the Government, which she cared about slightly more, in particular taxation levels.

When they had been served with the main course, Piers smiled and leant across the table, lowering his voice.

'Have the police got any further with finding out who killed my dear friend?' he asked.

'I'm not in their confidence, Piers,' she replied. 'Have you been questioned? They seem to be casting their net wide.'

He laughed. 'It sounds as though they're at a loss. They asked me what I was doing there, the day Rick died. But I have my wife's alibi, and that of her parents, of course, since I was at their house.'

'This second tragedy seems to have made the whole problem more difficult. No one knows why the girl was there, what her connection was with any of us.'

'But I thought she was one of Rick's discarded women?'

'Really? How did you hear that?'

He shrugged. 'I have no idea. Perhaps it

was Serena. Or maybe it was on the news, in the papers, about the suicide note.'

'Perhaps. She was a writer too, I believe.'

'Now that I didn't know. Published? I hadn't heard the name before.'

'Not published, but hoping to be. As I am, Piers. About my idea, what do you think? Could there be a market? Isn't that the term?'

'Memoirs are normally good prospects, and an autobiography of someone like yourself, my dear Dodie, especially as you have led such an interesting life, and particularly since you have met many famous people, such as the Hollywood stars, would give us an angle for promotion.'

'Put in lots of scandal, you mean? Inside knowledge about them? Wouldn't that lead to possible libel writs?'

He shook his head. 'I'd have my lawyers check it out thoroughly. And most of the time a court case only leads to bigger sales.'

Dodie smiled back. 'That would be a relief.' She talked about the ideas she had committed to paper the other day, in preparation for this meeting, and was amused to see his eyes glaze over slightly. 'Well, do we have a deal?' she asked quietly, and he snapped back to attention.

'Send in an outline, Dodie, and a few chapters, so that we can get a feel for your style, and then we can know whether it will be suitable for us. I'm sure it will be, of course, but I'm always wary of making promises on unseen books.'

'Yes, and you must be very disappointed that there won't be a second one from Rick, when the first has been so successful.'

'Oh, I'm not so sure. We may still find the typescript,' he said, but his smile had become fixed.

'Yes, of course. Well, thank you for the lunch, Piers, and I do hope we can do business.' Dodie stood up.

'Won't you have a pudding? And coffee?'

'No thank you,' Dodie said sweetly. 'I really have to watch my figure. And if this book of mine does get published, I'll no doubt be invited on to lots of TV chat shows. I shall depend on you to organize all that for me. Who knows, I might even make another career of it. Goodbye, Piers, and thank you for a delicious lunch.'

When Dodie stepped from the train she was expecting to find Elena waiting for her. Instead, a smiling Detective Inspector Morton came forward and took her arm to guide her out to the car park.

'I offered to meet you,' he said quietly. 'Elena's busy, and I have to go to Markenlea in any case, to see Dr Dean.'

'Is Elena OK? There's nothing wrong, is there?' Dodie asked, suddenly worried that this might be a way of breaking bad news gradually.

'Of course she's OK. I met her in the middle of town, she had several people to see, printers and florists, she said. She was looking harassed. Something to do with a Mrs Burroughs, one of her clients, I understand.'

'Oh yes, the one who expects miracles. Wants a wedding arranged in less than two months.'

'Does it take that long to arrange a wedding?' he asked, looking horrified.

Dodie chuckled and glanced at him speculatively. 'A year is the ideal time. I take it you're not married?'

He blinked rapidly. 'Not now,' he said shortly. 'Here's the car.'

The young woman constable was waiting on a double yellow line outside the station, and smiled at Dodie as she got in the back beside the Detective Inspector.

'I'm glad to be able to have a word with you,' she said quietly. 'There are several things I need to know, and the police can find out much quicker than I could.'

He looked at her in amusement. 'You're turning detective?'

'Heaven forbid! But I do have another theory, and I think I might be able to prove it. But I need more evidence. At the moment it's speculation. Will you humour me?'

'If I think your idea's viable, I'll do what I can.'

'Good.' Dodie proceeded to outline her theory and explained what she wanted him to do. Morton looked startled, but eventually agreed to do what she suggested.

'Thanks. Now, did Rachel Dean bring Anna back with her?' Dodie asked.

'Yes, and she's fully cleared.'

'Good, I'm glad. I never could see her as a calculating murderer. You found someone who saw her on the train?'

'Yes, and better still, she drew out some cash from a machine, and their records prove she was in Paddington when she said she was.'

'What about the second Sunday? She was with us in the morning, visiting that shed, but later?'

'She was with us at the police station, and while she was there she fainted, so we took her to hospital. She was there until late evening. And according to the post-mortem, Felicity Matthews was killed at some time in the middle of the day.'

'I thought they couldn't be too accurate about the time of death?'

'They can within limits that satisfy us Anna wasn't responsible. In any case, Charlotte insists she saw Felicity during the time we were with Anna.'

They were approaching Markenlea when

WPC Crossley slowed down.

'That's Dr Dean's car,' she said. 'Do you want to try and catch her now? It might be better than where Charlotte could be around.'

Morton nodded, and they drew up behind Rachel's car as she emerged from a house, carrying her bag. He opened the car door and stepped out to meet her.

'Would you mind answering just one question for me, Doctor? Shall we get into the car?'

Rachel looked surprised, but agreed, and while Morton took the front seat she sat beside Dodie.

'Where's Charlotte?' Dodie asked Rachel. 'She isn't on her own?'

'Of course not. She's safe at the Manor with Emily's people,' Rachel replied. 'Don't worry about her. They know the position, and have hired a security guard to patrol outside. What's this?' she asked the policeman.

'Just something I didn't like to ask you while we were talking to Charlotte. Her evidence may be crucially important. Let me recap. She saw a couple, she insists the girl was Felicity, on the day Rick Wilbraham died, at about the time he died. They were on the far bank, and she saw them cross over in a boat. It looks a good possibility that man was the killer. It becomes even more likely when we hear that the following week Charlotte saw the same couple, on the far bank again, and later on the man only. I have to ask you this,' he said apologetically, 'but is Charlotte given to romancing? Has she a vivid imagination?'

Rachel shook her head. 'Was she telling the truth, you mean. I've always found her truthful, even when she's in the wrong and expects to be punished. Her imagination is more to do with science than people, and she does have keen eyesight. She would have known the girl, been able to identify her.'

'Then we accept what she says. He might have killed the girl then, hidden her body, and in the evening after the boatyard was shut, borrowed a boat and moved her to the end of Wilbraham's garden. But we don't know who he was.'

'Or how he knew Felicity,' Dodie added.

'So we're back to motives, who benefits with both of them dead? Thank you, Doctor Dean.'

'Is that all?'

'Yes, thank you for your help. Now we'll let you get back to work, and Mrs Fanshaw can go home.'

Dodie set to the moment she was alone. She had several telephone calls to make. She fetched her large address book from her room, and flicked the pages, considering options thoughtfully. Then she made three calls to the journalists she knew best, who had in the past given her favourable publicity, and explained what she wanted. They promised to do what they could, she made several other calls, and then telephoned The Plough and asked whether Anna was still there.

'She is? Thanks. I'll come round soon, but please don't let her know. I don't want her to vanish, it could be dangerous for her to be on her own. If she does want to go out, please try to stop her.'

She was wondering whether to go right away or wait for Elena when Elena arrived.

'Good, you're back. Did Jamie – Detective Inspector Morton, meet you?'

'As you ordered him to,' Dodie replied. So his name was Jamie, was it? It suited him. And full marks to her daughter for discovering it. There was hope for her yet.

'He volunteered. But none of that,' Elena said sternly. 'First I want to know what the specialist said.'

'What could he say?' Seeing Elena about to erupt, Dodie relented. 'He'll know the results soon, and he's pretty sure, from the indications of the other tests, that they'll be able to control it with pills.'

Elena hugged her. 'I'm so glad. I know you hate the very thought of hospitals. Did you have lunch again with Gran?'

'I had lunch with a publisher, to talk about my memoirs,' Dodie said calmly.

'Who?' Elena demanded suspiciously. 'And what were you doing having a secret lunch with a publisher? You've no intention of writing your memoirs!'

'It wasn't secret, it was very public,' Dodie protested innocently. 'It was in a very famous restaurant in Greek Street. And an expensive one,' she added with a grin.

Elena was staring at Dodie in considerable alarm. 'Rick's publisher? He's the only one you know,' she said accusingly. 'What was the idea?'

Dodie preened herself. 'I was eating the most extravagant things I could find. And drinking champagne. You see, he thinks he might be publishing my memoirs. With lots of revelations about Hollywood people, and others,' she added in explanation.

'You always insisted you'd never write any, you don't approve of these kiss-and-tell books.'

Dodie became serious. 'No way is he getting his hands on them, even if I write them, which is highly unlikely. But I wanted an excuse to talk to him. This whole affair is so bound up with authors and agents and their books, I needed some background. Besides, I'd had an idea, and your Jamie Morton is going to follow it up.'

Elena coloured. 'He's not mine!' she

protested. 'What idea?'

'I'll explain later, first I must go and see Anna before she decamps again. Did you know her alibi's been sorted? And do you have any idea where Serena is? She isn't at home or the office.'

She explained her ideas as they walked across the green towards The Plough. This time Anna was there, and they went up to her small room. She got up from where she'd been lying on the bed, and smiled at them rather shamefacedly.

'We didn't know you'd had to go to hospital,' Dodie said, crossing the room and sitting on the bed beside her. 'I feel guilty, we ought to have called a doctor when you first got back. Are you quite better?'

'Yes, I'm fine. I was hungry, I think, and frightened. There was nothing else wrong, but they kept me there for ages. Did you know that helped clear me over Felicity?'

'Yes, and that your alibi for the Sunday before is OK.' Dodie reached for her hand. 'Anna, my dear, you can't be accused of any murder, but there is a murderer out there, and I believe it's all to do with that book. You have to tell the truth, child, or you'll be in danger until he's caught. And if we know what you know, the chances of that get better.'

'I feel so guilty,' Anna whispered.

'Never mind that. Tell us. First of all, did you ever introduce Felicity to Rick? We know you met her on the same course where you met Kevin. Was it possible she'd come to see Rick?'

Anna shook her head. 'How do you know that? Oh, never mind,' she added tiredly. 'No, I didn't. After the first time, on that course, I never saw her again. Neither did Kevin, so I've no idea how she knew Rick. If she did.'

'Good. Now let's try and do this chronologically. Anna, I'm convinced your friend Kevin wrote the book, which was subsequently published under Rick Wilbraham's name as his. Is that true?'

Anna nodded reluctantly. 'I suppose you'll all have to know, now. Kevin did write it, but Rick changed a few names, and made the hero a clerk instead of a building worker.'

'How did Wilbraham get hold of the script?'

'I believe Kevin gave it to him to read. He – Rick, that is – had shown an interest in what Kevin was doing, and offered to help correct his spelling and grammar. Kevin missed a lot of schooling when he was a child, through his own illness first of all, and then because his mother was terminally ill and there was no one else to look after her.'

'Why didn't he ask you to do it?' Dodie asked.

'I offered, but he said I was working on my own novel, and I had a full-time job too, so it would take up too much time. And I think he was flattered that his boss was taking an interest.'

'Do you know how long before Kevin died this happened? That he gave the typescript to Wilbraham?'

'About a month, I think.'

'Right, then. We've got all the other dates. Kevin died, and a few weeks later Wilbraham showed Serena Coates the typescript, as his own work. She sold it for a large sum to Wallaby Publishing. That made the national press. Did you see it and wonder?'

'I didn't see it then. I'd gone to America for three months. I was devastated by Kevin's death, we were planning to marry, you see. So I took a job out there to get away. I have an aunt in Houston who runs a secretarial agency, and I worked for her. The fuss about it had died down when I came back.'

'So when did you know?'

'A friend who writes book reviews for some of the local papers couldn't go to his launch party, so she gave me her ticket. She'd lent me her copy of the book, too, but I only read it that same day. I spoke to Rick and threatened him with exposure, at the party, but he persuaded me to see him afterwards, said he had an explanation.'

'What was it?'

Anna sighed. 'I suppose I shouldn't have let myself believe him. He said no one would be interested in a book by an unknown, dead author, and he intended to reveal the truth if the book was a success. Then he said Kevin had given him a rough draft of a second book, and would I help him write it? He'd tried, and found it wasn't as easy as he thought. I agreed, provided I got half his royalties, and moved down here to live. That was all, I swear. We weren't lovers.'

'Was there really a rough draft of a second book?' Elena asked.

'No.' Anna shook her head. 'I had just a page or two of notes, and Rick suggested I did a fuller synopsis, fleshed it out. That took more than a week, and he was never satisfied, he kept asking for changes. I was dumb, but it wasn't until then I accepted there wasn't any rough draft. We had a dreadful row, but eventually I gave way, we thought that between us we could write something. I'd tried to write a novel before, and he encouraged me to try and finish that too. He was very complimentary, and I was so eager to be successful myself. But I only agreed if he drew up a contract setting it all out, and because I'd then found out that Elizabeth was taking half his income, I wanted forty percent of what was left. And in the contract I made him put that he was leaving me the bulk of his estate if he died. I didn't expect him to, and when he was killed I was terrified. I thought everyone would think I'd done it, if they knew. I didn't really want the money. At the time I just didn't want Rick to profit, and I knew Kevin had no relatives to benefit.'

'Weren't you afraid of Rick?' Dodie asked.

Anna shook her head. 'No. You see, he needed me. He was even less competent than I am, he'd never have produced a book without me.'

Twenty-One

They persuaded Anna to return to stay with them.

'You'll be safer, and it's not good for you to be here on your own, brooding,' Dodie said briskly.

Looking worried, Anna permitted them to organize her, pack her clothes, and pay her bill. They walked back across the green, ate the cold supper Elena had prepared, and were sitting in front of the television watching the news when the front doorbell shrilled.

Startled, Dodie went to answer it, putting

the chain in place before she opened the door. It was Elizabeth, and she was in a furious temper.

'Don't be ridiculous, let me in!' she shouted. 'I'm not about to knock you all on the head!'

'No? You look fit to kill somebody,' Dodie replied, but she took off the chain and Elizabeth marched in.

'Where is the little slut? I've been trying to find her for days. And Serena's vanished too, no one knows where she is.'

'Who can you mean?' Dodie asked in her coldest grand duchess manner.

'Anna, of course! That devious little hooker who got her talons into my husband, and conned him into leaving her money which ought to have come to me! Then murdered him. She won't get away with it! I'll make sure of that. Where is she?'

Anna was standing in the doorway to the sitting room. 'I'm here,' she said calmly. 'And if you repeat those lies I'll sue you. Maybe then I'll get all Rick's money from you!'

Elizabeth spluttered in indignation. 'Listen to her! What did you do to earn so much of his cash? You must have been very inventive in bed. That was all Rick cared about, variety and some new perversion!'

Anna stepped forward, her face flushed, and as Dodie stepped between her and

Elizabeth, Elena appeared behind Anna and grabbed her arms.

'Don't let her provoke you,' Elena said firmly.

Anna breathed deeply. 'You're right. She's not worth it. For your information, Mrs Wilbraham, your husband and I were never lovers. I let it be believed because I thought that would be a reasonable explanation for any money I had. But now the truth is being told, and you'll soon find out what a cheat your precious husband was!'

Dodie intervened. This could go on all night. 'Rick didn't write that wonder book, Anna's boyfriend did. And there are still questions about whether Rick had anything to do with his so-called accidental death.'

Elizabeth gaped at her. 'That's slander!'

'No, just a question.'

'What do you mean, he didn't write the book? Of course he did!' she said, rallying.

Dodie sighed. 'No. He duped everyone. Rick scooped that advance which Kevin should have had, and Anna, who would have married Kevin, thought she was entitled to some of it. You have no claim at all on that part of his estate. I expect most of it will have to be returned to the publisher, and you may find you're liable, you might have to put your hands into your pockets to pay it back out of what Rick legitimately left you.'

'The publisher can whistle for it! I don't

believe you.'

Suddenly Elizabeth flung round, glared at Dodie, and marched out of the house, slamming the door behind her viciously.

Anna gave a shuddering sigh. 'My God, I thought she was going to claw my eyes out! Rick used to say she had an uncontrollable temper.'

'She's gone now, and she'll soon find out we were telling the truth. Now, my dears, I think we ought to go to bed. It's been quite an eventful day!'

They met for a late breakfast, all rather subdued and disinclined for conversation. Anna was reading the paper, Elena her letters, and Dodie was deep in thought. Then Anna gave a startled laugh.

'Listen to this! Can you ever believe anything the papers say? There's a short bit in the Diary about the script of Rick's second book being found. Where did they get that from?'

Elena looked up. 'Could someone else be trying to cash in?' she asked. 'No, that's unlikely. I've been brainwashed with conspiracy theories. Do they say where, or who has it?'

'No, but they imply it's somewhere in the village. Here, look. Do you think this will bring loads of the press down here? They'll have to know what I did. I don't think I can face it.'

Dodie patted her hand. 'Don't worry, child. I suspect other things might have happened before then.'

She refused to elaborate, and only five minutes later Detective Inspector Morton arrived, demanding to know what had happened. Elena brought him and WPC Crossley to join them in the kitchen, poured coffee and put more bread in the toaster.

'Anna, you'd better put them in the picture,' Dodie said, and Anna once more told her story.

He looked suspiciously at Dodie. 'That should flush out a few people we want to contact,' he remarked neutrally, and Dodie, unrepentant, grinned at him.

'You mean the elusive Serena will appear to try and claim it?' Elena asked, also looking suspiciously at her mother. 'Do you know where she is?' she asked, turning to the policeman.

He held up his hand in mock surrender. 'No, I swear. Her husband thinks she has a lover, and has gone to ground with him. He didn't seem to care, either.'

'Could it be Piers?' Anna asked. 'Even Rick was surprised when she wangled that huge advance, there was a lot of speculation about them, he said, but of course he pretended not to believe any of it.'

'We'll soon see.' Morton was enigmatic,

for which Dodie was thankful. She didn't want to be forced into making explanations too soon.

Then the doorbell rang. 'Saved by the bell,' Dodie muttered to herself, and looked on, amused, as Morton gestured to Elena to remain where she was, and went to answer it himself.

He came back escorting a puzzled-looking Serena.

'So you've seen the paper?' Dodie couldn't resist asking, and Serena glared at her. Then she turned to Anna.

'You've had it all the time,' she accused. 'What were you trying to achieve? Did you hope to get even more from someone else? Well, I can tell you, no one else has the right to it, it belongs to Piers, and me. It'll just about save the agency.'

'Do sit down, Ms Coates,' the Detective Inspector said, and Dodie noticed WPC Crossley move her chair back, and unobtrusively slide her notebook out of her handbag.

'Why? What is this? Where is it? It is here, isn't it?'

'Just a little information first, Ms Coates, if you please.'

She frowned, then subsided on to a chair, and wordlessly took the mug of coffee Elena placed in front of her. 'Go on, but be quick. I haven't time to waste. If anyone else gets that script first I'll be cheated out of my percentage, and I can't afford that.'

'There's just one question.'

He was suave, and dangerous, Dodie thought admiringly. Just the sort of man she liked herself. If she'd been twenty years – even ten years – younger, she'd have been tempted to try her luck. Then she remembered her daughter, and a wave of sadness at the passing of the years swept over her. She took a deep breath. Perhaps she was condemned to the Harry Keetons of this world now.

Morton was speaking again. 'Did you know Felicity Matthews? We know she approached your agency once.'

Serena was startled. She clearly hadn't expected this. 'I – yes, she did,' she said slowly. 'But what has that to do with anything? We have hundreds of hopefuls sending in scripts every week.'

'We're concerned with her, not the rest. What did you think of her work?'

'Are we having a literary seminar now? If I'm recalling the same work, I thought it had a certain naive charm. It needed work, of course, but most scripts do. Daniel wouldn't take her on. He wants life easy, the polished, ready-to-be-printed scripts.'

'And you? Did you take her on?'

'He didn't choose to permit it! I'm not allowed to make my own judgement, even though I negotiated the biggest advance the agency has ever achieved!'

And which you might have to hand back, Dodie thought.

'But you still believed she had potential?' Serena nodded. 'Did you, by any chance, introduce her to Piers Walls-Farmer?'

She began to look frightened. 'What if I did?'

'Did you?'

She gulped the coffee. 'Oh, what's the use? But I can't see how that's important. I sent him her script. That's all, I swear. He said he couldn't use it, and I returned it to her. That was the last I heard. What does it matter? I know she sent it to dozens of publishers who turned it down. They didn't see the potential,' she added defiantly.

At that moment the doorbell rang again, and whoever was there kept a finger on the bell until the Detective Inspector, who seemed to have taken on the role of butler, opened the front door.

'Come in, Mr Walls-Farmer,' he said smoothly, and ushered the publisher into the by now crowded kitchen.

'Good heavens, what is this? A prayer meeting?'

'A conference, perhaps, and I'm so glad you've come. It's just what we need to complete our investigations.'

'Investigations?' Piers shrugged. 'That's

your job, Morton. The only one I'm interested in is who's been hiding Rick's new book from me, and what they hoped to gain by it. It was you, I suppose,' he said, turning to Anna. 'Well, your cover's blown, as I think they say, so please will you give me my property? It's caused enough trouble already. And I have schedules to maintain.'

'How often do I have to tell you I don't have it?' she demanded.

He glared at her, then turned to go. 'I'm too busy to stay and argue.'

'A moment,' Morton said. 'Please sit down, Mr Walls-Farmer. I think you can answer some questions. Spare me just a few minutes of your precious time.'

To Dodie's surprise Piers complied. Morton allowed no hint of satisfaction to appear.

'Thank you. Just a few simple questions. Ms Coates has been telling us she sent you Felicity Matthews's novel. Did you ever meet the girl?'

A wary look had come into his eyes, and he tensed. 'No, I didn't. I don't make a habit of meeting authors whose work I've rejected.'

'Then perhaps, Mr Walls-Farmer, you can explain why she once worked in your office for a few weeks?'

'She didn't!'

'We have her bank records to show the

salary payments. One of your employees.'

'Oh, a temp! I can't recall all those sort of people.'

'Paul Maitland recognized her. He'd even taken her out a few times, which is why she knew his address. I suppose when she needed a false one for Harry Keeton it was the first she thought of. And several of her neighbours have identified your photograph as that of the man who frequently visited her, and spent the night there on many occasions. Were you her lover?'

He looked appalled. 'I didn't! They must have been mistaken!'

'And why the boatyard owner, or to be more correct, his son, identifies you as the man who dropped her off to hire a boat on the morning Rick Wilbraham was killed?'

'He must have been mistaken! I have an alibi – my wife, her parents, they can vouch for me!'

'Your wife was at church. Which presumably was why you organized that river crossing. You daren't risk her seeing you at Wilbraham's house, and asking why you were with another woman.'

'Her parents–'

'Her parents merely assumed you were in the house, Mr Walls-Farmer. They didn't see you. It's a very large house, and you'd told them you needed to read a script.'

'That's what I was doing!'

'You went out for a couple of hours that morning, and again the following Sunday, when Miss Matthews was murdered.'

Piers closed his eyes momentarily, then sighed deeply. 'Very well, I was with Felicity that first Sunday. It had only been a fling, Inspector. She was so persistent, but I'd tired of her.'

'Really?' The policeman's voice dripped scorn and disgust.

Piers glanced round at the others, and swallowed. 'She only wanted me in the hope I would publish her book.'

'So if you no longer wanted the girl, why did you meet her that Sunday?'

'She'd telephoned, in a dreadful state, wanting to see me. Little idiot. She'd got it into her head I was getting a divorce and would marry her. I didn't want her coming to the house. You don't have to let Chloe know, do you? It's got nothing to do with Rick's death.'

'Hasn't it? If that is so, Mr Walls-Farmer, we have no interest in your marriage or your extra-marital adventures. But Felicity was killed by someone the following week.'

'Well, I expect it was the same man who killed Rick.'

'You met her. You persuaded her to hire a rowing boat while you went to park on the far bank. She then took you across the river to see Mr Wilbraham. Why, Mr Walls-Farmer?'

'He'd phoned, wanted to see me. But with that wretched girl coming too, I had to keep her away from my in-laws, and I couldn't go through the village. I had to get across the river somehow.'

'And when you got there, what happened, Mr Walls-Farmer?'

He shook his head, and when the Detective Inspector didn't speak looked round at the circle of faces.

'You were seen,' Dodie said quietly. 'You can't deny it any longer.'

'Oh, God! I didn't want any of this coming out. Chloe will be furious.'

'And perhaps stop supporting your business?' Dodie asked. 'That is what she does, isn't it?'

Miserably he nodded.

'What happened?' the Detective Inspector repeated.

'Nothing. We just talked, Rick said he'd give me the script the next week, he promised.'

'That is not how we think it happened. There is no second script, for all you've been pretending you wanted to find it.'

'What?' Serena exclaimed. 'No script? But Rick said it was coming on well. Did he destroy it? And what about this in the paper?' she demanded, tapping the newspaper.

'Hush!' Dodie said.

'Mr Walls-Farmer?' Morton said.

Piers bit his lip, and suddenly slumped on to one of the chairs, hiding his face in his hands as his shoulders drooped.

'It was an accident,' he whispered. 'He fell, he hit his head on the side of the pool, and he was dead before we could get him out. Felicity dived in after him, but it was too late. That's the truth, I swear it!'

'Why not call for help? Why did you drag him down to that lower lawn?'

'I didn't move him!'

'Do you mean me to believe Frank did that, and stabbed him?'

'He must have done! I was too anxious to get away. Chloe mustn't know! That was all I could think about! I was terrified I'd be blamed, and Felicity was screaming. I had to get her away before Frank or somebody found us and assumed the worst!'

'Did he tell you there was no second book? That in fact he had not written the first one?'

Piers suddenly appeared to crumble. His shoulders shook and his voice trembled. Then he took a deep breath and looked the Detective Inspector straight in the eye. 'I – I went to have it out with him! Damn him, I've spent a lot of money on that book! I didn't believe him! He even wanted me to stop the publication of the paperback, and we've printed tens of thousands! It would have ruined the firm! That book had to be a success. Chloe was going on at me, threatening to withdraw her money! I couldn't let that happen.'

'You could still have published,' Serena, who had been staring at Piers in horror, said. 'He'd signed the contract.'

Piers rose to his feet and took a couple of steps towards the window, then swung round to face them. 'You don't understand! He said he would tell everyone. He refused to do any of the interviews I'd set up. He even...' He paused, and swallowed a couple of times, and brushed his hand across his face.

'He what, Mr Walls-Farmer?'

'He – he threatened to tell everyone I'd known all along about Kevin. He was the chap who wrote the damned book. He died. Rick said he'd tell everyone I was involved. With his death, I mean. There was some sort of accident on one of Rick's building sites. I didn't even know Rick when Kevin died!'

'Yes you did. You'd met him at one of my parties,' Serena said softly. 'I introduced you.'

Piers glared at her. 'Even if you did I don't remember! That was the first time I'd known about him, or Rick's deception.'

'So he threatened to involve you in this other death, did he? And you lost your temper and hit him?' Morton asked.

'No! It was an accident!'

'And the girl? Was her death an accident too? Or was she perhaps demanding marriage as the price of her silence?'

Piers stared at him, then suddenly lunged out at Morton. The policeman dodged the wildly thrown punch, and the publisher ran for the door, throwing down a chair behind him.

'Get after him!' Serena screamed. 'Go on, chase him! He did it! It was him, after all!'

The Detective Inspector smiled calmly at her, smoothed his lapels, righted the chair, and strolled slowly towards the front door. 'Don't worry, he'll be caught.'

Two burly constables proved him right, appearing with a struggling Walls-Farmer held firmly between them.

'This the man, Guv?'

'Yes. Thank you. Now if you can take him to the station, I'll follow as soon as I've cleared up a few matters here.'

They left. He returned to the kitchen and sat down again. Slowly the others joined him round the table.

'How did you suspect him?' Elena asked at last.

'Thanks to your mother. You were right, Felicity's neighbours recognized him, and then it was easy to get his wife's parents to amplify their statement. It's what Mrs Fanshaw deduced, and no doubt we'll discover she was right. Would you care to explain?' he asked Dodie.

She took a deep breath. 'It may be wrong in a few details, but what I worked out fits the facts, and he's just confirmed some of them. Suppose Piers Walls-Farmer met Felicity somehow, perhaps gave her a job, which seems to be what happened. He was her lover, she was probably besotted, but the fact she followed him here in a state implies he may have tired of her and she knew. He stood to lose money and, perhaps more important, he faced ridicule if it became known he had sponsored a fraud, which we now know Rick's book was. He may or may not have known the truth. If he didn't, why kill the golden goose? But as Felicity worked for him at one time it's quite possible she saw Rick's book and recognized it as the one Kevin had written. Perhaps she blackmailed him. In any case it seems as though Rick confessed, after Anna had left that Saturday, and wasn't there to keep him firm. I think he despaired of ever writing the second book and was tired of the whole thing.'

'I shouldn't have tried to make him,' Anna exclaimed, and burst into tears. 'It's all my fault!'

'But it was his idea at first. You didn't know until the book was published,' Dodie said, patting her shoulder.

'I know, but I helped him. I tried to help him. But we couldn't do it. I wanted it for

Kevin's sake. If we hadn't pretended, Rick wouldn't have been killed.'

'Nonsense, it was his own doing, trying to pass off Kevin's work as his own. It wasn't your fault he was killed, Anna.'

Anna looked unconvinced, but she subsided and Dodie continued her explanation. 'Piers would be very afraid for his business if Rick threatened to reveal all, especially if Rick could throw suspicion about Kevin's death on to him. And apparently small publishing houses like his are very vulnerable to takeover bids. If he stopped publication of the paperback as Rick demanded, he'd have lost a lot of money, and he'd be scared silly he'd lose his business too. It may have been temper, an accident as he says, but if Rick were no longer there he could publish the paperback and make enough, probably, to survive. Why, the death of the promising author could even have been a bonus, generated more sales. And if Rick died, no one would expect a second book. His reputation would be intact, and he could quietly recoup any money Rick had been paid for the second book. Felicity was hoping to get her novel published. She'd had lots of rejections, she wasn't much good. He could have promised to publish it if she helped him. But he has to keep up the pretence of looking for the second typescript to deflect any suspicion he knows there isn't one.'

'The slimy snake!' Serena exclaimed. 'And to think I trusted him!'

Dodie smiled sympathetically at her. 'You weren't the only one. So he plans to approach Rick in secret, by crossing the river. But he can't be seen hiring the boat, so he gets Felicity to do that, and take it back. She'd probably believe some story about a secret conference, which no one must know about. She was dropped off by someone in a Jag, and he drives one. But from what he said she was there during the quarrel. I wonder if she was meant to be? She even tried to save him. She got wet, which may have been why she pretended she'd capsized, to explain that away.'

'It may not have been deliberate,' Elena said. 'She was hopeless at handling the boat. She had been in the river, judging by the weeds.'

Dodie nodded. 'I suspect he sent her to take the boat back. But I don't believe she'd have stuck that stake in, unless she meant people to suspect it was murder. She was shocked more than afraid, I think, when she came to us. And she went to him, where they'd planned to meet after she returned the boat, in that car park near Charlotte's field.

'Later, I imagine, she starts asking questions or even threatening him. And he decides he has to get rid of her. He kills her, gets into her flat and leaves a suicide note, and makes sure she has identification on her so that the note is found.'

'What suicide note?' Anna demanded. 'Was there one?'

'Yes, but no one but the police, and Mrs Fanshaw and Elena, knew,' Morton said quietly.

'And he mentioned it when I had lunch with him to discuss my memoirs. How did he know unless he'd planted it himself? Have you really gone through all her papers?' she added, turning to Morton. 'He might not have had time to destroy all the evidence. There might be something else there. And you could check her phone calls, and see if there's a note in her diary.'

'I'm sure Jamie – the Detective Inspector knows his job, Mother,' Elena said, laughing.

'Oh. Sorry.'

'Why did he abduct me? It must have been him,' Anna added. 'Was he intending to kill me? And where did he get the van from?'

'His in-laws had one for the use of the outdoor staff. We found his fingerprints in it. He may have thought Rick had told you he meant to confess. Or he may even have hoped to persuade you, by threats, to carry on with the deception, writing the book yourself. He might not have realized how very little there was.'

'Why did he leave me there for so long? I could have died!'

'I expect he didn't have time, or couldn't get the van again, and didn't want to risk his own car being seen there.'

'Never mind that. What were you doing in the lion's den?' Serena demanded of Dodie. 'Are you really writing your memoirs? That would be a wonderful book. Do let me see some sample chapters, I'm sure I could get you a good figure.'

'No one could do that at my age,' Dodie murmured, pulling in her stomach. 'Don't get your hopes up, I've no intention of writing anything except cheques. It was a ploy to talk to him.'

'Perhaps I can persuade you to change your mind. I see it all. He would be a loser from the whole thing, and he would have been angry with Rick. In fact, it could have been an accident, a sudden fight, as he said.'

'Except that it was too well prepared,' Dodie reminded her. 'We knew that once Charlotte had told us she saw Felicity with a man. It must have been premeditated, and I'm becoming fairly sure he used that stake to make it obvious it was murder, once he knew there was no hope of a second book, and in the hope that Anna or even you, Serena, would be accused. After all, he was furious with both of you too.'

'He must have felt very certain he wouldn't

have been suspected. He had the nerve to come to Rick's while the police were there.'

'I imagine he's the kind of man who has to be in total control, so has to know what is going on. That's what brought him here today.'

'He came there after Felicity met him, that morning she left in the taxi. Where was she?'

'Maybe he sent her home by train, though as she had no shoes that would have made her a little conspicuous. I expect he dumped her somewhere and told her to wait while he came here.'

The Detective Inspector stood up. 'I must go, lots to do. I'll come back to tie up loose ends and ask questions later.'

'I must go too,' Serena said reluctantly. 'Let me know if you change your mind about those memoirs.'

Anna stood up too. 'I'll go too. I feel so guilty.'

Elena closed the door after them. Dodie sat staring out of the window, to where it had all begun with a mermaid. The phone rang and Elena picked up the receiver. A moment later she came into the kitchen.

'That was Gran. She's at Paddington. She read about the manuscript being found, and thinks we may be in more trouble. She's coming to make sure we don't get involved again.'

The publishers hope that this book has given you enjoyable reading. Large Print Books are especially designed to be as easy to see and hold as possible. If you wish a complete list of our books please ask at your local library or write directly to:

This Large Print Book, for people
who cannot read normal print,
is published under the auspices of

THE ULVERSCROFT FOUNDATION

... we hope you have enjoyed this book.
Please think for a moment about those
who have worse eyesight than you ...
and are unable to even read or enjoy
Large Print without great difficulty.

You can help them by sending a
donation, large or small, to:

The Ulverscroft Foundation,
1, The Green, Bradgate Road,
Anstey, Leicestershire, LE7 7FU,
England.
or request a copy of our brochure for
more details.

The Foundation will use all donations
to assist those people who are visually
impaired and need special attention
with medical research, diagnosis
and treatment.

Thank you very much for your help.